Uddhav J. Shelke (1931–1992) was born in Hinganghat in the Vidarbha district of Maharashtra. After his school education, he joined the Amravati daily, *Hindustan*, as associate editor. Then he moved to Tapovan, Dr Shivajirao Patwardhan's colony for people affected with leprosy where he worked as proof-reader, compositor and finally manager of the printing press. He won himself a place in the Marathi literary canon with his first novel, *Dhag*. His prodigious output of long and short fiction thereafter pandered exclusively to popular taste. However, it allowed him to live as a professional writer.

Shanta Gokhale (1939) was born in Dahanu and educated in Mumbai, London, Bristol. A writer, translator and theatre critic, she began her career as a college lecturer, moved to a multi-national corporation as P.R. executive and was then appointed Arts Editor of the *Times of India*. Her novels in Marathi, *Rita Welinkar* (1992) and *Tya Varshi* (2005), both won the Maharashtra State Award and have been translated by her into English. Her play *Avinash* (1988), also translated by her into English, was staged in Marathi, Hindi, Kannada and Malayalam. She has translated several other Marathi plays and scripted many documentary and feature films. She has authored *Playwright at the Centre: Marathi Drama from 1843 to the Present* (2000) and edited *Satyadev Dubey: A Fifty-year Journey through Theatre* (2011), *The Theatre of Veenapani Chawla: Theory, Practice, Performance* (2014) and *The Scenes We Made: An Oral History of Experimental Theatre in Mumbai* (2015).

Kautik on Embers

A Novel

Uddhav J. Shelke

Translated from the Marathi by

Shanta Gokhale

SPEAKING TIGER

SPEAKING TIGER PUBLISHING PVT. LTD
4381/4, Ansari Road, Daryaganj
New Delhi 110002

Originally published in Marathi by Popular Prakashan in 1960
Published in English by Speaking Tiger 2017

ISBN: 978-93-86050-65-6
eISBN: 978-81-933073-0-4

10 9 8 7 6 5 4 3 2 1

Typeset in Adobe Jenson Pro by SÜRYA, New Delhi
Printed at Thomson Press India Ltd.

TRANSLATOR'S NOTE

Uddhav J. Shelke (1931–92) was born in a family whose traditional occupation was tailoring. This made him a Shimpi (tailor) by caste. Kautik and Mahadev, the protagonists of *Dhag*, are also Shimpis. When their younger son Nama is withdrawn from school to help support the family, he too is apprenticed to a senior village tailor to learn the family trade. Shelke's story is thus about people he knows best. They live within the rigid grid of caste and poverty that binds rural India. Their caste allows them to do only certain kinds of work if they cannot do their own. It forbids them from doing work that has been traditionally assigned to lower castes. However, hunger has a more strident voice than caste. If stomachs are empty, the poor must do whatever comes their way. Mahadev cannot swallow his caste pride and submit to practical exigencies. Kautik, whose first priority is feeding her children, has no use for such pride. While she struggles hard to win through, he is ever ready to give up and lose. Her fight then is not only against the hostile circumstances that beset the family, but also against the negative force that her husband exerts.

Dhag is set in the Amravati district of Vidarbha in

northern Maharashtra. Shelke himself was born and grew up there. Besides location and caste, *Dhag* draws on Shelke's life in other ways too. Like Nama, he too had to give up his education in order to support the family. However, though he could not go to college, he had friends with literary ambitions like him. In a sense, they were instrumental in his establishing himself as a young writer of promise. In the late forties and fifties, the highly selective literary magazine *Satyakatha* was considered the ultimate arbiter of literary merit in Marathi short fiction. Egged on by his friends, Shelke sent his short story 'Maay' (Mother) to the magazine. The story was accepted and published. Based on Shelke's mother's life, 'Maay' became the seed from which *Dhag* grew.

Another factor that contributed to Shelke's self-education and eventual decision to become a professional writer, was his job as compositor in a printing press. The press was part of the training and rehabilitation programme started by Dr Shivajirao Patwardhan in Tapovan, the home for leprosy patients that he had founded in Amravati district. In time, Shelke rose from composing to proofreading to managing the press. More importantly, during those years, he had access to Dr Patwardhan's large collection of books. They opened up to him the wider world that lay beyond Amravati and helped him grow as a writer. The knowledge that Shelke gained about leprosy at Tapovan was obviously the source on which he drew from for a major turn of events that occurs in *Dhag*.

Published in 1960, *Dhag* was immediately acclaimed as an important work and went on to take its place in the Marathi literary canon as a modern classic, alongside novels like Bhalchandra Nemade's *Kosla* (1963) and Bhau Padhye's *Vasunaka* (1965). The searing tale of suffering and grit that *Dhag* told came from areas of experience that were totally new to the largely middle-class readers of Marathi literature. Shelke's terse narrative style did nothing to shield them from the harsh life that India's poor were forced to live. Although Shelke's dialogue was in dialect, his narration was in standard Marathi. Yet the prose struck readers as alien. There was a reason for this. Shelke's prose was sparse and unadorned. He had no use for the self-indulgent word-love that many contemporary writers displayed. Further, unlike the sentimental view that urban writers took of the poor, Shelke's approach to them, coming as it did from personal experience, was direct and down-to-earth. So if readers found his prose unfamiliar, it was only because his subject and his approach were unfamiliar. Language, after all, is what it does and how it does it.

Translating *Dhag* has been both challenging and rewarding. My friend, playwright Mahesh Elkunchwar, born and bred in Vidarbha, gave generously of his time, reading, correcting and commenting on the translation. A great admirer of *Dhag*, his opinion of the translation, forthrightly expressed, was that it did not have the force of the original. But he did concede in the same breath, that it was a beast of a novel to translate into English anyway.

Fully aware of the challenges that *Dhag* presented, I tried to do what every serious translator aims at doing. I made choices that came as close as they could to the original, in substance, sense, spirit and yes, sound. It is not only vocabulary but also sound that sets dialect apart from the standard language. The cadences and lilt of Shelke's Varhadi dialect give it a musicality that is absent in standard Marathi. In *Dhag,* some lines are extended beyond their immediate meaning with the addition of 'o'. This seems to intensify the emotion of what is said, making it an urgent plea. When I encountered such a line for the first time, I found myself instinctively adding 'o' to the English rendering. That brought me up short. What was I doing? Could I do this? Should I do it? When I read and re-read the line, I found it lent something of the cadence of Varhadi to English without loss of meaning. So I decided to go with it. That explains the presence of some 'o's in this translation.

Amravati, where *Dhag* is set, abuts Madhya Pradesh, a Hindi-speaking state. The influence of Hindi on the local dialect is pervasive. A prominent borrowing from Hindi in *Dhag* is the colloquial form of address, 'bey'. This is the equivalent of the colloquially used 'man' in English, as in, 'What are you doing, man?' I have chosen to retain 'bey' to give the translation a local colour.

Village people's conversations tend to be peppered with proverbs and sayings for which there are no English equivalents. The proverbs come from lived experience that speakers of English do not share. I found that translating a proverb and making it as epigrammatic as the original, was a better solution to the problem than looking for an equivalent English proverb. Epigrammatic translation not only made the proverb authentic, but gave the text an interesting texture that was not native to English. With all this, it was vital that I retain the fluidity of the original narrative. One of the great strengths of *Dhag* is the seamless way in which the narration and dialogue segue into one another and flow without pause, like a stream. If I have managed to achieve a similar flow in *Kautik on Embers,* I shall count myself happy.

Kautik on Embers

ONE

Those days, Kautik was staying at her brother's. Brother Govinda, sister-in-law Ganga, Ma Godubai, husband Mahadev and she and her two little ones, Bhima and Nama, all lived together. Govinda owned a sewing machine. It was set up way back in the corner of a cloth shop in the market street. A lot of sewing came the way of the machine, some from people Govinda knew, some from people Godubai knew. Those weren't shirt, bush-shirt and jumper days. Just common crossovers, vests, knot-blouses. Not to say that one or two jumpers didn't turn up. But the big load was caps and coats.

This was where Mahadev worked. He sewed these things. Govinda made the buttons and buttonholes or hemmed. Those days no garment was 'pressed'. But if someone wanted theirs to be pressed, Govinda would fold it and put it under his butt. After sitting on it the whole day, he'd hand it to the customer 'pressed'. Sometimes it was he, sometimes Mahadev who did the 'pressing'. The two brothers-in-law toiled together in one place. The two brought home a tidy sum. Eighteen or twenty rupees a week in those days when living was cheap. Plus there was Godubai's salary. She got paid ten rupees in the mill. It was enough and more for everyone. They ate wheat and rice. Wore clothes that covered them from head to foot. Owed nobody money. If anything, others owed them. With the household balanced on these firm shoulders, the rest of the family could relax. Kautik and Ganga would sit on the verandah, legs stretched out before them, picking dal and rice. Rolling out wheat-strings and rice wafers. Chatting and teasing each other. Nama and Bhima went to school. Bhima was in the third. Nama in preschool.

It was all nice and smooth. All pots together but no noise. Not that pot didn't clash with pot once in a while, but you didn't hear them. The noise was muffled by an underlying goodwill and good sense. There came a day, however, when the noise was heard. Nobody was sure what had happened but Govinda came home alone for lunch. Kautik asked, 'Bhau, hasn't he come home with you today?'

Govinda sprinkled water ritually around his plate. Said nothing. Swallowed his food, mouthful after mouthful. In silence.

Growing more uneasy and even fearful, Kautik began again, 'Brother...'

'You think I sit with my eyes on him all day?' Govinda said, pushing the mouthful he was chewing into his cheek.

Kautik didn't say anything. She looked at Ganga, trying to cover her uneasiness. Both lowered their heads, stunned into silence. Govinda finished eating in this silence. Then, wishing to give it a stir, he wiped his mouth on his dhoti, belched and spoke to the air, 'Nama, go look in at the Maruti temple on your way to school. If his lordship is there, tell him he must meet me and come clean if there's something on his mind.' Then he put a piece of areca nut in his mouth and set his cap firmly on his head.

This kind of thing went on for four or five days. On the sixth day Govinda met Mahadev. Lunch was eaten like it was the thirteenth-day-ritual meal of mourning. Taking a piece of areca nut from his wife's hand and blowing on it before putting it into his mouth, Govinda spoke to the air as usual.

'Mahadevrao, if there's something bothering you, let's at least hear what it is. Why all this sulking?'

Mahadev lowered his his head. Touched by her husband's state, Kautik's eyes blazed at her brother. Unaware of her look, Govinda repeated what he'd said. Mahadev was forced to look up then. 'I can't work on your machine, that's what.'

'Why not?' Govinda suddenly fixed his eyes on Mahadev. 'You got to do something for your stomach, no?'

'That I got to.'

'So then?'

'I suppose I'll do it when I have a mind to do it.'

'Oh! When you have a mind to do it,' Govinda began sarcastically, but quickly controlled himself, and said, 'And if you don't have a mind to do it for six months, then?'

Mahadev didn't speak. He sat twirling the nutcracker in his hand. Govinda turned to address the air again, his voice agitated. 'If people don't know what they should do, how much can I alone do? How long can I slog for others?'

'Now what's this about slogging?' Mahadev's hurt ego sounded pathetic. 'Who asked you to slog for anyone?'

'Do I need to be asked?' Govinda said. 'If you wander around like this when there's work to do, a mature man must slog, mustn't he? There's half-a-dozen people eating here. How can I cope on my own?'

'But who asked you to cope?'

'I have to be asked?' Govinda got up like a shot. 'Can't I see?'

'Look here, Govindrao. Let me tell you this straight one and last time. I don't like anybody talking to me like that. Not even my own father.'

'Who's been saying anything to you now?' Govinda said, pulling himself together. 'D'you have to serve anybody here or ask anybody for anything?'

'Better if I did. If I had to serve someone, I'd have the right to ask for what I wanted.' Mahadev heard the sharpness in his own voice and suddenly stopped.

Govinda made a face to show he understood much more than was said. As he left, he said dejectedly in a final kind of way, 'Well, think about it...'

Govinda left. Mahadev continued sitting where he was. Kautik and Ganga exchanged looks. They continued like this for a long time. If Ganga hadn't taken Kautik by the hand and led her to her plate, most likely she wouldn't have eaten the whole day. She only ate half a chapatti anyway.

Things went on in this way till Monday dawned. Mondays the mill was closed for the weekly Hinganghat market. Godubai was at home. She'd got to know what had happened. So she stopped Mahadev on the verandah and asked him in a warm, caring voice, 'Mahadevbapu, did Govinda say, do something to hurt you?'

As usual Mahadev didn't answer. So she coaxed, 'Would you like to set up another shop?'

'What do I have to set it up with?'

'You may or mayn't, but first say if you will...'

'I will,' Mahadev said, bashfully but brightly. 'If it's possible.'

Godubai worked hard at it. A brand new machine arrived home from the Singer company. She pleaded with Govinda to give Mahadev his pair of broken-pointed scissors and to fetch down for him an old wooden seat from the loft. Mahadev didn't have a tape measure but he made himself one with a cloth band of two arms' length and one finger's width. He marked it with black thread at intervals of four fingers' breadth with equal divisions in between. Mahadev measured clients with this 'tape'. Cut cloth with the broken scissors. And soon the machine was whirring.

It whirred at home. Mahadev had to pay the company five rupees a month to pay off its cost. The company would own the machine till he paid fifty rupees. Then he'd be the owner.

That was going to be a long time yet.

The day the machine arrived on the verandah, Mahadev separated from Govinda's family. One Monday he asked Godubai to get him four rafters and bamboo matting from the market. Using them, he made a lean-to with his wife's and son's help. What had been one home was now two. Two cooking fires burned in two corners. Ganga still roasted wheat chapatis on her griddle; but Kautik made bhakris of coarse millet, roasted on hot embers raked out of the cooking fire. They might be accompanied by vegetables, and then again not. When they were not, she gave her children red chilli powder mixed with yellow linseed oil instead, and threatened to hammer them if they breathed a word about this in the outside world. Namya, the younger one, would still kick and stamp at the sight of the chilli and oil. On Nagpanchami day he threw an all-out tantrum. He kicked away his plate of bhakri and chilli and oil and screamed, 'In other people's homes they're eating karanjis and papdis and you…'

Kautik didn't wait to hear the rest. She pushed her bangles all the way up to her elbows and shouted, 'Are you going to shut up and eat or not?'

'Not going to eat.'

'Watch out.'

'Yes, yes, yes! Won't eat.'

But he couldn't speak after that. Words got mixed with tears. Kautik was thrashing him. With every blow she raged, 'Won't eat?'

Finally she broke his will. He could barely breathe for crying. He looked to his father for help. Every time before this, when Kautik had beaten the boys, he had gotten angry with her, and felt sorry for them. He'd said things like, 'You're a monster! Why not kill the boys off once and for all' and held them close. But that day he didn't say a word. Not only did he support his wife, he incited her by saying to Nama, 'With fancy ideas like yours, you should've been born to a rich Marwari; why to a pauper like me?'

Finally Ganga, who'd been hearing the battle cries issuing from behind the bamboo matting, came to Nama's rescue. Freeing him from Kautik's grip and wiping his nose and face with her sari-end, she said, 'What's this, sister? Why pour your rage on the child?' Then she took him to her part of the house, saying, 'Come with me. I'll give you anarasas and papdi. Come.'

And truly she fed Bhima and Nama on rich fried savouries and sweets till their bellies ballooned. On top of that, she gave Bhima and Nama a standing invitation for all festivals to come. But it wasn't their luck to accept.

One day soon after, Mahadev, who'd been acting dispirited since the morning, dragged on somehow till the afternoon. But once he was sure there was nobody at Govinda's, he leaned his elbows on the machine top, hid his face in his hands and began to think. When he continued sitting that way even longer than expected, Kautik, who'd been hovering around, asked in a tearful voice, 'What's it? Does your head hurt or something?'

Mahadev shook his head heavily.

Kautik looked even more tearful. 'Then why are you sitting like this?'

'Why make me say things, woman?' he said. 'I don't know why, but my heart just won't settle here.'

'Why? What's wrong now?'

'Everything,' Mahadev's voice suddenly rose in anger. 'The machine doesn't work. Four mouths to feed here. The company to pay off there. How's one man to manage?'

'So what do you say we do?'

'I'm not going to stay here,' he couldn't stop himself from blurting out.

'Then where will you go?'

'I'll go anywhere. Whichever way God takes me.'

'Let's go then.'

'Why should you come?'

'Then what should I do here?'

'Stay with your brother.'

'Dear Lord, did I marry to stay with my brother?'

Mahadev bent his head. Kautik said, 'What do you say?'

'What can I say?'

'I'll go.'

'Where?' Mahadev said, rousing himself.

'Wherever you go.'

'Give me up,' Mahadev said, his voice trembling worse than before. 'I can go live anywhere.'

'I'll come wherever that is,' Kautik said, pulling her sari-end off her head. 'I'll be where you are. If you cut grass, why should I feel ashamed to tie sheaves?'

'And the brats?'

'Where we go they come. What've the poor souls seen yet that we should leave them behind and go?'

They continued talking like this, husband and wife, for a long time. Occasionally he'd tell her to keep quiet. At other times she'd plead with him not to weep. They stopped only when they heard people stir on the other side of the bamboo matting.

All of them were ready now. Mahadev wore a coat and cap; Kautik a pair of old slippers. A ragged cotton scarf, nibbled here and there by mice, was wound round Bhima's ears and neck. Even then he shivered in the cold. He'd go to the door every now and again and peer out into the dark. He was carrying two cloth bags stuffed tight with an assortment of things. Kautik's share of the luggage, a large cloth bundle, sat before her. Having inspected all the arrangements keenly and made sure everything was the way he wanted it, Mahadev moved towards the iron trunk which he was to carry, signalling to his wife along the way to wake up the sleeping Nama. So she went to the thin, coarse woollen rug he was sleeping on and began to shake him awake. She'd been shaking him long and hard, when he suddenly yelled, still half-asleep, 'What you want, o?'

Clenching her teeth, Kautik clapped a palm to his mouth and hissed, 'Don't yell, wretch. Get going, no sound...'

Lifting her cloth bundle to her head, she hoisted Nama up by his armpit and dragged him behind her. The others picked up their loads too and started walking in silence. After trudging through a dark dirt path they came out into the half-light of the metal road. They continued to walk in silence along the road, the municipal streetlights making their shadows short or long as they approached or passed them. Even the policeman patrolling the road in style in his warm kit looked like a shadow. He blew his whistle once. That made Nama jump. Bhima snickered.

They'd trudged along like this for a whole hour or more when they came upon an iron fence. One of its slats was missing. The ground on either side of the gap was flattened hard, because of the number of people who went in and out of there all the time. Mahadev had thought he and his family could also slip in through there, but their assorted baggage wouldn't go through. Kautik thought of a way. She went through the gap first. Mahadev passed all the bits of baggage to her one by one over the fence. After she had lowered them on the other side, he went through and they set off again, balancing their bundles on their heads.

Soon they were stumbling across the railway tracks gleaming under the station lights and scrabbling their way onto the platform. They had to weave through the untidy heaps of other people's luggage before they could find a bit of empty space for themselves. Settling his family by the luggage, Mahadev went off to the booking window.

Excited by the sights of the station, the boys kept darting around, leaving their mother to mind the luggage. Nama bent lower and lower, looking in the direction from which the train was expected to come. But he was too scared to go to the edge of the platform. He stood a whole manlength away from it, taking in all the sights while his heart thudded. But Bhima wasn't scared. He stood at the very edge of the platform. If Kautik hadn't been keeping an eye on him, he'd have been on the tracks by now.

A little while later, Mahadev came with the tickets. At the very moment that Kautik turned to look at him, Bhima jumped onto the tracks. In one lightning move, he had picked up an empty cigarette tin lying gleaming between the tracks and climbed back onto the platform, his face glowing with triumph. He looked at the tin inside out. Then, on a sudden impulse, aimed and threw it at a goods wagon lying in a siding far away.

The second bell clanged. The sluggish crowd on the platform suddenly sprang into action. The monster train came thundering down the tracks, swallowing them up, till it slowed down to a halt at the platform. Stuffing the boys into a brightly lit compartment, Kautik said to her husband, 'Now either I get in and you pass me the stuff or you get in...'

Mahadev got in. Kautik fetched two loads of luggage a trip. Mahadev carried them to where the boys were. Once all the stuff was stacked up, Kautik climbed in, her loose sari-end tucked in at the waist. She looked around with troubled eyes for a place to sit. She made a Marwari woman who was reclining sit up. She made her boys sit in the empty space. She told Mahadev to clear himself some sitting space on the luggage stack while she herself stood, hands on hips. Her eyes stared daggers through the sheet that covered a person sleeping on another seat further away. Meanwhile she was saying to Bhima, 'Sleep if you want to, son. You can lean against that trunk.'

'No, I want to watch the fun,' Bhima said, fiddling with the sliding window. He kept trying to open it, till he finally managed. He poked his head far out to look at the engine, unmindful of the coal dust flying back into his eyes. Nama nodded off where he sat while Mahadev and Kautik sank into their own grim thoughts.

Soon, the train had left Hinganghat far behind, and was steaming into Wardha. Kautik shook Nama awake. He blinked at the dazzling lights all around. Blue, red, green lights like stars come down to earth, he thought. He poked his head out of the window, gaping with curiosity and wonder. Just then a giant engine came out of nowhere and thundered down the neighbouring track. Nama started, and was about to pull his head in, when the window came down on his neck. Even before he could cry out, Bhima burst into titters. Kautik warmed Bhima's back with a couple of whacks before lifting the window off Nama's neck. Getting up, she said, 'Come on, you ghouls. Get off.'

'Is this our village?' Nama asked, sad that the journey was over. 'You said we'll travel the whole night.'

'In the next train.'

Kautik began moving their things out. When all the stuff was on the platform, they picked up their loads and began to climb up to the bridge, Bhima trailing his hand along the iron railing. Halfway along the bridge a sahib in a blue uniform coat asked them gruffly, 'Tickets?'

Mahadev made an eye sign to Kautik. She held out the tickets that were grasped tight in her hand. The sahib examined them this way and that a few times under the electric light. Then, looking at Nama, he said in Hindi, 'How old is this one?'

Mahadev's lips moved but Kautik's eyes told him not to speak. She said quickly, 'He'll be seven this Ganpati.'

'Then show me his ticket,' the sahib said sharply as he punched the other passengers' tickets. 'He needs a half-ticket.'

'Let us go, Sahib. So many others must be going through in this crowd everyday,' Kautik pleaded.

The sahib didn't seem to have heard her. He continued with his work.

Seeing this, Kautik made an eye sign to Nama to move

on. She too shuffled forward and said, 'Let us go, Sahib. We've no money. We're poor people.'

The sahib lost his temper then. He held out an arm barring Nama's way and said harshly, 'Don't give me any of that. Wait here, all of you.'

Kautik thought hard. Mahadev tried his best to plead with the sahib, but the man ignored them completely. He was absorbed in dealing with the other passengers' tickets.

Kautik and Mahadev stood by with their little ones. Passers-by glanced at their abject faces, some with suspicion, some with pity, till all the passengers had gone. Then, handing over his post to a boyish-looking colleague, the sahib said in the same harsh voice, 'Come with me, all of you.'

'I'm a poor man with wife and children, Sahib. I'll swear by anything I haven't another paisa on me.'

'No money?' the sahib said, pushing ahead, 'Then why did you get on the train? You think it's your father's train?'

Kautik dabbed at her eyes. Looking around to make sure nobody was watching, she quickly bent down before the sahib. Touching both his feet, she said, 'Let us go this once, Sahib. We won't do it again.'

The sahib stepped back deftly and continued walking. As he walked, he pulled out a notebook and pencil from his pocket and began asking Mahadev for his name and village, his voice filled with menace. Mahadev's lips moved, showing his willingness to answer the questions. But Kautik interrupted him once again. Wiping the tears from her eyes, she asked the sahib, 'How much more money will it be?'

'Two rupees one anna.'

Kautik thought hard. She asked Mahadev softly, 'How much money d'you have, o?'

'Maybe five-six annas.'

Kautik lifted the iron trunk off Mahadev's head. Took a key out of her cloth bag. Opened the trunk with her back to her husband and children. Pulled out two British-period rupee coins, took an anna from Mahadev and handed over the full amount to the sahib. He gave her a square smudgy slip from his notebook in return.

The train set a few passengers down on the Talni platform and steamed away. People whose villages lay nearby, set off for them straightaway. But Mahadev and his family had to spend the night on the platform with only the dim, flickering station lantern for company. Mahadev piled up their luggage in its light and was about to settle down and relax against one of the bundles when a sahib arrived. He was dressed like the sahib on Wardha station, but with less style, maybe because of the old square kerosene lantern he was carrying. Glancing around at the untidy scatter of Mahadev's luggage and family, he asked, 'Where are you going?'

Mahadev felt a stab of fear. His legs became stiff. He stammered, 'We got tickets. Got one even for the boys.'

'That's okay,' he said in a voice cooler than air. 'Which place are you headed for?'

'Talegaon.'

'There's no Talegaon this way.'

'Not Talegaon Thakur, sahib,' Mahadev said more confidently. 'Talegaon on the Nagpur road.'

'Oh that?' he said. 'Then why didn't you get off further, at Chandur? That would have been nearer.'

'We didn't have enough money for tickets to Chandur, sahib.'

'You mean you'll go to Talegaon on foot with these children?'

'Yes, sahib,' Mahadev said simply. 'What else can we do? We know the road. We'll get there in no time.'

The man in the sahib's uniform, moved by their plight, muttered something but soon went on his way.

So Mahadev's family got ready to wait there all night as planned. Leaning against their bundles and bags, legs pulled up to the chest, they thought about their future. Mahadev didn't want to tax his mind too much about it, but Kautik wouldn't let hers be free of worrying thoughts. In between, she'd keep glancing at Nama and if she found him dozing off, she'd say, 'Don't sleep now, Nama. Day's about to break.' Or she'd yell at Bhima who was busy inspecting every nook and corner of the platform unafraid. 'You deathhead! Don't run around this godforsaken place like some idiot ghost.' Then back it was to Mahadev, forcing him to think, thinking herself. Forcing him to say something, saying something herself, listening, compelling him to listen.

The night seemed to go on and on, till finally something seemed to stir in the trees. Crows began to call. The grating burr of a handmill they'd been hearing from a distance for several hours stopped now. It was difficult to say whether the grinding had stopped or its sound had been swallowed by the other noises of a village waking up. Now a cock could be heard crowing from the same direction. Soon after, a faint light began to show in the east. As it grew brighter, Mahadev's anxiety, repressed till then, suddenly surfaced. He said to his wife, 'What do you say, o? Everything's worked out for the best, but what'll we do for tea now?'

'Go take a look in the village.'

'What for?'

'Could be a shop.'

'What shop in this beggarfucking place?'

'So what d'you say I must do?'

Mahadev said nothing. Kautik said spiritedly, 'Don't sit around—let's go. We'll have tea in Shendurjana or Chandur.'

'I can't move a step without tea, I'm telling you.'

'No? Then keep sitting here,' she said bitingly. Mahadev was not a bit affected by her reply. He settled down nonchalantly to a smoke. Then Kautik lost her temper. She poured her anger against Mahadev on the boys. 'Pick up your stuff, you ruffians, and get going. And if that doesn't suit you, then sit here like beggars, you too.'

Nama and Bhima picked up some of the baggage. Kautik fiddled with the bundle Mahadev was leaning against, and snapped, 'Let me take this, o. Or I'll go without it.'

Mahadev lifted his head off the bundle with painful effort. Stubbing his bidi on the ground, he began to mutter placatingly, 'What I was saying was...'

'Then why don't you lift your butt off the ground? Or

you think you can just sit there saying come fruit fall into my mouth and it will?'

Mahadev found some reassurance in Kautik's words. He picked up his cap that had got crumpled under him and said, 'Let's go wherever you say.'

When they got to the village, Kautik told the others to sit under a tree while she herself went straight to the house ahead of her nose. 'Is nobody at home?' she called out.

A woman peeped out of the door, her hands covered with cowdung plaster. 'Who might you be looking for?' she asked.

'No person,' Kautik replied. 'I was only asking if there's a shop around here.'

'What shop could there be in this place, my dear?'

At this, Kautik's face filled with extreme surprise, almost as though she'd been certain a shop did exist nearabouts.

Noticing her expression, the woman asked. 'Why then? What were you needing?'

'I was needing tea-jaggery, what else, sister?' With that she turned away muttering to herself, 'We'll get nothing now till we reach Chandur…'

Just then a man of about Mahadev's age, who'd been cleaning his teeth with burnt tobacco, looked out and asked Kautik sympathetically, 'Where do you come from, lady?'

Kautik narrated her tale, then muttered angrily, 'I can go without anything at all, but my man's legs won't move without tea.'

'Is that all?' The man's voice carried the hospitable warmth of Varhad soil. 'Go bring the man of your house here. So much talk about such a small thing—tea!'

Mahadev could hardly wait for Kautik to reach him before he was asking, in a timid voice, 'Have you fixed something, o?'

'I'm not tongueless like you,' she retorted, picking up her share of the luggage. 'Arms and legs hanging helpless all the time. Come on. Lift your butt...'

Mahadev smiled weakly at this, rolling his tongue in his cheek. The gesture was an involuntary admission of his wife's capabilities and his own weakness. In his enthusiasm, he picked up more than his share of the luggage. Taking Bhima and Nama along, he followed behind Kautik. They walked to the house that stood directly before them. The man who'd spoken earlier, was spreading a coarse cotton rug on the newly cowdung-plastered floor. 'Please come in,' he said courteously, standing before Mahadev. 'This way. Why don't you sit on the rug?'

Mahadev sat on the cotton rug. Kautik went quietly indoors. Nama and Bhima found a spot to perch on. As they settled down, their host started a conversation to put Mahadev at his ease. When Mahadev told him his father's name, the host's face flooded with the joy of reviving an old and precious acquaintance. 'Really?' he exclaimed. 'He wouldn't be the one who sells areca nut pouches and cloth bags?'

'Yes, yes. That's the one.'

'The one with the crooked face?'

'The same. The old man got that crooked face from a stroke.'

'Of course I know the old man. Raghunath Tailor. But he comes here every Wednesday for the weekly market.'

'Yes. He does.'

'Well, it turns out we're close acquaintances then. If I'd known earlier...' Now the host's voice and demeanour changed. He said, 'Mahadevrao, don't mind my saying so, but the old man has a foul temper.'

'Don't even talk about it,' Mahadev responded contentedly. 'It's his temper that's brought us to this pass. Why else would we have left our own home to wander like this through heat and sun?'

'Is the old man the same way with you?'

'With us?' Mahadev began talking now as though inspired. 'I'd say he's all right with outsiders like you. But we don't get on even for a little tick of time. He's my father only in name.'

By now everybody had had tea. The older people were chewing on their bits of areca nut. It was when Mahadev, chatting away happily, lit his third bidi that Kautik could hold back no longer. She signalled Nama to come in. He listened to his maay and carried her message to his father.

'Tatyaji, maay says let's leave soon.'

'How can you leave soon?' the host said, looking in Kautik's direction. 'The food will be ready now. You must eat a few mouthfuls, relax, then leave in the afternoon. What do you say, Mahadevrao?'

'No, Dhondiba. We'll have to leave,' Mahadev said, adding without conviction, 'We'll soon be there.'

'That won't do,' Dhondiba said with the authority of friendship. He flung an order at his wife standing behind the kitchen door. 'Hurry up and make some bhakris.'

The sun was high overhead by the time everybody had

eaten, not just a few mouthfuls, but bellyfuls of lunch. Now Mahadev was ready to go. He said to Dhondiba what Kautik was saying to his wife—that they mustn't forget them now, but visit them in Talegaon soon. Finally then, they were on their way.

Bent under their assorted bundles and bags, Mahadev and Kautik trudged along the well-beaten road. Bhima raced ahead with a bag in each hand. When he got far away enough, he hid behind a thorn bush and when his mother-father came up, he sprang out shouting 'Bho!' That first time everyone was startled. Kautik screamed, 'Monster! You want a slap across your face?' That made Bhima laugh outright and he raced ahead again to hide behind a bush. This time when he jumped out with a 'Bho!' nobody got scared. Used to the trick, they continued to walk as if nothing had happened. But Nama soon began to wilt. He started muttering to himself and stamping his feet noisily. He began to fall behind the others. Kautik's feet grew heavy for him. She slowed down, increasing the distance between herself and her husband. Even then Nama fell half a field behind her at one point.

She had to stop then. Setting down her bundles under a tree, she stood with her hands on her hips looking back at Nama's little figure in the distance, her heart filled with pity. Noticing this, Nama's feet grew even heavier. He began to drag them deliberately. As he came within earshot, Kautik asked him with a pinched face like a sparrow's, 'Nama, are you tired then?'

Nama made a sulky face and stamped his feet a little harder. Kautik said, 'There's just a bit left now. Cross this patch of fallow land and we're there.'

'Oh yes. You said the same thing miles ago.'

'When was that?'

'When we got to Shendurjana.'

Kautik was tickled by his smartness. Wiping his face with the end of her sari, she said, 'Little rascal. You kept that in mind, didn't you?'

Nama didn't answer. Kautik glanced ahead. Mahadev was standing under a tree looking back at her. When they got there, Kautik asked him softly, 'How much further do we have to walk?'

'Maybe a few miles more.'

'That much, is it?' Kautik thought about it. 'Will you carry Nama then?'

He waved his hand over his bundles and said, 'And who'll carry these?'

Kautik glanced at Bhima. He was running back towards them. When he got there, he panted in fear, 'Maay, maay, there's a wildcat out there.'

'Where?'

'On that tamarind tree it was.'

'So will it swallow you?

'But he came after me, tatyaji.'

'You must have teased it.'

'No, truly. Just threw a pebble.'

'That's why.' Kautik turned to Mahadev. 'So will you carry Nama?'

'Yes. But the luggage?'

'Give it to me. I'll take it,' Bhima said.

'No, son. It's too much for you,' Mahadev said with concern.

'Too much? If you say so, I'll carry the whole stuff by myself all the way to Talegaon. Am I a sissy like our Namya? Give.'

Mahadev sensed Kautik's eyes full of foresight sending him a signal. Knowing what she meant, he put part of his load on Bhima's head. He lifted Nama to his shoulders. Held out his hand for the bags Bhima had picked up. Scolded him when he refused to hand them over. And so they continued on their way.

When they'd walked some way, Kautik couldn't stop herself from asking Mahadev a question that had been nagging her all along. 'Listen, o. We're going back to the village and that's fine, but what'll we do for daily work?'

'Let's see if the old man gives us his machine.'

'As if he's going to do that.'

'So he won't,' Mahadev drawled. 'The one who's given us life should worry.'

At this, Kautik heaved a loud sigh. Smarting, Mahadev asked, 'Now what's come over you?'

'What should come over me?'

'Then what's the matter?'

'Look,' Kautik said, irritated. 'Don't start nagging me for no reason now.'

'What's the matter then?' Mahadev said again. 'Every grain carries the eater's name. The one who cares and worries is up there.'

Kautik didn't say a word in response. She listened, and her feet followed Mahadev.

The sun was now preparing to set. The cattle, returning to the village from the forest, were in their path. They had to weave in and out through them to move on. The long haul had tired them so much, they could hardly speak. They walked in silence, and a long time later, Mahadev glimpsed the village huddled in a dip in the land. He slid Nama off his shoulders and said, 'Do you see that? That's our village. You'll walk now, won't you?'

Kautik answered instead of Nama, 'Of course he will! He's a good boy, Nama. He's not a donkey like Bhima. Isn't that so, Nama?'

'Yes.'

ೞ

Talegaon, covered by a translucent veil of smoke, had come into view. A distant beating of drums and ringing of a temple bell reached their ears. Every once in a while, a villager would go past, splitting his eyes to make out who they were. They saw more people as they entered the village. A face framed in a doorway would greet Mahadev and Kautik, asking them how they were and what brought them there. When they'd gone on, another person, who mightn't know them, would ask the first who they were and what they did. The first would give him all the information he had. Mahadev and Kautik continued walking towards their home, past houses of mud, wattle and clay, past faces known and unknown. Nama, quite exhausted, walked behind them like a pony behind a mare.

Their house stood on the bank of the village river. All the houses here were built in a row, like shops, on a man-high plinth. When the river was in spate, the plinth stopped it from bucking into their homes. People climbed the plinth on rough-hewn steps gouged out of it. Householders who owned farm animals, bullock-carts and handcarts, had beaten the foothold into a sloping path. Others had retained it as it was, neither step nor slope. Mahadev's house also had one of these footholds.

Bhima had already landed up at the house before Mahadev and Kautik got there. He sat leaning against the locked door, his feet resting on the bags and bundles he'd been carrying. He was spinning yarns about his exploits to the group of children playing there. By the time Mahadev and Kautik had climbed the plinth, the neighbouring womenfolk had begun to gather around. They chatted with Mahadev and Kautik, asking after them as if they had known them through many lives. Sita, the barber woman, said, 'Tell me, Kautik o, how old was Nama when you left us?'

'Can't say for sure,' Kautik replied, 'But he'd just begun to walk maybe.'

Sita looked at Nama admiringly. 'And look at him now. You wouldn't know him from what he was.'

Then Mahadev said to her, 'Sister, where's the old man gone?'

'What day is it today?'

'Saturday.'

'He must've gone to the Mozri market then, where else?'

Mahadev examined the shape of the padlock on the closed door and said, 'Let's take a look at your keys, sister.'

Not a single key in Sita's bunch worked in the lock. Keys were fetched from a couple of other homes. They too were tried and returned. Finally Mahadev broke open the lock with a pestle from Sita's house, and everybody went in.

They entered the verandah first. An ancient Pfaff sewing machine stood there. With its top wrapped in an old piece of cloth, it looked like a respectable man who'd been arrested and had covered his face as he walked down the road handcuffed to a policeman. A thin film of dust covered the table-top worn smooth with years of use. Only a small patch of space under a pair of scissors was dust-free, taking on the shape of the scissors. There was another clean patch, thin and long, where a strip of cloth must have lain. Nama spotted it and wrote his name, N-a-m-a, below it. He wiped his dusty finger on his shorts. He put his feet on the pedal of the machine. As if on cue, the large beltless wheel began to spin. Nama made the wheel whirl round and round till Kautik said stop.

Kautik who had gone indoors came out to the verandah. The inner room was so dark it frightened her to step in. She drew an oil lamp from a niche in the wall. She blew the dust off it and shook it. It was empty. Kautik took Mahadev's matchbox. She struck one of the sticks and entered the inner room by its light. When she came out again, she was carrying a kerosene bottle. She held it up to the light. That too was empty. Kautik said to Mahadev, 'Better send for an anna's worth of crude oil.'

'Who's got the money around here...'

Kautik tugged at the little purse hanging at her waist. She said to Bhima, 'Son, go run to Tukya's shop and...'

A little girl pulled a chewed-up wad of petticoat out of her mouth to say, 'Tukya's dead, aunty.'

'So who runs a shop in the village now?'

'Ganpat Brewer.'

'Where's it at?'

'The upper end.'

'I haven't seen it,' Bhima said.

'Go ask around.'

'I'm not going and all,' Bhima replied. 'My feet hurt.'

Kautik said to the girl, 'Will you go, dear, this one time?'

A short wait later, Kautik's efforts were rewarded. The yellow oil the girl brought produced a reddish flame at the top of the lamp, just visible enough to prove its existence.

TWO

It wasn't long since Kautik had come to Talegaon. They were living off the rations they'd brought from Hinganghat. As soon as they ate, Mahadev would go into the village and the boys would start playing with the other children. It was on one such day, when the boys were out playing and Mahadev was about to go out loafing, that Kautik asked him hesitantly, 'Listen, o! Are you worrying about work or are you simply…'

'God! D'you think I don't have even that much sense?' he said. 'Let's wait. At least till the old man comes back. I wanted to ask him about the machine.'

'Oh?' she said. 'And if the old man doesn't get back for a month, then?'

Smarting at Kautik's tone, Mahadev said, 'Are you starving or something?'

'No,' she retorted with equal spirit. 'You can dig the well when we're thirsty.'

Mahadev said nothing. He went his way. Once he had gone, she too was free. She would sit chatting on Sita's verandah or call Sita over to hers. That day the two women were sitting on Kautik's verandah, cutting and chewing areca nut and chatting. Glancing at Sita's stomach, Kautik smiled to herself saying, 'So, you've eaten on the sly, eh?'

'It's nothing new, sister,' Sita said, shaking her head resignedly. Then she noticed Kautik's stomach. Judging its dimensions, she said, 'So I've eaten on the sly. And you've eaten publicly have you?'

'Could be, sister,' Kautik said, making a wry face. 'People cry if you die once. But if you die every day, who'll cry for you?'

'Fed up already, hunh?' Sita said. 'You haven't had a quarter of the full measure yet. Just two boys. They didn't come in heaps like mine.'

'What would I do with them coming in heaps? It's bad enough worrying about feeding two twice a day.'

'You say that now. But if God had given you more, would you have thrown them away or what?'

While Sita and Kautik chatted, their children romped all over the plinth, playing catch. Nama was the den. Janrao closed his eyes with his palms. Just then the old man, Raghunath Tailor came huffing and puffing up the plinth, carrying a square bundle on his head. As he came up, his sharp gaze fell on Nama and fixed itself there. Noticing this, Janrao's grip over Nama's eyes loosened. Nama stood watching the strange, crooked-faced old man with grave curiosity. The old man came right up to him. Steadying himself and his wavering gaze, he said, 'Is that Bhima?'

'No. Nama.'

'Oh? You've grown very big, bey.' When the old man's surprise wore off, he asked, 'When did you come?'

'Saturday.'

'Who all have come?'

'I, maay, tatyaji and my big brother...'

'I see...' The old man's words became slurred.

'Who're you?' Nama asked.

The old man muttered to himself as he moved towards the verandah, 'Why would you know me, my child?'

When she heard the old man's footsteps, Sita slipped away. Kautik too went indoors to the kitchen. The verandah was empty. The old man lowered his bundle in its corner. Leaning against it, he allowed his eyes to travel the whole length of the verandah, resting in turn on the machine, the mud wall, the faded coat that always hung on a peg. They took in the wooden box kept behind the machine for the user to sit on, its lock, the pair of scissors and the cloth-cutting board. The old man's eyes did more. They pierced and rummaged through the heap of leftover rags. Finally, though it was winter, the old man began to fan himself with the loose end of his turban.

Kautik signalled Nama to come into the kitchen. Handing him a water pitcher and tumbler, she whispered, 'Take that to him.'

'The old man on the verandah?' Nama asked loudly.

'Don't call him old man, you ghoul,' she said through clenched teeth. 'Can't you say abaji?'

The old man grew thoughtful when the water was brought out. He looked in turn at the pitcher and tumbler, at Nama and at Kautik standing hidden in the darkness of the kitchen. Then he sighed feebly and finally took the pitcher and tumbler from Nama's hands. He moved out onto the plinth and moistened his hands and feet. He wiped his face with the same wet hand. Nama would have burst out laughing if Kautik had not made warning eyes at him from the kitchen. When the old man had dried his face with his turban end, he asked Nama, 'Do you go to school or not, bey?'

'Yes. I go.'

'Which class're you in?'

'Pre-school.'

'Shame on you. And Bhima?'

'He's in the second.' Then Nama added colour with his brother's other exploits, saying, 'And abaji, when there's nothing to do, Bhima picks fights.'

'With who, bey?'

'With the boys at school. He beats up the big boys too. Maay curses him all the time. And aba, he....'

The old man turned his face away. A while later, he put his hand to the waist-fold of his dhoti and asked, 'You like eating snacks?'

'Yes.'

Nama took the coin the old man gave him. Kautik called him in. When Nama came out, he said, 'Abaji, take off your outdoor clothes. Maay says she's served lunch.'

The old man sighed again. Taking off his turban, he asked, 'Where's Mahadev?'

'Which Mahadev?'

'Your father, bey. What's his name?'

'He said he was going to the Brewer's shop,' Kautik said, taking this chance to speak to the old man.

The old man didn't respond. He said to Nama, 'Come.'

'Where?'

'To eat.'

'I'm not hungry.'

Kautik snapped at Nama from the kitchen, 'Why say no if he wants you to eat? Have a couple of mouthfuls with him, can't you?'

The old man and Nama sat together to eat. The old man gulped his food down in silence, without raising his head. When the rice helping was over, Kautik brought out the bhakri. Holding off her hand with a gesture, the old man said to Nama, 'I'm through. See what you want.'

The old man washed his hands. Wiping his mouth on his dhoti as he returned to the verandah, he muttered to himself but loud enough to be heard, 'I wasn't hungry anyhow. But I ate a couple of mouthfuls because we shouldn't turn our back on food.'

In the morning everybody had tea except Kautik. She had left her father-in-law's and her own share on the fire and was waiting for him to get back home. But he hadn't come even an hour after he should have. So she drank her tea at last, leaving his to simmer on the fire.

The old man returned a couple of hours later with small quantities of tea leaves and jaggery knotted up in his shoulder cloth, and a mix of rice and lentils knotted up in his dhoti. He dumped everything on the verandah. He shifted the tin trunk from its usual corner to another. He set up three stones where it had been to make a cooking fire. As he shoved twigs into it, he asked Nama, 'You want a sip of tea, bey?'

'I've had,' Nama said truthfully.

'I see. So you don't want any now, is that it?'

Nama grew thoughtful. He looked towards the kitchen for counsel. Following Kautik's signal, he said to the old man, 'I'll have some.'

'Watch it. Think hard,' the old man said pointedly. 'No one's forcing you. Ask someone if you want to.'

Nama didn't answer. The old man said, 'Go get a pan from the kitchen.'

Nama brought a pan. Kautik had sent water in it but the old man threw it out. He made tea with the water he had fetched from the river. After tea, he set his rice and lentil mix to cook in the same pan. From then on, that's how it was with Raghunath Tailor.

Kautik, who'd been growing more and more worried, faced Mahadev squarely one day. 'So, what do we do now?'

'About what?'

'About work, what else?'

'Oh yes. I should've asked the old man about the machine, I suppose.'

'You're not going to, now,' Kautik said in a huff. 'Can't you see how he's been with us from the day we came? He's the sort who'll let rot but not let grow.'

Mahadev fell silent. He sat staring at the ceiling as if he'd been struck dumb. Seeing her chance, Kautik pressed on.

'That's why I was saying. Unless we work for someone on daily wages, we can't fill our bellies.'

'That's for anyone to see now,' Mahadev said helplessly. 'No need to say it.'

'But can you cope with farm work?' Kautik asked plaintively, watching her husband's face. Mahadev didn't answer. When Kautik repeated her question, Mahadev muttered angrily, 'Which son of a shit's going to care if I say no? Man's belly has screwed him twelve ways anyway.'

'When will you start looking out?'

'When?' Mahadev said, grinding the butt of his bidi into the ground. 'If it's now, it's we who must look; if it's later, it's still we who must look. So it's best I go now to the village to ask.'

Kautik could not bear to speak. Mahadev returned from the village in good spirits. 'If the bhakris are ready, wrap some up for my lunch,' he said.

'Why, o? Has there been a call?'

'No lack of work in this season,' he said. 'I'm off to Ragho Gawai's field for the cotton.'

'By weight or by the day?'

'By the day.'

'How much?'

'Five a day.'

'And for women?'

'Three annas.'

'Then I'll come too.'

'No.'

'Why, o?'

'Isn't there enough work in the house?'

'So what if there is? Don't village women finish house work and run to work in other people's homes?'

'Why come today? We'll see about it another day.'

And so Mahadev 'Teller' was on his way to the cotton

field with his bhakris tied in a piece of sari and a strong length of coarse cloth to gather cotton in. Kautik watched him go and when she could see him no more, she dabbed at her eyes with the end of her sari.

ᔕ

Some five or six days later, Mahadev said there was no more work and stayed home. Kautik's anxiety rose when he continued staying home. She began making moves to find work. One morning she hurried home from the shit-place outside the village. The instant she stepped in, she asked Mahadev, 'Have you taken on anyone's work?'

'No. Why?'

'Then let's go to the Patil's field,' Kautik said happily. 'He'll pay by weight he says.'

'How much a maund?'

'Four annas.' Kautik made her voice extra joyful to put some enthusiasm on Mahadev's face. 'I said I'll ask you and send word. So?'

'Come,' Mahadev said dejectedly. 'What use am I sitting at home anyway?'

Kautik's spirits stayed high. She said to Bhima, 'Son, go to the Patil's big house and tell the manager we're coming and not to send for anyone else.'

ᔕ

The sun was blistering hot now. The lentils had begun to shed their blossom and put out pods. The fragrance of the blossom wafted all over the field. The farhadi pods dried and popped open under the white heat of the sun. The cotton plants bent low to the ground. They hung heavy. Shed their burden. Fluffs of cottonwool dropped off of upper branches to hang on lower ones. Kautik thought ruefully of her boys doing nothing but romping around at home. She started bringing them with her to pick cotton. She'd tie a sling round their waists. They would pick the cottonwool off the branches, drop it into their slings and empty the swollen slings onto the cloth that their maay had spread out at one end of the field.

The first day Kautik brought them along, she told them the work was going to be fun and games. Nama and Bhima weren't so sure. But there was no time to think. They simply worked alongside their tatya and maay everyday. As the slings round their waists filled, they'd trot off to where Kautik had made place for the cotton heap. Bhima's sling would fill faster than Nama's because, once in a while, Nama would scuttle away to hug the shadow of a tree to escape the sweltering heat. Similarly he'd make a trip now and then to the river at the edge of the field, out of earshot, even when he wasn't thirsty. Kautik's sling would also fill faster than Mahadev's. Once in the shade, he wouldn't budge till he'd smoked two or three bidis. Even when he did budge, his heart was not in picking cotton. Kautik and Bhima worked like they were possessed. Kautik was possessed by her concern for the family. No such reason drove Bhima. He worked because his schoolmates worked.

During Diwali week, it took all of Kautik's stubborn willpower to keep the boys working. She held out all kinds of bribes before their trusting eyes to snatch work out of them. She promised Nama a new pair of shorts one day and on another, held out to Bhima the hope of a new shirt. On Tuesday, she was going to do something she'd never done before—take them to the Shendurjana market. The boys, their eyes fixed on these temptations, worked with the full weight of their will thrown into their small bodies. They waited for Tuesday.

That was the Tuesday before Diwali. Kautik, Mahadev and their sons were on their way to Shendurjana. Kautik carried a wicker basket with a piece of Mahadev's old dhoti to tie millets and other foodstuffs in; and two empty bottles, one for coconut oil and the other for cooking oil. As they walked, Kautik and Mahadev worked out what they wanted and could afford to buy in the market. Their boys walked behind them, looking around at the trees and bushes.

Suddenly Bhima halted. He also stopped Kautik who was busy talking. Pointing to the branch of a tree, he said, 'Ma, look, up there...'

'Where? What is it?'

'Hey, blind-eye!' Bhima blurted out. 'Look where I'm pointing.'

'Get going smartass!' Kautik flung at him. 'You blind-eye me and I'll bash your face in.' She hurried on to make up the distance between herself and her husband. Nama was like her tail, running after her. Barely had Kautik fallen in step again with Mahadev when Bhima, who had stayed back, came running up to them, blood spurting from his finger. 'What happened?' Kautik asked.

'It's nothing,' Bhima said, removing the finger he was sucking from his mouth for a moment. 'The parrot bit me.'

'What parrot?'

'The one I showed you back there. It was in a hollow of that gonni tree.'

'On the tree? And how did it bite you from there?'

'I went up to catch it!' Bhima said, dejected. 'But when I put my hand in the hollow, the arsefucker bit me and flew away.'

'Good,' Kautik said, her face blank, as if she wasn't one bit surprised at what had happened. 'Why go meddling with that gonni tree in the first place?' she demanded, and continued walking.

They arrived in Shendurjana in good time. As usual, they went first to the public water tank in the market. But the space around it was already occupied by many families. Several wagons had been unharnessed in the dense shade of the surrounding mango trees. The bullock-carts had been emptied. Lunch bundles had been opened and people were eating seated on the ground or in the empty wagons and carts. Some people were eating puffed rice and roasted gram instead of a meal. A couple of measures of puffed rice and gram were spread on a quilt, like cattlefeed in a cowshed.

There were water pitchers nearby and pails and earthen pots. Everybody had one or other of these things. By the time people finished eating, their water vessels were empty. They sat back then, unrolling their betel leaf pouches, belching and smoking bidis.

Kautik opened her bundle of food as soon as they'd settled down in a bit of shade. Bhima went off to the water tank with their water pot. There was a wriggling mass of people around it. Many hadn't washed their hands and mouths yet after eating. Many needed water to quench the fire of chillis burning on their tongues. The people who were serving water looked harried. They couldn't serve everybody at once. Everybody would get water in the end but according to the servers' convenience. Some people drank from cupped hands, others wanted their water pots to be filled. Those who'd come with buckets and pails could draw water from the large well nearby.

As soon as Bhima returned with the pot of water, Kautik's family began to eat. There was a single bundle of bhakri and onions between them from which they ate their fill.

Then Kautik began the buying. Nama got his shorts and Bhima his shirt, as promised. Mahadev bought a large measure of wheat for Diwali.

While Kautik got busy tying all the stuff in bundles, Mahadev gave the shopkeeper a five rupee note. After waiting a long while for the change, he finally said to the shopkeeper, 'Can you give me my change quickly?'

'What?' the shopkeeper suddenly exclaimed. 'Are you trying to fuck me up? Hand over the money for your wheat, no tricks.'

Mahadev's face fell. Hitting his forehead with his palm, he said pathetically, 'What is a man to do now...'

The shopkeeper's voice grew sharper. 'Give me that money. I don't want your acting. There's customers waiting here.'

Mahadev poured his whole bleeding heart into explaining, 'Oh sahib, I just gave you a note. I'll swear by anything you say...'

'Get out, you. Put the wheat back in my sack.'

Mahadev felt fear at the menace in the man's voice and face. He said to his wife, 'Dump the wheat. Let's go.'

'Am I a fool to dump the wheat?' Kautik said threateningly, handing her bundles to Bhima. 'That money didn't just fall in my lap. It was earned with sweat.'

The shopkeeper suddenly lunged at Bhima's head across the sack of golden wheat, pulling at the bundles. When Bhima wouldn't let go of them, he gnashed his teeth and raised his fist at Bhima, saying, 'Swine, let go or you want some hammering?'

In a trice, Kautik was facing the shopkeeper. 'Come on, hit him. Let's see you do it.'

Now Mahadev too found courage. He thought of the value of the five rupee note and went to Bhima's aid. The shopkeeper gave him a hard push. Kautik hurled a richly spiced obscenity at him. It found its mark. The shopkeeper now called her all kinds of names. Mahadev's honour had now been attacked. He rushed at the shopkeeper and tried to grab his wrist. But one jerk of that massive wrist and all of Mahadev's anger melted away on the spot. The shopkeeper grabbed his collar and the two went at each other. They wrestled. The shopkeeper's rugged frame won the day. Mahadev crashed to the ground. The shopkeeper sat astride him and began raining blows on his face.

While this was going on, Kautik had handed the basket on her head to Nama. She had tucked her sari-end in at her waist and had rushed, raging, to her husband's aid.

She hammered and kicked the shopkeeper on his back, hurling abuses and curses at him all the while. Every bangle on her wrist broke. Her wrists bled from the broken glass pieces. Bhima ran to his father's aid from the other side. He bit the shopkeeper's arm twice. Getting a hold on his leg, he was now concentrating all his strength on pulling it.

Nama who was looking after the bundles and baskets, just stood and wept, calling out in an agony of fear, 'Tatyaji, maay o.'

A crowd gathered, gradually growing denser. A couple of people suggested that the shopkeeper let Mahadev go. One or two even attempted mildly to pull the enraged man back by the arms. But the shopkeeper, driven by fury, wouldn't move. Finally, a fellow pushed his way through the fat crowd. He was wearing a Bengali tussar-silk kurta. A wad of notes was clearly visible, folded into the hang of his pocket. The watch on his wrist was of the same flashy yellow as his kurta. He used all his strength to pull the shopkeeper off Mahadev's chest, and said quietly to the cursing Kautik, 'Calm down now will you, lady...'

Then he said to Mahadev, 'Did you really pay him?'

'Yes, yes. I did, lord sir,' Mahadev replied. 'I'll swear by anything you say, I did.'

Now the silk kurta man said to the shopkeeper in Hindi, 'And you say you didn't get the note?'

'I'm telling you honestly, sir, this fellow didn't give it to me.'

The silk kurta man bent to peep into Mahadev's pocket. 'Just check your pockets and all properly, see...'

Mahadev started turning his pockets out. Kautik put her hand on Nama's head and said, 'I'm swearing by my child, sir. He put the note on that cadaver before my eyes. If you like, we'll hold a cow's tail; or tell him to do it.'

The silk kurta man took the wad of notes out of his pocket and pulled a five rupee note out of it and held it before Mahadev. Instantly Kautik said, 'Why should you give the money, sir? Keep it. We put our note on that corpse. Warmed him up with it.'

By this time, Kautik had finished undoing the bundle of wheat. Flinging the wheat on to the shopkeeper's sack from where she stood, she said to him, 'Take that. Put it on your corpse. Let's go, children.'

They set off. Their minds were like ashes smouldering after a house has burned down. For a long time, they didn't know where they were coming from and which way they were going. But soon enough, it was Kautik who found her wits. She muttered almost as if to herself, 'It would have been better if we hadn't bought clothes for the boys first.'

Mahadev said, 'But who was thinking such a thing would happen?'

'Will you do something?'

'What?'

'We'll return the clothes.'

'As if he'll take them back.'

'He will. We could offer to take a few annas less, what d'you say?'

'We could try.'

'Come,' Kautik said. 'We can't serve the children bhakris on a festival day, can we? Clothes! We can buy them any time. But Diwali's not going to wait for us, is it?'

Kautik glanced at the boys' faces. They looked crestfallen.

She tried to make them understand. 'You choose. You want the clothes or the festival?'

'The festival,' Bhima took a quick decision.

'And you Nama?'

'I want my knickers,' Nama said, sulking.

Kautik fondled his cheeks, stroked his head and promised to buy him knickers next week. He reluctantly agreed.

The shopkeeper in the clothes section wouldn't hear of taking the clothes back. Goods once sold stayed sold. Not eight annas, not even a rupee less would make him change his mind. Defeated, Kautik and Mahadev gave up. They began to retrace their steps through the clothes section in despair, past the shops one by one. Just then, a voice called from a shop. 'Isn't that Mahadev then?'

Mahadev recognized the man who had called. 'Sheshrao, isn't it?'

'Who else? Remember me or not?'

''Course. Why wouldn't I?'

'When did you come from Hinganghat?'

'A month or more ago.'

'So sit. Why are you standing?'

'There's things to buy.'

'They'll get bought and all!' Sheshrao now turned to Kautik saying, 'Sister, you recognize me, I hope.'

'Why wouldn't I?'

'So tell me my name then.'

Kautik fumbled. She'd even forgotten the name Mahadev had called him by a moment ago. At last he said, 'So you don't recognize me, see?'

Meanwhile they had walked to the back of Sheshrao's shop and sat down.

He and Mahadev had begun chatting. Betel-leaves were made up and eaten. Kautik had one too. She told her husband something as she took hers from him. When Sheshrao heard what it was, he wasn't one bit keen. While he was still making negative sounds, Kautik said, 'You've got to do this for us, brother.'

'All right. If you insist. Give me those clothes.'

Moved, Kautik thanked him profusely. When she asked for the money though, he said, 'How can I give it now? You can come for it in the evening.'

Evening it was, but Sheshrao did Kautik the favour. The market was emptying fast by then and Mahadev and Kautik had just begun to shop. By the time their Diwali shopping was done and they returned to Talegaon, the clock in the village office had struck ten in the night.

Kautik's Diwali began from the thirteenth phase of the waning moon. She woke up before dawn and sat down to hand-grind her soaked wheat in Sita's house. The flour for chaklis and then the washed rice followed into the handmill. She spent the whole day milling and pounding. The semolina was separated from the flour. The bran got ground into wholewheat flour. The preparations for the festive cooking were now over. The sweeping and the cleaning of the house and yard remained. She plastered the walls after filling up the pits and holes. She washed and cleaned the cooking pots, dusted, swept, swobbed. At last she was ready to make a dinner of bhakri and pithla for the night.

When everybody had eaten, the deep fryer went onto the cooking fire. Bhima was sent to fetch the press-mould from Sita. The coconut grater was called for. The mortar and pestle followed. Bhima started pounding the jaggery in the mortar. Nama raked the dried coconut halves hard across the back of the grater. The black-flecked white flakes of coconut began to drop and gather on the paper below like tea leaves mixed accidentally with sugar. When the jaggery was pounded smooth, Kautik kneaded it into the wholewheat flour along with oil and a pinch of salt. The dough was done. Kautik pushed the ball of dough, the rolling board and pin towards Bhima, saying, 'Here, roll out disks, cut them into diamonds with this cutter. I'll fry them.'

Bhima demonstrated a sample. 'Like this?'

'Can't you make them thinner, you wretch? Or are you in some hurry?'

Bhima got it right the second time. Kautik fried the diamonds that Bhima cut. When the first lot was done, she put a couple of shankarpalas each in the boys' hands. 'See how they're turning out.'

'Great,' Bhima said. Nama couldn't eat his because they were still hot.

It was the same with the karanjis. One was broken into two halves for the two of them. And then Kautik said, 'That's enough. Now go sleep.'

Bhima said, 'But I'm not sleepy.'

'Of course you aren't!' Kautik said, stirring in the

deepfrying pan with her slotted ladle. 'Hustle in the house and bustle in the heart.'

Nama said, 'Can't we help you with the festival, o?'

That's how half the night went by. The boys didn't budge.

Finally Kautik covered the chakli dough and put it away. When she began to douse the cooking fire, Nama couldn't help crying out, 'Ma, aren't you making the chaklis?'

'I might in the morning, and I might not.'

Bruised in their hearts, Bhima and Nama rose painfully. Their legs were all pins and needles after sitting for so long. Kicking in the air to bring them back to life, Nama made his way to his mother's mattress and Bhima to his father's and both lay down. As Bhima pulled his rug over his head, he called out, 'Ma, wake me early in the morning—to help with the chaklis.'

It was still dark. The shehnai playing before the Patil's house could be heard the village over. Kautik hauled Nama off her mattress by his armpit. 'Get out of that shirt and get on to that rangoli.'

'I'm feeling cold. Let tatya go in first,' Nama said, rubbing his fists into his eyes.

'Oh he's still hanging around unwashed like you, is he?'

Soon the shirtless Nama squatted on his haunches over the rangoli pattern, wearing his father's cap. Kautik brought out the salver for the aarti. There was kumkum in it and damp rice soaked in vermillion. A wick flickered in a small earthernware lamp filled with linseed oil. Kautik made circles with the salver before Nama's face. Then she bathed him, scrubbing and scouring his body with a piece of scented soap. Then she put him back into the same soiled, sweaty clothes in which he had slept. Bhima too was wearing his everyday clothes.

When Nama was dressed, Kautik made everyone, including her husband, sit in a row. She served the festive sweets and snacks to her husband in a china plate, Bhima in an aluminium plate and Nama on a sheet of paper. When they had eaten, Bhima and Nama began to burst crackers. Nama was scared of them. But Bhima would hold a cracker, however large, straight to the flame, while Nama ran to hide in a corner of the house. Once, when Nama was least expecting it, Bhima burst a cracker right beside him. Nama jumped out of his skin and began to howl. Bhima roared with laughter, 'Old sissy,' he mocked. 'Go wear bangles.'

On Lakshmi Pooja day, Mahadev managed to get marigold flowers and mango leaves from somewhere. Nama and Bhima strung them into garlands for the doors. They hung them up on the verandah and kitchen doors. Bhima was about to hang one in front of the gods when Mahadev shouted, 'Not there, bey...'

'Why not? Janya's hung one before Sitakaki's gods...'

'Maybe so. Their gods and ours are different.'

At night, Kautik made a rangoli pattern on the floor.

Mahadev placed a flat seat over it and spread a piece of red waste-straw matting on it. On this, they set out Kautik's earrings, Bhima's and Nama's silver waistchains and ankle hoops, and a rupee and four annas. They worshiped these as Laxmi, goddesss of wealth. Then they burst crackers and distributed popped rice and sugar discs as prasad.

It was almost a week after Diwali. By then people should have shed the languor of those days and returned to work. At least that's how Kautik thought it should be. And so she had packed Mahadev off to the village common first thing in the morning. Returning from there, Mahadev asked Nama, 'Where's she gone?'

When he heard she was at Sita's, he sent Nama to call her back. Nama was entering Sita's house, when her children stopped him on the verandah. Kautik heard his voice and asked from the shadowy interior of the house, 'Is that you Nama? Why're you here? Has he come back home?'

'Yes. He's asking for you.'

'Go tell him I'm coming,' Kautik called back. She said to Sita, 'I'll be back. I'll see what the man wants. But you don't worry. I don't see trouble coming for another fifteen days at least.'

When Mahadev saw her, he pulled an anxious face and said, 'What do we do now?'

'Why?'

'Ganpat Basketmaker has already called in some women.'

'And what about Vishnu Brahmin?'

'He finished his picking long ago, they say.'

'So there's no work on anybody's field?' Kautik looked at her husband in disbelief. 'Are they saying there's no work at all?'

'Not that. There's twigs to be picked for Bairam Maratha.'

'That swine!' Kautik spat out scornfully. 'As if he'll pay!'

'So what do we do?'

'We'll go, what else?' Kautik said. Then stopped herself, 'Tell me, o. Whose basket measure is he paying by?'

'His own. He showed it to me.'

'How big is it?'

'Big as the one we put bhakris in.'

'That's all?'

'Then what...' Mahadev was happy at the prospect of being let off.

'Whatever it is,' Kautik said, 'we'll go. What'll we do sitting at home anyway?'

Mahadev was pained. He said, as a last effort, 'Are you going to break your back all day for the scraps he'll pay?'

'Even that's hard to come by,' Kautik said, unaware of his reluctance, or perhaps guessing at it but deliberately ignoring it. 'Go tell him we'll do it.'

Kautik entered the kitchen to make bhakris. She bustled around to make up the cooking fire. Mahadev didn't move. His butt stayed fixed to the newly cow-dung plastered verandah. He lit a bidi. A while later, Kisna Gardener came by in a great hurry, asking Mahadev, 'What's your Bhima doing, eh?'

'Must be on the common. What's up? What d'you need him for?'

'Well, I don't know how to put it,' Kisna said, making a show of being worried. 'I was thinking suppose you took it badly, then?'

'At least tell me what it is.'

'Er...it's like this. Will you send Bhima in place of Yesonta?'

'Cattle grazing?' Mahadev said, rubbing his bidi butt there and then into the ground. 'Hell! You got to think before you speak. Think of our caste and all. Or you think because we're poor we'll do any work for the belly?'

'Now you're upset, aren't you?'

'The way you're talking,' Mahadev said, his voice still raised, 'will upset anyone.'

Just then Kautik's voice came from inside, 'Brother Kisna. What's that you're saying?'

Kisna told her what, ending apologetically, 'And so Daji lost his temper with me.'

'What's there to get angry over?' Kautik said, coming out to pacify her husband. Then she asked Kisna, 'Wasn't Yesonta Mahar grazing your cattle.'

'He's not well, poor soul.'

'What'll you give per day?'

'What I gave Yesonta.'

'So how much's that?'

'Ten paise.'

'How many animals?'

When Kisna told her, she said as she went indoors again, 'I'll send Bhima if you pay three annas.'

'I'll pay eleven paise.'

'I don't talk twenty things.'

'Oh all right. Send him. With his lunch.'

'And listen. You're going that way, so send Bhima back will you?'

'All right.'

Once Kisna had gone, Mahadev said to Kautik, 'What? You're now sending Bhima to mind cattle, are you?'

'And so?' Kautik said. 'What's the shame in it? Human beings have to be ashamed of only two things—thieving and slutting. What shame is there in working for the belly?'

'You think up good belly work,' he muttered angrily. 'Your people will stuff dung in my mouth the way you're going. They'll say...'

'Sayers will only show span-long teeth,' Kautik said in a huff. 'It's months since I left Hinganghat. If they're really my people, have they asked after us? Have they wondered how their sister might be doing and their sister's husband?' She continued to mutter angrily to herself, 'Nobody cares for anybody. There's nothing like blood brother and sister-in-law. They're all good-time kin. Let them come to my door now...'

She went into the kitchen trembling with rage. She banged pots and plates as she cooked. She packed three lunches, two for the two of them, one for Bhima. He hung his from one end of his cattle prod. On the other end, he hung a pair of his maay's old slippers.

He balanced the stick across the back of his shoulders like a milkman carrying milk cans. This work was just up his street. So off he went with a spring in his stride. A little while later, Kautik too was ready to go. Nama got after her then to go with her. Cajoling him, she said, 'Why d'you want to come little one? The field's very far away.'

'Let it be.'

Nama sulked. Threw a tantrum. Petting him, Kautik said with a woebegone face, 'Stay home just for today, little one. Play with Surya. Have a good lunch. There's bhakri and dal in the basin. Have some oil from the cup if you want.' But Nama was still sulking. So she took a paisa out of her bag. Giving it to him, she said, 'Will you play now? And listen, play outside. Don't gather all the neighbouring kids here. Don't touch the old man's things or sit spinning the machine wheel. Now can I go?'

Nama merely nodded. Kautik started walking down the path with her husband and baskets and lunch. But her labour was wasted. She had to come back. As soon she got back, she went straight to Sita's house first. 'How is the pain now?' she asked her.

'Better.'

'I knew it. Didn't I say it was just the baby turning?'

'Didn't you go to cut twigs?'

'I did and all,' Kautik said sharply. 'But that rotter whom even dogs won't eat says he doesn't want women. Only men. Says women don't work fast enough.' She smiled ruefully.

'Will you have a betel leaf?'

'I don't know about a betel leaf and all,' Kautik said, laying out the leaves on the betel leaf pouch. 'My mind's not easy with the daily wages going down.'

Even before she could spread lime on her betel leaf, somebody called from down below. 'Who's that?' she called back.

'It's me, Godi Shepherdwoman.'

'Come up then.'

'Not now,' she called back from below the plinth. 'You want to come cotton picking?'

'Yes. Is it by the day or by weight?'

'Who'll pay you by the day this season?'

'I suppose there isn't much to pick.'

'Whatever it is.'

'I'll come what else. Even if it's just to make enough for salt and chilly powder. What am I doing at home anyway?'

Kautik, Bhima and Mahadev were now away, each at their own work. Nama was left at home alone, playing with Surya. It was afternoon when Raghunath Tailor returned from one of the weekly markets. He was carrying the usual load of goods on his head. He lowered the load to the ground. The old man always rested awhile against the bundle till he got over his fatigue. He had just done that when he shot up again. He went to his trunk and began to feel around it and undo the assorted bundles that lay on top of it. He muttered to himself, 'The moment something's left outside, there's mischief for sure! That jaggery I bought the other day, hadn't made one cup of tea with it. Next time I want it, half of it's gone!'

Nama, who didn't know people could talk to themselves asked, 'Who are you talking to, abaji?'

'To nobody.' Then the old man had an idea. 'Namya, you want snacks?'

'Yes.'

'Can I ask you something?'

'What?'

'Will you tell the truth?'

'Yes.'

'Did your mother come near my trunk?'

'What for?'

'Just tell me if she was here.'

'She was.'

'Why?'

'She lifted the trunk.'

'And what else did she do?'

'She plastered cowdung under it.'

'What did she do after that?'

'Nothing after that.'

'Tell me the truth. You want money for snacks, don't you?' the old man said. 'Did she open these bundles?'

'Which? Yes.'

'How much jaggery did she take from here?'

'This much.'

'Hmm. Go play now.'

'Money?'

Nama was on his way to Ganpat Brewer's shop to buy roast gram with the money when he saw Bhima coming from the opposite side. He was stamping his feet hard as he walked and his eyes were streaming. He stopped Nama and asked him urgently, 'Is maay at home?'

'No.'

'And tatya?'

'Not him too.'

'Have the fuckers died on me, all of them?' Giving up on Nama, he hurried home. The moment he stepped onto the verandah, he kicked his slippers off his feet letting them fall any which way. He shredded the cloth in which his lunch had been tied, the dried crumbs of bhakri and dal falling on the ground. He lay his cattle prod on the ground, put his foot at the centre of it and, concentrating all his strength, arched it upwards till it broke in two. Then he leaned back against the verandah wall and sat there without moving. In the evening, as soon as he saw Kautik climbing the plinth, he howled, 'Ma, ma, that sisterfucker beat me, o!'

'Who did?' Kautik asked, scared.

'Bakhadya's wife-kept son-in-law.'

'And why?'

'Because my animals trampled his embankment.'

'And why did you let your animals walk over it?'

'Was it only my animals?' he asked glowering at his mother. 'You're a big one. Zhingya, Karpya...all their cattle went the same way.'

'Nobody said nothing to them?'

'No.'

'And why should only you get beaten?'

'Because my animals were the last and I was behind them. And the sisterfucker turned up from some shit place and began thrashing me.' Bhima couldn't say more. He turned his back to his mother, pulled up his shirt and said, 'Look at the welts he made with his chappal.'

Now Kautik flew into a fury. 'What? He beat you with his chappals?'

'Yes, o maay,' Bhima said. 'I kept telling the sisterfucker, you want to hit me, use your hands, not your chappals. I'm getting polluted. I'm a tailor by caste.' He swallowed a sob. 'But the bastard wouldn't listen. He went on hammering me, seeing I was smaller. Couldn't he pick on someone his own size! Now see if I don't tear his asshole a foot.'

By this time, Kautik had banged her basket down on the floor. Tucking her sari-end tightly at her waist, she said, 'Come along with me.'

Then Mahadev who was emptying the twigs from his basket asked her, 'Where?'

'I'll show that Bakhadya's son-in-law where he gets off.'

'Hey o, he's got money.'

'Maybe. Boys will be boys. That doesn't mean he can be beaten with chappals. If he had to beat him, he could have given him a couple of slaps. Even the cane if the damage was all that much. But not chappals just because he's a poor man's child! Oh no.'

Zhingya came up the plinth while Kautik was still hopping around in a rage. He'd gone cattle grazing with Bhima. Seeing him, she raised her voice even higher. He heard her out. Then said very civilly, 'It was Bhima's fault, aunty.'

'How?'

'That's what I'm telling you,' he said. 'When our animals had trampled the bank and gone on, Bakhadya's son-in-law came cursing and abusing. We kept quiet, aunty.'

'And what did Bhima say?'

'That's what I'm telling you,' Zhingya said. 'Bhima says to Bakhadya's son-in-law, "Does the field bank belong to your father?" It's just as well it belongs to the father-in-law.'

Kautik did an about-turn. Bearing down on Bhima, her hand raised, she said through clenched teeth, 'This span-high fellow said that to Bakhadya?'

To which Mahadev said, sarcastically, 'Easy! The child's timid, like a cow, right? Go on then. Fight for him with Bakhadya!'

Nagpanchami was over. The season was in its prime. The lentils were ripening. The millet was ready for harvesting. There wasn't a single free farmhand in the village. And in the middle of it all, rain clouds began to patrol the sky. A wild wind was playing aggressive games with the crops, scaring the farmers. They were making trip upon trip to farmhands' doors, pleading, 'Come to my farm first.' They were loosening their purse strings for daily wages. The farmhands were tugging the strings even wider. For their own yards and verandahs were also piled high with drying ears of corn. Boxes of lentils and huts of sesame stood rigid. Pods of mungbeans and mothbeans were drying in the sun.

Kautik and Mahadev too were busy squeezing farmers for all they could get. They tried to avoid working on far-flung fields that took hours to get to and back from. If they did agree to go, it was on piecework, not daily wages. The farmer looked helplessly at the sky, wringing his hands and gave in to the rates Kautik and Mahadev demanded. And why not, Kautik thought. 'There's nobody for hard work like me.' And she was right too.

When she had piecework, every person in her house was out working with her. On those days, Kautik would bake a span-high pile of bhakris before daybreak. She'd put the pile on Nama's head. Bhima would carry the water pitcher. Mahadev would carry the trowel and cloths, and Kautik a stack of four basins on her head. The retinue was now ready for the road. Occasionally, leaving home at daybreak, they would return only as the morning star rose.

That's what happened one day. The moon in its fourth

or fifth phase had risen while they worked. Little Nama had been nodding off on his feet. He'd told his maay again and again that he was sleepy. Each time she'd said, 'That's it now. Just four basinfuls to winnow and then we'll all sleep.' And after those four basins, she said, 'Give us four more. There's a good breeze. We'll get through fast.' And then she added after a pause, 'Or we'll have to waste another day finishing the job.'

Scared of his mother, but stamping his feet angrily, Nama continued to carry basinfuls to his father, standing atop a three-legger. Mahadev would throw the pods onto the ground and fling the empty basin down with a bang, waiting for Nama to come up with another basinful. Each time Nama was delayed, he'd instantly lean back and light a bidi. When Kautik noticed this, she scolded, 'Either work or sit smoking.' To which Mahadev's wary reply was, 'Why're you telling me? The boy isn't coming with the basins fast enough.'

At one point, when this had happened a few more times, Nama, who had gone to fetch a basin, did not return at all. He simply pulled a cloth under himself and one over from near the stubble heap and fell fast asleep. Mahadev smoked two bidis; then, fearing Kautik, shouted from the top of the three-legger, 'Nama, are you coming with the basin, bey?'

Nama heard him well enough but he pulled the cloth over his head and muttered inside, 'Oh yes, I'm coming. Keep waiting now.'

When a couple more shouts from Mahadev still brought no answer, Kautik climbed down from her three-legger and headed for Nama muttering, 'Has the low-born wretch spread himself out?'

Seeing his chance, Mahadev said, 'Let him be if he's asleep. He's only a boy. Must be tired working all day.'

'Only a boy, is he?' Kautik said. 'Isn't only a boy when he's eating! He puts down two man-sized bhakris, doesn't he?' Pulling the cloth off Nama's face, she shouted, 'Only a boy, is he? Well, are you getting up or you want me to show you what's what?' When Nama didn't make a sound to show he had heard, Kautik gave up and strode back to her place. She said to Bhima, 'Boy, you get on to my three-legger.'

'And who'll fetch me the basins?'

'I will. Who else?'

'And for tatyaji?'

'Yes, yes. I'll supply both of you,' Kautik said in a rage. 'A centipede who loses one leg doesn't become a cripple. That's how it is and what!' She immediately scolded her husband, 'Now don't sit smoking bidis. Go on. Get on to that three-legger. Up.'

'I will if you say so,' he said. 'I was thinking we'd do the rest tomorrow.'

'And who'll go on the next job?'

'Bakhadya's?' Mahadev suddenly remembered. 'Ye-es. I suppose we'll have to go there tomorrow, eh?'

That's how Kautik got through the rest of the work that night. Then she went and shouted at the sleeping Nama. He woke up and rubbed his eyes open. The crumpled ball of the moon that had been over his head when he slept was now hanging by his feet. It was reddish when it rose.

Now it was setting silver. He woke up fully when Kautik snatched the cloth roughly from under him. Suddenly he said, 'Where's my basin?'

'In heaven.'

His tatya said to him, 'Coming home? Get up then.'

She was on the plinth. She had taken the key out of her cloth bag and was struggling with the lock. Mahadev stood by yawning, with bidi smoke coming out of his mouth. His exhausted body was aching. So was Kautik's. She had worked harder than any of them. So she must have been more tired. At the very moment that the lock creaked open, a voice called from the plinth, 'Vahini, when did you come?'

'Who's that? Sukhdev Bapuji. Come in.'

'I can't. You'll have to come.'

'We've only just returned from the field,' Mahadev was beginning to explain.

'Then better sleep!' Sukhdev said helplessly.

'You sleep,' Kautik said to her husband. 'I'll just take a look at Sita and be back. She's got nobody to help her out. Just a brood of little ones.'

Then she asked Sukhdev, 'Haven't you sent for the Mang midwife?'

'She's not there. Gone to Tivase.'

'Never mind if she isn't. Don't worry. I'll come in a tick.'

Primed with the courage Kautik had given him, Sukhdev turned to go home. As soon as he did that, Mahadev began to grumble. 'Don't go,' he badgered Kautik.

But she wouldn't hear of it. On her way out she said, 'Today she's in need. Tomorrow it might be me. You got to help out a cow who's stuck in mud. It doesn't cost you a hand.' And she went to Sita the Barberwoman's house without waiting for her husband's reply.

Kautik hadn't returned even when the sun was an armlength up in the sky. Mahadev, fed up with smoking bidis and waiting, finally sent for her. Even then Kautik didn't return for almost an hour. As she came onto the verandah, Mahadev rubbed his bidi into the ground and said, 'I suppose you were up all night there?'

'Oh no! I've just woken up.'

'Oh yes? Now how are we going to get through Bakhadya's mountains of lentils, I'm asking. I don't understand anything. And the clouds are playing up. And that man, he's like a dog's tail, he'll be after us.'

'Don't worry,' Kautik said as to a child, holding up a reassuring hand. 'I'll manage it all right. I'll bake half-a-dozen bhakris and be with you on the threshing floor in no time. You go ahead.'

'And your sleep?'

'Sleep is not important.'

'Huh! Kill yourself here all night, then go kill yourself there. And if something happens to you?'

'How'll anything happen? Am I made of wax for things to happen?' Kautik jerked the rug from under Mahadev saying, 'Come on. Get up. Let me take that.'

That's how Kautik had run around to scrape what she could out of the season. A mountain of corn lay drying around the tulsi shrine in her backyard. Her grain bin could barely contain her lentils. The groundnuts and sesame had been stored in a drum. Mungbeans and mothbeans spilled out of every pot, stacked one on top of the other, largest to smallest. Verandah and kitchen, inside and out, were packed to overflowing with grain. The only thing lacking was cash. But that didn't matter too much. When cash was required, Kautik would send a basinful of millets or lentils or mungbeans with Bhima, Nama or her husband to sell in the market. Others also came with their baskets. Not all had grain measures. They used the couple that were available turn by turn. With the money the grain fetched, they'd buy their provisions. Sometimes Kautik struck deals sitting at home. She might get betel leaves from the betel-leaf seller in exchange for millets. Or mungbeans, sesame or whatever else and however much she thought she should give to the itinerant beads-and-bangles seller for a mirror and comb or a box of wax to stick the vermillion powder on her forehead. And yet, with all that, the bounty in her home was hardly depleted.

Yet Kautik's spirit wouldn't let her rest. She continued to roam the fields, dragging her boys with her. When the boys complained of the heat, she bribed them, especially Nama, with the promise of school. Her promises didn't take Bhima in, but Nama got taken in each time and went along with his maay. Out in the fields, she made them pick harvest litter, beat down the soil around the stubble, weed out tubers. She got them to collect cotton tree twigs and dried dung pats from the jungle. She tied the firewood and dung fuel in great big bundles and loaded them onto the boys' small heads. At times when Nama's headload weighed down terribly on his neck, he'd complain. Or even cry. If he couldn't bear the weight and Kautik wasn't paying attention, he'd fling it down. Then Kautik would undo the bundle. Baring her teeth at Nama, cursing and abusing him, she'd lessen his load, dividing the rest between herself and Bhima. Now Bhima would complain and Kautik would coax and cajole him all the way home.

She wouldn't let Mahadev alone either. She'd keep needling him with such barbs that home became an impossible place for him. Fed up, fuming and fretting, he would go out looking for work. He'd take whatever work was going. If a wedding was on at some Patil's home, he might help store drinking water there; or he might sprinkle water to settle the dust in some Marwari's pandal; help erect the poles for the pandal or lay out beddings for wedding guests. At times he'd bring home a bundle of wedding food—puris and vegetables, jalebis and bundi ladoos.

The boys hardly ever finished the food. Kautik would send the leftovers to Sita's house. But this kind of work was rare. Most times, Mahadev would trudge from field to field. He'd carry thorn bush twigs by bullock cart for somebody's fencing. Fetch loads of dung manure for someone else. He'd work the sower in one field or plough another and smooth down the soil in a third. Ploughing and smoothing meant leaving home before dawn, as the morning star rose. By the time the sun stood overhead your blood would turn to water and your bones to powder. Then you tied up the bullocks in the farmer's shed and came home in sweat-drenched clothes. Until the first mouthfuls of food went down, every word was a curse and talking was shouting. Lunch over, it was time to stretch out on your rug, smoke a chain of bidis and sink into sleep which lasted till the morning star rose next day.

The brutal heat of the Varhad summer had settled with its scorching arms locked around the village. The deep black earth spewed steam as if it was on fire. No form of man or animal was clearly visible even when they were within calling distance. Behind the heat haze, figures trembled like reflections in flowing water. All living things lay inert wherever they found shade. Animals chewed the cud slowly. Human beings dozed off and on.

But Kautik's toil knew no end. She trudged as usual through fields, trailing her sons behind her, looking for firewood. Wandering through the forest, reassuring Nama when he complained, 'Just today, that's all.'

'You're always saying that.' He spoke the truth.

'But not this time. These three headloads and our drum's full. Then we don't worry about fuel through the rains.'

Mention of the drum made Nama curious. 'Won't water get into that drum, maay?'

'No, dear,' Kautik took the chance to keep his mind busy.

'After this round, we seal it off.'

'What with?'

'With dung.'

As she spoke, Kautik's face was transformed. She stood rooted to the spot. Her gaze fixed itself on Talegaon lying in the dip. She remained standing and gazing for so long that Bhima had to say, 'Come on. My feet are burning.'

'Wait.' She couldn't control the rapidly changing expressions on her face. She stopped even trying, saying to her boys, 'Go wait under that kavath tree if you like.'

'And you?'

'I'll come too.'

The next moment she and her children had dropped down under the tree heavy with raw kavath fruits, every branch bent under their weight. Kautik was biting on her tongue as she lowered herself, her hands gripping her low, bulging stomach to support it. Her eyes were sightless, their light turned inwards into her stomach. Almost before she had touched ground, she shot up again supporting her stomach with her hands. She grabbed the cloth coil on which her basket was balanced off her head, poured water on it and threw it to Bhima. Then she moved swiftly behind the broad trunk of the tree. Frightened at the way his maay had disappeared, Nama bent over to catch a glimpse of her. Sensing his movement, Kautik straightened her disarranged sari and snapped, 'Yes, come, there's stuff to eat here.'

Nama straightened up. After a while, when Kautik came back from behind the tree trunk, Bhima asked, 'What happened, maay?'

'What can I tell young children like you, dear God?' Then, looking at the village again trying to take a measure of the distance, she said, 'Let's go home.'

'Why, o?'

'Stop whenning and whying. I'm saying let's go so we go. Fast.'

Kautik set off towards the village. Ripples of pain surfaced on her face with every step she took. She kept a firm hold on her stomach. Again and again her tongue shot out of her mouth, then slipped back in. When it came out, she'd screw her eyes tight; when it slipped in, she'd open them again. Resting under a gonni tree after they'd covered a field's distance, she lashed out at herself, 'What made you leave home, you bone-head? Best if you'd stayed in.'

'Why, o? What happened?'

Kautik was in no state to answer. When she got her wits back, she said to Bhima, 'Son, run home fast and tell your father I want him here quick.'

'Yes.'

Bhima set off but at a leisurely pace. Kautik shouted after him, 'You skull-head, run, can't you? Other times you got seven horses' strength in you.'

Bhima remained unaffected by this. Since he didn't quicken his pace, Kautik rose and said to Nama, 'Let's go, son. When's that skull-head ever helped me that he's going to do it now?'

They hadn't walked more than two fields when Kautik needed to be in the shade again. Even as she sank down, she was raising her heels to look towards the village. When she sat down, she said, 'Namya, whose cart is that coming this way?'

'Can't make out.'

'Looks empty though, doesn't it?'

'Yes.' Soon afterwards Nama said, 'It's Brewer's, ma.'

'Which? Ganpat?'

'Yes.'

'Who's on the shaft?'

'Looks like Sadashiv.'

'Not Ganpat though?'

'No. I'd make him out.'

As soon as the cart was close enough for recognition, Kautik rose, supporting her stomach. Looking at Sadashiv, she forced a smile of recognition to her face.

'Please can you take me up to my place?'

'Where's the time?' he said, smiling.

'I'm not joking. I really need to be taken home.'

'Why?'

'You're going to get a nephew.'

'What? Is that right?'

'Swear on you, I've got stomach pains!' Kautik was grimacing again. 'Will you take me?'

'Won't I just,' Sadashiv said, turning the cart round and straightening out the crumpled cart-rug for her. 'Get in quick. But why did you stretch it to the last moment, sister? Or is it your first time?'

'Well, brother,' Kautik said, settling down on the rug, 'There was nothing wrong when I left home.'

'Oh really! So that's the sign, is it?' Sadashiv said, in righteous indignation.

Mahadev had just about got into his slippers and was looking around for his cap when the cart touched the plinth. As Kautik stepped on the verandah, she said, hiding the pain on her face, 'At this rate you're not the one to get water to the dying man in time.'

'But Bhima just...'

'Your son after all. Like wheat, like bread.' Kautik paused, then said, 'Stop gawping at my face. Get the cot from the yard and set it on my corpse. Then go ask for a cotton carpet from Sadashiv Brewer's place.'

'Will he give it?'

'Try asking,' Kautik said, glaring at him. Scared of her, he quickly escaped. Taking a four anna bit from the waist-fold of her sari, she threw it at Bhima and ordered, 'Take that, boy! Go get two paise each worth of stuff from Ganpat's shop.'

'What stuff?'

'He'll know what. Go fast.'

With Bhima on his way, Kautik sent Nama to Sita's. Sita left the dough she was kneading and arrived on Kautik's verandah. She asked when the pains had started and whether something had been ordered to make a shelter on the verandah. She reminded Kautik about sending for the midwife. After a while, Mahadev returned with the carpet. He hammered in a couple of nails, strung a rope and hung it like a curtain. A shelter was made. A while later, the midwife climbed up the plinth carrying her bowl. As she approached Kautik, she casually mentioned her generosity in leaving her tea half-drunk to come running to her. As a result, despite the frantic pressure of the moment, Kautik asked Sita to put water on the fire for tea. Everyone got a share of jaggery-sweetened tea, brewed in the midwife's name. The midwife began to make her demands now. A basin, cowdung cakes, embers, she kept on and on asking for things. And Sita kept providing them. When Kautik didn't have something, Sita would ask Bhima or Nama to get it from the market, or from some neighbour's or from her own house. At night, she took flour and other stuff from Kautik's place and made food for the family. Sitting under the light of the moon, Mahadev and Nama polished off a potful of yoghurt and a span-high pile of the reddish bhakris made from newly harvested millets. For the only oil lamp in the house was behind the carpet shelter.

At some late hour of the night, Sita called out to Mahadev to wake him up. When he awoke, the midwife was beating a metal vessel behind the carpet. When its echo died down, he asked what it was. Smiling, Sita said, 'What would you like it to be, brother? Boy or girl?'

'Whatever God gives,' he said blushing.

'Well then, God's given you a girl.'

The end of summer heat was on when Yasodi was born. That's why Kautik kept her wrapped up in banana leaves the first five days. That reddish ball of flesh swaddled in green leaves used to lie on Kautik's cot. Dark-skinned Kautik hadn't turned pale after delivery as light-skinned women did. She looked purplish, wrapped in an oily sari, its loose end wound around her forehead, its tail covering her ears. When she spoke, her mouth, always red like a parrot's beak, smelt of carom seeds.

Every hour or so, Kautik would change the leaves swaddling the bundle lying beside her on the cot. She'd fling the old leaves into the mess under the cot and wrap fresh leaves around the lump of flesh. While doing so, she would talk to the lump with helpless regret. 'I'm doing all I can for you, poor soul. Beyond this, it's up to you. If you can survive, you will. If you can't, you won't.'

This was how it continued till the relentless rain of the fifth constellation came hurtling down. When Kautik saw that first shower of thundering rain, she folded her hands heavenwards and said gratefully, 'Father God, it is only because you are there that my lap has remained full. I hope you will always answer the prayers of this senseless woman.'

Within a few days, the air grew heavy with monsoon wetness. Little black clouds camped immovably in the sky, putting dire fear into the lethargic farmers, who fell over themselves to get their sowing done. Those who owned bullocks and had enough men to work the land, were the first to finish their sowing. Those who lacked manpower fell at the feet of servants and farmhands, coaxing them to work. Yet Mahadev had no work. He'd spend his time sitting on a rug on the verandah puffing away at bidis. Unhappy about this, Kautik aimed barbs at him over the boys. Mahadev understood what she was driving at but pretended not to. Finally one day, Kautik lost her patience and burst out, 'What's this? You tell me not to talk but nothing happens if I don't.'

Mahadev did not answer. Merely looked at her. She changed the suckling Yasodi from one breast to the other and pressed on, 'How long should a man sit around?'

'So, what should I do? You say.'

'Will you look for some work or not?'

'I will I'm saying.'

'When is that?'

'Somebody'll come to call me.'

'Ganpat Brewer came. Why didn't you go?'

'There was a pain in my head.'

'And why did you turn down Bakhadya's manager when he came around yesterday?'

Mahadev's voice grew angry at the tone of Kautik's questions which were putting him in a spot. 'Listen, o. If I said no to one, does it mean nobody else will come to call me?'

'And if they don't?'

'If they don't, they don't.' Now it was Kautik's husband talking. 'Are you starving right now that you're badgering me like you have nothing else to do?'

Kautik simmered down. She muttered to herself as she changed Yasodi's vest, 'Suit yourself. Find work after we starve. What's hurting your eyes is the bit of grain we've got laid up. So let's wipe that off once and for all and then we can pray.'

At this, Mahadev lost his temper and got up. Putting on his cap, he roared, 'Now shut up with that nagging of yours. I'm going. That's what you wanted.' He climbed down the plinth rapidly and went off where he could hide his face from Kautik.

Muttering angrily, Kautik got down to her work. Hitching up her sari, she lay Yasodi on her bare legs and put drops of linseed oil, warmed up with a flake of garlic, into her ears and nose. She rubbed some oil into the soft spot on her head. Next she put a wide basin under her legs and bathed Yasodi, scrubbing her with a piece of washing soap till she was squeaky clean.

Throwing away the water in the basin, she wiped Yasodi and put spots of lamp-black on her palms, the soles of her feet, her stomach, back and cheeks, to ward off the evil eye. Then she put her to her breast. That quietened her and she began to suckle contentedly. She gave up the breast of her own accord once she was full. As Kautik was lowering the little bundle into a cradle made of rug-and-rope hung from the ceiling, Nama, who had been watching all this time with wide-open eyes, blurted out, 'Ma, she looks so nice now.'

Kautik instantly made as if to spit on the air. 'Shut up, pest. Never say that. It brings the evil eye.'

She put Yasodi in the cradle. Pulling the string, she sang,

The sun rides up in the sky,
Widen the cradle
He's fond of cradles, don't cry.

She had to sing more such songs before Yasodi closed her eyes, sucking on her fist. By the time Kautik entered the kitchen, set a pot of water on the fire for the dough and poured a mountain of flour in a basin to knead it, morning had turned into noon. Just then, Mahadev who had left in such a huff earlier returned defiantly and asked in a brave voice, 'Now will you tell me, whose field has work for me?'

'Nobody's,' Kautik said to herself. 'That's how it is. When you don't want to live with someone, that someone is bad.'

Mahadev kept quiet. He began to whisk the dust off the rug on the cot. Picking up the bidi butt he found there, he got Nama to get it lit and sat down calmly smoking and puffing. Mahadev's coolness would not let Kautik remain silent. Without taking her eyes off the griddle on the fire, she said, 'Then at least do something else.'

'Now what've you got to say?'

Deliberately ignoring the irritation in his voice, she said, 'At least take the boys to the school and get them in.'

'I'll have to go all the way to Tivase just for that.'

'Will that also be too much for you?' Kautik was now properly angry. 'Then stay home and bake bhakris. I'll go to Tivase.'

Mahadev smiled secretly at this. Kautik straightened her shoulders angrily. 'I don't find it funny.'

After they had eaten, Mahadev got ready to take the boys to Tivase. As they left, Kautik said, 'On your way back, get an anna's worth of opium.'

'What for?'

'For the girl,' Kautik said in frustration. 'How much longer can I sit at home like a queen?'

'What? You'll leave her at home and go to the fields?'

'No. I'll sit right here swinging her cradle and shoving clods of earth into my belly.'

The boys arrived in Tivase with Mahadev. This was the first time after they'd left Hinganghat that they were seeing a car, eateries, shops. Nama put letter and letter together painfully to read a shop sign that said 'Rambharose Hindu Hotel'. He also noticed the name Tivase at the bottom. Bhima's eyes had darted into the hotel and were now on the goodies laid out in the glass-fronted counter, on the customers eating them, on the cups and saucers in front of them. Nor was just looking enough. He couldn't resist saying to Mahadev, 'Tatyaji, let's go in, can't we?'

'Got something in your pocket? Or is it pebbles and we're off to buy gold baubles?'

Bhima's joy disappeared like water into sand, and he followed his father in silence. A while later, they got to the school. Mahadev searched for and found the headmaster's room. The headmaster was in. He sat with his hairy legs, bare up to the thighs, stretched out on the table in front. A book lay crumpled under his feet. His head lolled on the back of the chair. His mouth hung open staring at the ceiling. From it issued a continuous 'sirrr…phook' sound. When he heard Mahadev shuffle into the room, he woke up with a start, pulled his dhoti down and asked, 'What's it?'

Mahadev, even more confused than the headmaster, muttered, 'Nothing.' Then, waving his hand in the boys' direction, said, 'I wanted to put their names in the school.'

'What were you doing all these days? Sleeping?' The headmaster was now taking care to speak very clearly. 'Why didn't you admit them till now?'

'We did.'

'Which school?'

'Not here. In Hinganghat. The little one was in the first and this bigger fellow in the third.'

'Have you brought their certificates?'

'No, sir.'

The headmaster scratched his legs noisily and said, 'Go get the older one's certificate first.'

'Can't it be done without that?'

'Why not? He'll have to sit in the first. That's all.'

'So he will if he must.'

The headmaster pulled out his books. After he'd entered Nama and Bhima's names he asked, 'What are their birth dates?'

'I wouldn't know that.'

So the headmaster looked at the boys' faces, gauged their height and breadth and decided on their birth dates, which were duly entered. Then, pulling his betel-leaf pouch out of his pocket and unstringing it, he said, 'Tomorrow's Tuesday. Half day. Send them from the day after. They must come to school every day.'

'Yes, sir. Can I go now?'

'Don't you eat betel leaf and all?'

'I do.'

'Then sit down.'

Mahadev sat down. The headmaster peered deep into the insides of his pouch and said, 'Looks like the catechu's over. What's your name? Nama, isn't it? Go to that shop across there and get a paisa worth of catechu.'

Nama didn't say anything. But Bhima did. 'I'll get it teacher.' And he was off to the shop with the anna bit he took from the headmaster. When he came back, the headmaster and Mahadev ate their betel leaves with lime, catechu and areca nut. When they had said goodbye and Mahadev was out of the school, he said to Bhima, 'Didn't we have to get opium?'

'I'll get it. Where's the shop?'

Mahadev told him how to get to the shop. It was on the

other side of the school. Walking in the opposite direction, Mahadev called out, 'Come back fast. I'll be down there, see? In Sheshrao Tailor's shop. You'll find it?'

'Yes.'

'Can I go with Bhima, tatyaji?'

'Why not?'

Nama and Bhima set off for the opium shop. When they were out of their father's earshot, Bhima said, 'Nama, let's have bhajias.'

'Where?'

'The tea shop.'

'Money?'

'I have three paise.'

'How?'

Bhima boasted, 'I squeezed three paise out of the teacher.'

'How?'

'I didn't return the change from his anna.'

Shocked at this, Nama said, 'No, no. I don't want to eat bhajias from that money.'

'You sissy!'

At this point, they stopped to join the crowd gathered around a snake charmer on the side of the street. The snake charmer stood at the centre of a circle of children and grown-ups. He rattled his clatter-drum with one hand, and blew a tune from the bulbous pipe he held in the other. His fingers danced over its holes to the beat of the clatter-drum.

The music attracted more and more youngsters and grown-ups, Bhima and Nama amongst them. When they joined the crowd, the snake charmer stopped playing his pipe and began to untie the string round his basket. As he did so, he chanted his practised rigmarole. 'Boys and girls, sit down on the ground.' Bhima pulled at Nama's shirt, 'Down, idiot.'

'Boys and girls, I want you to clap loudly, once.'

The children clapped happily. Imitating the sound, the snake charmer teased, 'Great. That was some applause nobody heard. I want to hear it. Loud and clear.'

There was loud applause again. The snake charmer was satisfied. He threw his head back to shake the hair over his forehead into place. He dug into his sack and pulled out two equal-sized rings, an empty cigarette tin, a human skull and two bones, each two feet long. With his head still stuck in his sack, he said, 'Do we have a smart boy around here?'

Nobody responded, not even after he had repeated it a couple of times more. Not a single child stepped out of the crowd. Seeing this, the snake charmer taunted all the boys in the crowd with practised sarcasm. 'What? Not a single boy in this huge crowd who's man enough to step out? Shame on you!'

Bhima could hold back no longer. While Nama said, 'Don't, don't, don't,' Bhima walked up to the snake charmer with his chest stuck out. The man slapped Bhima on the back and told him to sit down at a distance. Then, peering into his sack again, he asked in his mechanical chant, 'Son, what is your name?'

'Bhima.'

The man put his hand to his ear, 'Let's have it loud and clear.'

'Bhima,' Bhima shouted from the centre of his navel.

Not expecting him to shout so loudly, some of the bystanders laughed. The snake charmer was happy. 'Bravo! And where do you live?'

'Talegaon.'

'And why have you come here?'

'Because you called me.'

Everybody including the snake charmer laughed now. The snake charmer publicly declared Bhima to be a smart boy and asked him, 'Will you marry?'

'Yes.'

'Who will you marry?'

'You.'

The snake charmer slapped his forehead with his palm and looked around helplessly at the spectators. A moment later he said, 'I see. So you want a wife.'

'Yes.'

'Young or old?'

'Young.'

'One with milk or with children?'

'With milk,' Bhima said, confused. Then he tried to make amends and said, 'No, no, with children,' and got even more confused.

That's when Mahadev pushed his way through the crowd. He spotted Bhima near the snake charmer and called out to him. Bhima came out, very scared. Mahadev boxed his ears hard. The snake charmer winced. Mahadev paid no attention to him. Then he bought opium from the Brewer's shop and they returned to Talegaon.

They passed Ganpat Brewer's house on the way home.

He called out to Mahadev as he walked past, 'So will you do my work from tomorrow at least?'

Mahadev said, 'Oh? I thought you were taking your mechanical sower out today?'

'Don't I need men? What do I do just taking the sower to the field?' Ganpat paused. Then said, 'Your woman came to the shop a while ago.'

'What for?'

'Jaggery.'

'You didn't tell her or anything did you?'

'What about?'

'That I refused your work.'

'Sadya was in the shop. Not me. What's wrong?'

'Nothing. I told her there's no work.'

'You're the end, aren't you?' Ganpat said smiling to himself. 'So you tell your wife fibs, eh? Why don't you sit down for a bit? Have a betel leaf.'

Mahadev sat down. Bhima waited, but Nama ran away. When he came home, he saw that the stream below the plinth was in spate. Standing on top, he asked Janrao, 'What's up? It hasn't rained so why is the stream flooded?'

'It must have poured upstream.'

'What's that?'

Just then Kautik rasped from the verandah, 'Come here, you butcher. I'll explain everything to you.'

Kautik's eyes were on fire. Her father-in-law was sitting on the verandah. Nama had barely got there when Kautik grabbed him by the arm and rained two resounding blows on his back. Then standing him before her father-in-law, she said, 'Now, you bastard, tell me when did I take jaggery out of his jaggery?'

'I...I don't know.'

The old man widened his eyes and said, 'Why, didn't you tell me that day?'

Nama grew scared. Kautik roared at him again, 'Listen! Tell the truth now or I'll throw you into that flood. My name isn't Kautik if I don't do just that.' With that, she began to lay into the boy again.

The old man shouted, 'Stop it! Don't you put your hands on that child, you witch. I know what a fine daughter of a fine, upright father you are.'

Nama and Bhima started school on Wednesday. That day, they made friends with the other boys from the village. They'd known them earlier, but walking to and back from school together brought them closer. On the road to Tivase, they had to pass the Tivase bus terminus. A few days after they'd started school, they were on their way home as usual. As they passed the bus station, they noticed a bus that had just arrived from some place and was spouting people onto the road. Another bus was all set to drive off.

A third was empty. It stood at the edge of the road like a discarded box of matches. The schoolboys looked at it with curiosity as they walked past. But Bhima's feet faltered. He went right up close to it, touched the mudguard, passed a hand over the glass face of the headlights. Trembling with fear for him, Nama looked around quickly and said, 'Why are you touching it, bey? They might beat you.'

'Run off, little sissy,' Bhima said and climbed on to

the footboard of the bus. He looked in and around the bus. Moving forward a little at a time, he reached the blow-horn. He squeezed it. No sound came. He squeezed harder. The horn instantly went 'po po'.

Hearing the sound, a man in a roadside tea shop yelled, 'Who's that, eh? You want me to come across there?'

The other boys who'd gathered around the bus fled.

But Bhima didn't budge from the footboard. He grinned in triumph as he continued to squeeze the horn 'po po po', his eyes fixed on the man drinking tea in the tea shop. Meanwhile, a coarse-faced boy in grimy clothes was approaching the bus stealthily from the opposite side. Suddenly, as Bhima continued to grin and blow the horn, he was grabbed by the scuff of the neck and marched to where the bus conductor sat drinking his tea. The conductor boxed Bhima's ears, gave him a few tight slaps and told him to run along after making him promise that he'd never touch a bus again.

The moment the conductor relaxed his grip, Bhima laughed hee-hee in his face and ran off to join his companions. Nama, who was waiting for him, asked, 'Did he hit you hard, bey?'

'Never. He was just joking.'

And so they set off for the village. At the fork, Sudhakar, the Brahmin's son, asked, 'Which way?'

'We'll go by the dirt path.'

'No. By the road.'

'But that's way longer.'

'If a bus comes by, we'll get a ride, see?'

'We don't have money,' Nama said.

'What d'you want money for? They'll take us for free.'

'Really?'

''Course. We've gone free lots of times, eh Doma?'

'Plenty.'

'Come.'

They set off down the metal road. Sudhakar waved his hand at every bus that came up from behind. Three or four went by without paying attention to him. One stopped. Everyone piled in quickly. There were no empty seats, so they stood. When the bus started, the conductor pulled a solemn face, winked at a passenger and said to one of the boys, 'Where do you want to go?'

'Talegaon,' they said in a chorus.

'Two annas each, if you please.'

Nobody said a word. The other passengers smiled secretly at the sight of their faces. The conductor continued as gravely as before, 'Come on, hurry. Don't waste my time.'

'We don't have money.'

'If you don't have money, off with your clothes.' Looking pointedly at Nama's new shirt, he said, 'Take off that shirt you.'

'But maay will scream,' Nama said, his eyes brimming with tears.

'Then why did you get into the bus?'

'I won't do it again.'

'That's something else.' The conductor said, pursuing Nama now as the main source of amusement. 'Take off that shirt, quick.'

Nama began to cry. He began to plead to be set down and allowed to go on foot. That made the conductor happy. Just then, the driver stopped and called out to the boys, 'Come on, off you go, you little mites.'

The boys jumped off quickly through the door held open a crack by the conductor. Wiping his eyes, Nama said angrily to Sudhakar, 'And what if he'd torn the shirt off me?'

'Never. He always jokes like that.'

But such jokes in exchange for a free ride didn't come their way too often. Perhaps a couple of times a month. But going and coming, they regularly took the road instead of the shorter dirt path, trudging the two extra miles in the hope that they'd get a ride. Even on the Shendurjana market day when they knew for sure no bus would pick them up, they did not give up the hope of a free bus ride. They waved to every bus that came along till they had walked all the way to the village.

One day, Mahadev saw Nama return from school alone. 'What's this? Where's Bhima?' he asked.

'He hasn't come.'

'So where is he?'

'At the Tivase bus terminus.'

'What? When's he coming?'

'I don't know.'

'What was he doing?'

'Standing by the bus.'

'Didn't you tell him to come?'

'I told him.'

'So what'd he say?'

'He abused me.'

'What for?'

'Because I said let's go.' Nama was telling the story in all innocence, exactly as it had happened. 'He said why don't you run off, you arsefucker, or you want a kick in the arse?'

'Where's his schoolbag?'

'In the tea shop.'

Enraged, Mahadev spewed all the abuse meant for Bhima before Nama. 'Let the sisterfucker come home and I'll show him.'

'He won't come, he says.'

'Never?'

'No.' Nama continued innocently, 'I said I'll tell tatyaji so he said I'm not scared of even tatyaji's old man, so go yell.'

'The arsefcuker's head's got swollen,' Mahadev muttered to himself.

'I don't know,' Nama was still being helpful. And then, because it was Tuesday and Mahadev was at home, he asked him, 'Why didn't you go to work?'

Mahadev snapped at him, 'Keep your nose out. Light this bidi, go, if the fire's alive in the stove.'

Nama lit his father's bidi and went back to the kitchen to get his lunch. He served himself some leftover mungbean curry and stale bhakri. Kautik, who had gone to the market, came back just then. She and Yasodi were drenched through. She peeled off her sari as soon as she stepped in and hung it over the hot stove to dry. Then she squeezed the water out of Yasodi's dress and bonnet. As she wiped the baby dry, she asked, 'Where's he gone?'

'He was out on the verandah just now. Isn't he there?'

Kautik didn't answer. She was looking anxiously at Yasodi, shaking her now and then or holding open her heavy eyelids to peer into her eyes. Once in a while she'd say to the baby, 'My little Yasodi, why aren't you talking to me?'

Even after Nama had finished eating, Kautik was still there. Yasodi lay on her lap, motionless, eyes closed. Kautik heard Nama move about. Without shifting her gaze from Yasodi's face even for a moment, she called out to him to bring her a ladle from the house. She held the ladle to her breast with one hand. With the other she squeezed her milk into it till it was half full. Then she described a circle with it over and around Yasodi, still motionless, and muttered something. Repeating the same sounds a few times more, Kautik went to the stove. Picking out an ember of dried cow dung, she put it on the griddle. She carried the griddle to the verandah and set it down on the left side of the threshold. Then she wrapped raw-cotton string around the ladle and placed it on the ember. Kautik returned to her place feeling drained. She lifted Yasodi onto her lap with a heavy heart and a deep sigh and tried again and again to thrust her nipple into the baby's mouth. Yasodi would not take it. Every time the nipple was thrust into her mouth, it would slip out again. At last Kautik asked Nama for a page from his school book. Her lip trembling, she said to him, 'Son, go call Sita aunty at least.'

Sita wet her feet with water from the earthen pitcher outside and came in. 'What's wrong?' she asked.

'My girl won't have milk, o,' Kautik said, swallowing the sob in her throat.

'Why not?'

'I don't know, poor soul.'

'It must be the evil eye. You should've tried the charm.'

'I did that too, poor soul,' Kautik waved her hands towards the ladle on the ember behind the door.

'Did you circle it over her body?'

'That too, poor soul.'

'And she still won't take it?'

'That's what, poor soul.' Kautik dried her eyes on her arm and pleaded, 'Tell me what to do now, o.'

'Don't cry, sister. If she won't have it now, she'll have it later.'

Kautik muttered something. She was drying her eyes. She looked intensely at Yasodi's motionless form, not believing what she saw. She mopped a drop of milk from the baby's cheek. Watching all this with minute attention, Sita said, 'Don't say she's had more opium than she should?'

Kautik's lips trembled. Pronouncing each word with great effort, she said, 'I too was thinking that.'

'How much did you give?'

'Just a jot more than usual.'

'What for?'

'The girl wouldn't stay quiet with the usual amount. She troubled me in the field. So I gave her just a spot more.' The sob she was pressing down from her throat made her whole body tremble.

'Don't cry like that,' Sita consoled her. 'Try giving her paper-pulp water.'

'Tried that too. That too, sister.'

'It'll wear out in a while. Hush. Don't cry like that. Here, let me hold her.'

Sita tried shaking Yasodi. Turned her head about, forced her eyelids open to look at her eyes. Watching her, Kautik burst into a wail. 'What made God put the thought into my devil mind? Was the little one my enemy from the last birth?' Raising her folded hands skywards, she said in a voice of surrender, 'Shadulbuwa, my God, if I, foolish woman, have done something wrong, take me away in a single night, but don't snatch away my fruit, so tender, so raw. If it helps, I will fast five Thursdays in your name from next week's Thursday.'

Meanwhile Sita was trying to help Kautik take a hold of herself. 'Don't say such evil things, you poor soul. If you go to pieces, who'll look after that mite? Hush, Nama. Don't cry now. Nothing's going to happen. It'll wear off in a bit. These things happen.'

This state of affairs continued for a long time. The first surge of Kautik's pain had been washed away in the flood of tears. Sita rose and tidied things around the house. Then she asked quite casually, 'Where's bapuji?'

'Where else?' Kautik shook her head in rage. 'Must be in that exorcist-Bodya's house spinning long yarns.'

'Why? Didn't he go to work?'

'No,' Kautik's tone was sarcastic. 'He feels ashamed, don't ask me why, to do weeding work. And he can't drive a weeder…'

'He can't drive a weeder?' Sita covered her lips with a finger in surprise. 'But that's too much! My little Janya, no higher than my knee, can drive a weeder and you're telling me that…'

'When you don't want to do, you can't do.'

When Sita had left, the pain of Yasodi hit Kautik even more sharply. At last, unable to stop herself, she sent Nama off to fetch Mahadev to be with her. Standing before his father, Nama blurted out, 'Tatya, our Yasodi's going to die.'

'Get off, you arsefucker.'

But when Nama put together an account of Yasodi's state in what words he could find, Mahadev set off for home. He walked fast, kicking up clods of mud. He called out to his wife from the verandah, 'Why? What's happened?'

Kautik didn't reply. When Mahadev asked the third time over, she flared up at him. Then she told him. Showed him Yasodi. Mahadev felt afraid. He put Yasodi on his lap. He shook her. Swayed her. Not a sound or movement came from her. Then he lost his temper with his wife. 'But who told you to do all this, to take that little thing with you to work in the field?'

'I'm supposed to eat air? Or clods off the wall!'

'Were you going to starve today itself?'

'Why should I?' Kautik's grief was edged with anger. 'I'll go roaming from one house to another in the village like you.'

'So why don't you tell me straight what you mean,' Mahadev said agitated, knowing full well what she meant. 'Nama, go get Janya over.'

A little while later, Mahadev asked Janrao who came back with Nama, 'Listen, whose field are you working in now?'

'Today I was in Bakhadya's field.'

'Does he need someone else?'

'Don't know,' Janrao said. 'But you can't drive a weeder.'

'I'll drive the bastard as I can,' Mahadev answered dejectedly. 'So will you ask?'

'Yes.'

Night came. Kautik served everyone their dinner. Nama ate enough to burst. Mahadev was through after half a bhakri and went out to wash his hands. Kautik didn't touch a thing. She and Mahadev began taking turns to sit by Yasodi. She was passed from lap to lap. Sita would drop in now and again, make inquiries, shake and dandle Yasodi, return home and lie down by her own baby. As soon as he slept, she'd put him down next to her husband and go back to Kautik's. This went on till the morning star rose. When she went back to Kautik's after a short nap, she found her nursing Yasodi. She took in the sight till her eyes were sated and asked happily, 'When did the opium wear off, Kautik?'

'Now, as the star came up.'

'You two must have stayed awake all night, no?'

Casting her eyes on Mahadev sleeping soundly on a rug nearby, Kautik said, 'There was just me, alone. Who else in the house is of the child's flesh and blood to stay up all night?'

When Sita lifted Yasodi onto her own lap, the baby was smiling. Sita said to her, 'Smiling now, are you girl? Scared us all last night.'

Again Yasodi did an eager little leap and smiled. Turning away from her, Sita said to Kautik, 'So, will you be coming out weeding today?'

'What will I eat if I don't?'

'Bapuji was saying...'

'Doesn't cost him anything to talk. I'll take Nama with me today. He'll keep an eye on the girl.'

That morning, Mahadev went weeding with Janrao in Bakhadya's field. Kautik got ready to go out to her work with a coir rope and a large piece of cloth, taking Nama with her and enough lunch for the two of them. Nama carried the lunch basket on his head. She carried Yasodi under one arm and a water pitcher under the other. She went to the field. There were several trees on the embankment—thorn and hivara. She hung a length of cloth from a branch of a hivara tree and looped it up again to form a cradle. She put Yasodi in it, sat Nama down beside her and got down to her work. The line of women Sita and Kautik joined began working its way slowly towards the opposite bank, digging and weeding. Both had young children on that bank minding their little ones in cradles hung from trees. Sita's Gunji said to Nama, 'Nama, will you play tamarind seeds? I'll loan you four for now.'

'Then I'll play.'

So Nama walked over to where Gunji was minding her baby brother in a cradle strung up on a thorn branch above her head. Gunji loaned him the promised tamarind seeds and they began to play. Nama kept interrupting the game every now and again to look over his shoulder at Yasodi's cradle in the distance to make sure she wasn't crying. Once in a while, he would throw a glance towards his maay weeding with the other women. But this division of attention didn't last long. Soon he became completely absorbed in the game. He could think of nothing apart from winning more and more tamarind seeds to add to the heap growing beside him.

Half an hour or so later, when least expecting it, Nama felt a hard slap on his back. He looked up. The punishing hand was Kautik's. 'You skull-head!' she said. 'I brought you along to play, did I? Can you see that? The crows are tearing up the girl.'

Drying his eyes, Nama looked at the cradle. A flock of crows had gathered on the hivara tree. Their cawing surrounded Kautik's Yasodi, boding her ill.

Kautik drove the crows away and warned Nama not to move from there. She went back to join the other women again, digging up and pulling out weeds.

ꕥ

She got home rather early that evening. Mahadev was already there before them. He should have come back much later. To begin with, Bakhadya's field was far away. And Bakhadya's workers were always let off quite late. Their working day stretched to lamp-lighting time. By the time the workers walked home, it was dinner time. And here was Mahadev, back before Kautik and Nama. And, to tell by the bidi butts and burnt-out matchsticks strewn around, he'd been there quite a while. Taking in the situation, Kautik instantly asked, 'You went to Bakhadya's today, didn't you?'

'Uh...'

'What's the matter then?'

Mahadev still said nothing. Kautik became fearful.

Feeling his body all over, she pleaded, 'Tell me on my life, what's wrong.'

'What good will it do telling?' Mahadev blurted out in a single breath, like a child. 'That dog abused me.'

'Bakhadya?'

'No. His home-kept son-in-law.'

'And why?'

'Because I couldn't control the weeder. Maybe a few plants got knocked. But this sisterfucker starts off immediately abusing me over sister and mother.' With this, he pushed his head down between his knees.

'Is that all?' Kautik asked patiently. 'Why take such a small thing to heart? These things happen. That's the way it is. Did you eat?'

'I'm not hungry.'

'Is that any way to carry on? Come on,' Kautik said giving him a hand to sit up. 'Come, let's have a few mouthfuls. I haven't eaten all day myself.'

Mahadev was lost in his own thoughts. He muttered, 'I can't do this kind of hard work to start with. But I tell myself let me do it. Better people than me must run to survive. Who am I to escape it? And then someone talks to you as if you were a worm and you want to pick up your cane and bundle and walk right away, down any road God shows you. To hell with the whole motherfucking business.'

At the time, Kautik heard him out without a word. But after a week had passed, then two, Mahadev was still brooding and angry and hadn't stepped off the verandah. One day, serving him dinner and hearing him mutter to himself as usual, she said, 'How much money will you need if you buy goods to sell?'

'If I buy remnants and sew them up, ten rupees will do,' Mahadev said eagerly. 'But we don't have a machine to sew.'

'If you buy readymade clothes?'

'That'll be fifty or so.'

Thinking about that, Kautik said, 'Won't thirty do?'

'Why not, if I have to make do, even twenty will do.'

'It will?' Kautik sounded happy. Then, remembering something, she asked, 'That day Ganpat Brewer was looking out for millets. You think he bought any?'

'Don't know.'

'Why don't you go ask? If he didn't buy any, we can sell him some of ours. What do we want with so much? And the new crop will soon be up.'

A few days after that, Nama and Mahadev began to carry away baskets of grain to fill Ganpat Brewer's bins. They swept and washed their house down, Ganpat Brewer gave them fifteen or twenty rupees for the lot. Kautik added to it Bhima's silver ankleband lying in the trunk unused, and the silver chain around her own neck. She said to Nama, 'Nama, you want your waistband polished, don't you?'

'Yes, you going to do that?' Nama said, thrilled.

Then Mahadev prised open the waistband clasp with his teeth. He tied the rest of his capital along with it in a cloth bundle. He picked up a rug to cover himself and set off for Umravati.

That day Nama was on his way home from school with his village friends. As they got to the bus terminus, his eyes began to search for Bhima as usual. Every day after Bhima had stopped coming home, the minute Nama was ready for school with his satchel slung over his shoulder, Kautik would remind him of Bhima. She'd urge him to look out for him around the Tivase bus terminus. Nama would do as she said on his way to and back from school, trying to see as far into the teashop as he could without ever stepping in.

That day his search was more hopeful. A little while earlier, the schoolmaster had taken the roll and asked after Bhima. The students from Tivase had come up with a lot of information. One of them had seen him around the bus terminus, another had spotted him carrying loads, a third had seen him sweeping the bus, a fourth, cranking it up, and a fifth remembered seeing him washing the bus. When they asked him why he wasn't coming to school, he had abused them and charged at them. All in all, Nama's classmates from Tivase were fully aware of Bhima's existence. Those who had nothing to do with Nama outside the classroom had related Bhima's exploits with great confidence at roll-call time. So on his way home that evening, Nama looked out for his brother with greater hope than usual.

As soon as he arrived at the terminus, he began looking around for signs of Bhima. He wandered around in the neighbourhood, made inquiries in places which he thought Bhima was likely to have visited. The search seemed unending. His village companions got thoroughly bored and told him they wanted to get back to the village fast. Nama set off with them. They'd hardly walked a little distance when Sudhakar waved his hand towards a distant maidan and said to Nama, 'Look. It's the circus, I think.'

'Oh yes,' the others chorused.

Their feet turned automatically towards the circus tent. They looked carefully over the tent not sure whether it was going up or coming down. But it wasn't a circus tent at all. It was Bhika-Bhoya's tamasha tent. There wasn't much to see there, so the boys turned back towards the village.

When Nama arrived home, it looked as if his father had just got back from Umravati. He'd brought back a whole lot of goods. There were cotton socks and vests and mufflers; khadi caps, baby vests, baby-bonnets with ear flaps and other assorted garments in different colours. Mahadev was sitting on his haunches folding the clothes neatly, making separate piles of the bonnets and the vests and so on. When all the clothes were divided into little piles, Mahadev wrapped them in a square bundle. Then he put the bundle away gently in a corner of the verandah. He covered it with a piece of cloth with as much devotion as a Muslim laying his rich, green cloth-offering over a saint's tomb. Then, at last, he came back to earth and asked Nama, 'Boy, is there anything to eat in the house?'

'Maybe. After I ate in the morning, there was still a bhakri-and-a-half left.'

His appetite whetted, Mahadev went up to the food basket. He asked Nama to bring out the oil and chilly powder while he himself reached up to the basket kept in a sling hung from the ceiling. The basket was hardly out when Mahadev dashed it to the floor, shouting, 'There's nothing here.'

'No bhakri? There was some before.'

'She must have eaten it.'

'No. Maay went out to the field before I left in the morning.'

'So who ate it? A ghost?' Taking an anna piece from his pocket, Mahadev said to Nama, 'Go get me roast gram and puffed rice at least.'

Mahadev ate the roast gram and puffed rice and lay down in the verandah. He smoked bidi after bidi and waited for his wife. Kautik came home after a while. She too was shocked to hear that there was no bhakri left. She went on muttering in surprise, 'This is something strange. I had made two extra bhakris last night. I said to myself who knows he may come back from Umravati in the morning and maybe he won't have eaten and be hungry. And now you're telling me...'

'Tell your stories later,' Mahadev yelled, crazy with hunger. 'First boil up some water for tea if you can do that.'

Kautik hurried into the kitchen. She got Nama to fetch her some cow-dung pats from the backyard. She set the water to boil on the fire. She picked up the jaggery pot. The moment she took the lid off the pot, her hand flew to her mouth. Before she could stop herself, she shouted, 'Where's the jaggery from this pot gone, oh mother.'

Then a sudden thought flashed through her mind. She almost ran to the stack of pots standing in the dark corner of the kitchen. She lifted all the pots rapidly off the stack one by one and set them down on the floor. She plunged her hand up to the elbow into the pot at the bottom of the stack. She pulled out a piece of sari folded several times over. She felt swiftly around its every layer. Then she looked at Nama with eyes big with anger and said, 'Tell me the truth now, Nama. You've been up to things around the house, haven't you?'

'What things?'

'Oh?' Kautik said, taking a deep breath. 'I won't tell you what things now. Let that man go out and I'll show you your funeral pyre.'

Nama didn't understand. Nor did Kautik, in her usual way, explain. She angrily flung an anna piece from her bag at him and sent him to buy jaggery. Tea was made. Next she started cooking Mahadev's lunch. It was only when he was halfway through the meal that Mahadev found his voice. He told Kautik about the goods he had bought. She asked him how much he had spent. Dutifully, he gave her the accounts. Finally he spoke of his plan to start selling the goods in Shendurjana from that day itself. But Kautik didn't approve. She told him what she thought. According to her, Mohurrum was coming in a day or two. She suggested that they should make their annual offerings to their family god Shadulbuwa on that day and then start business. As it happened, the next day was Friday. Kautik thought he'd make a more auspicious beginning at the Tivase market which attracted lots of people and goods. Mahadev went along with her suggestion. He finished his lunch. Kautik handed over the wages she'd earned that day to him. She sent him to the Shendurjana market to buy the weekly groceries and wheat and rice for the Mohurrum festival. Mahadev set off for Shendurjana carrying a good large piece of dhoti cloth.

He could hardly have crossed the village boundary when Kautik's anger against Nama, held back so far, surged up. Clenching her teeth, she shouted at him, 'Now tell me, you skull-head, didn't you take the money form the pot?'

'Me? When? Who says?'

'Oh? Who says! Come here.'

Petrified, Nama began moving back, pleading, 'Maay o, really, I didn't touch the pot.'

Kautik was not convinced. She picked up a broom lying nearby and began to thrash Nama with its grip. He kicked his legs and cried as Kautik brought the broom down again and again on his back, saying, 'If you didn't touch it, did a thief get into the house? Bhima's not around. The old man's not been seen eight days. This man just got back from Umravati. So who took the money? The villagers? Are you going to talk or not?'

Nama wouldn't admit to the theft and that was an invitation to Kautik's tongue. She continued to thrash him. Nama's crying brought the water rushing from his eyes and nose. He was finding it difficult to breathe, but he would not say he'd taken the money. And till he did, Kautik wasn't going to stop either thrashing him, or talking.

The neighbourhood children stood watching the scene with fear in their eyes. The more timid amongst them ran away home, afraid they too would get thrashed. The bolder ones stayed to watch. Just then Sita came out of her house. She took Nama's side. Kautik fumed at her, 'Today, he's stolen money from our house. Another day, it'll be from someone else's. What then?'

With all this, Nama was still desperate to have his side heard. 'I…I didn't take it, aunty.'

Sita pitied him. She said to Kautik, 'If he says he didn't, he mustn't have.'

'Look, don't pamper him. Who came into the house, the villagers?'

'Maybe Bhima or someone else took it.'

'Have I even seen that devil's face in…'

'He was here just a while ago.'

'What? When?'

'When you had barely gone to the field, just then.'

'He opened the house?'

''Course. Took the key from me. I wasn't giving it but he said he wanted food so I gave it.'

'Is that so then?' Kautik beat her forehead in remorse. 'And here I was thrashing this child.'

Serving dinner that night to Nama and Mahadev, Kautik said to Nama with even more anxiety than usual, 'When you go to school tomorrow, look out for him.'

'For who?' Mahadev asked. 'Bhima?'

'Who else then?'

'He was seen in Bhika-Bhoya's tent, wasn't he?'

'Who said?'

'Sheshrao Tailor. Met him in the market.'

'What was he doing?'

'Pulling out tent pegs, he was. The tamasha was here. He hammered in the pegs too when it came, I heard.'

'The tamasha's gone?'

'Yes,' Nama answered. 'Coming back from school, I saw the tent was all down.'

Kautik said to her husband, 'Will you go take a look in Tivase? Or the child will go off with the tamasha.'

'Let the bastard go. He and his destiny. You think I'm going to run after that sisterfucker?'

Kautik pleaded, 'I was only saying because it's Mohurrum in two days.'

'Don't be saying anything. Mohurrum doesn't need him to be around to happen.'

When she heard this, Kautik suddenly became inscrutable. She moved around as if there was nobody but her in the house.

Kautik gave Nama a bath on Mohurrum day. She scraped and rubbed his body clean. She plastered his head with coconut oil and parted his hair neatly. Told him to get into his new shirt and made him wear shorts. Then she knotted up a bag made out of a brand new baby quilt from Mahadev's goods. She hung this on Nama's shoulder. She put a red and yellow cloth-tape around his neck and a metal bowl in his hand. Then she checked whether he remembered her instructions. 'How many homes will you ask for alms?'

'Five.'

'And what will you say?'

'Hassain Hussain dhulla,' Nama answered, embarrassed. 'But maay o, what if I don't go to five homes?'

'No, son. We got to. And what's to feel ashamed about it? If we don't serve our God, who will?'

'But Gujji, Janrao, they'll all laugh at me.'

'Let them. You tell them our Shadulbuwa told us to be fakirs. Nobody laughs then.'

'But you first tell them they mustn't laugh.'

'I'll tell them. Go now.'

'No tell them first.'

'I said I'll tell them,' Kautik snapped. Then she said quietly, 'And anything anybody gives, don't take it in your hand. Take it in your bowl and empty it in the bag.'

Nama went round five neighbouring homes with his bag, ashamed and reluctant. Some gave rice, some wheat, some millets and a paisa or two on top. The round done, Nama returned, light with relief. Kautik milled all the grain together. She bought milk and jaggery with the alms. Baked thick flat bread with the flour. Mahadev crushed it into the milk and jaggery and moulded it into round ladoos. He offered these to Shadulbuwa. He burned incense and smeared holy ash on the deity. He touched his head to the ground before the God. He made Nama do the same. Then it was Kautik's turn. She undressed Yasodi. Laid her on her stomach before the deity. She applied holy ash to her own and Nama's and Yasodi's forehead and stomach. Then, touching her head to the ground before the deity, she murmured, 'Lord Shadulbuwa, I am a fool who doesn't know or understand anything. If I've done any wrong, forgive me for it. This big world and its deeds are all yours. If you wish to save us, save us; if you wish to kill us, kill us.'

Later they all made a meal out of the ladoos offered to Shadulbuwa. They ate from the same plate, their hearts overwhelmed with faith.

On Friday, Mahadev put his bundle of goods together for the market as planned. Noticing this, Kautik said, 'I'll be your auspicious first customer. Undo your bundle, let's see.'

Mahadev undid the bundle. Kautik sat beside it, deeply contented. She picked a pair of socks from the bundle. Waving them in front of Mahadev like any other customer would, she said, 'What will you take for these?'

'Five annas.'

Kautik took five annas out of her pouch and put them in Mahadev's hand. He knocked the money on his goods. Cracked his knuckles over them. Murmured something to himself. Then he tied up his bundle and asked, 'Can I go now?'

Mahadev's buying and selling began. On Friday, it was Tivase; on Saturday Mozri. Monday, Shendolay. Tuesday, Shendurjana. Wednesday and Thursday, some other towns. He visited all these places on their weekly market days to set up shop, lay out his goods and sell them. Five or six such market days were enough to deplete his stock. So he'd make a trip to Umravati to replenish it. Then back he went to the markets to sell the new goods.

Mahadev had gone to the Shendurjana market one Tuesday. It was a dark night and he had still not returned home. It was very late and Kautik was worried. She walked restlessly from house to yard and back again looking out towards Shendurjana for some sign of him. She asked whosoever came by from that direction whether they had seen him. Some said they had; others said they hadn't and continued on their way. Kautik was getting more and more frantic every minute.

At last Mahadev emerged from the dark. Kautik saw him more clearly as he climbed the plinth. She also noticed in that instant that he wasn't carrying his bundle of goods on his back. She was on the point of asking him about it when he barked into the shadows over his shoulder, 'Come up onto the verandah, you sisterfucker.'

Bhima emerged from the dark, balancing the bundle on his head, hardly able to carry it. He trembled under its weight as he tried to lower it to the floor. Kautik instinctively made as if to help him, tucking her loose sari-end in at her waist, when Mahadev growled at her, 'No need to help him. Get me a rope from the house first.'

'Why, what's the matter?'

'Ask him.'

'What happened Bhima?'

Bhima swallowed a sob and turned to face the dark. 'But what's happened?' Kautik asked again.

Bhima still couldn't speak. When Kautik asked Mahadev, he told her once again to ask Bhima. A couple of times more of this and Kautik came to a decision. Appearing to have understood more or less what had happened, she dropped the subject and said to Mahadev, 'Let him be, the wretch. You come and have your dinner.'

'No. Let me tie up the sisterfucker first. Where's that rope?'

Kautik neither spoke nor moved. Mahadev strode angrily into the house and came out with the thick rope they used for drawing water from the well. He wound and tightened it hard round Bhima's ankles like a stud bull being trussed up for castration. Next he tied his hands together. Knotting the other end of the rope in a bull-knot round the verandah pillar, he muttered, 'Let me just see, you sisterfucker, which son of a bitch comes to untie you now. If I don't starve you to death right here, don't call me Mahadev Tailor.'

Then Mahadev straightened up and said to Kautik, 'Get going. Don't stand there. Give me my dinner. Now.'

Mahadev chewed his way through one bhakri. As Kautik served him the second, she asked him in a confidential tone, 'Now tell me, what did that monster do?'

'Why do you make me tell you,' Mahadev said, banging down the tumbler from which he was drinking water. 'That sisterfucker was running off with someone's wallet in the market.'

'This, this child?' Kautik asked furiously, waving her hand towards the dark outside where the unseen Bhima stood.

'Yes, yes. This same fellow.'

'And then?'

'Why are you asking? They got hold of him.'

'Did they beat him?' she blurted out the redundant question. 'Now what do I do with this corpse-head,' Kautik cried, slapping her forehead with her open palm. 'Life's not worth living in this devil's clutches.'

Mahadev said in a raised voice, 'The bastard's lucky it happened right in front of my shop. He'd have been in handcuffs otherwise.'

'Oh mother!' The thought shook Kautik.

'So, what did you think?' Mahadev said. 'I begged and fell at people's feet. Any other father in my place would have said if they're taking him to jail, good riddance, eh?'

'You should have let him go. He should pay for his sins.' Kautik was in despair now. 'What use is it anyway to have bittercane in a field of sugarcane? It's better God doesn't send us any children than give us these monsters.'

Kautik continued in this vein till Mahadev had finished his dinner. When she began covering up the leftovers, Mahadev asked about her dinner.

'I can't eat at all.'

'Go jump in the fire then!'

Kautik spread out their bedding. Seated on his rug, Mahadev smoked three bidis down to ash, one after the other. He wasn't speaking to anybody, just staring at the beams. Then he lay down. As he pulled his rug over his head, he took a deep breath and let it out in a long sigh.

Kautik took Yasodi out of her cradle. She lay down and put the baby to her breast. An hour passed, then two, but she couldn't sleep. She lay sniffing and snivelling. Cursing Yasodi occasionally for not letting her sleep. Sigh followed upon sigh. Once in a while, she would look at Mahadev's covered form. She called to him twice. He answered both times. The third time she called, he made no sound. Kautik got up instantly. Picking up the oil lamp from the niche in the wall, she tip-toed out onto the verandah. She went to the pillar and sat down. Leaning against it, she watched Bhima silently in the light of the oil lamp.

He was asleep. He had simply tipped over. His head rested on the base of the handmill. His mouth hung open. A string of saliva hung out of the corner, forming a little pool on the base of the handmill. He was breathing deeply, his stomach rising and falling with every breath.

Kautik wiped her eyes as she watched him in silence. She put the oil lamp down and began to caress Bhima's face, head, back, whatever she could reach, with her tender hands. Through her pinched mouth, she called, 'Bhima, oh my Bhima!'

Bhima woke up with a start and tried to sit up properly.

'No, no, don't,' Kautik assured him quickly. 'Don't be afraid. It's me.' She freed him then from the rope, held him close and began to caress him. Even the flower-light touch of her hand on his back made him whimper in pain, 'Maay o, not there.'

'Why, what's happened?'

'There's a heap of pain.'

'But why?'

Bhima didn't speak. Kautik held up the oil lamp in one hand and lifted Bhima's shirt with the other. Bhima's back was a mess of welts. Red and green ones. Span-long and finger-thick, entangled together. Kautik ran a finger soft as balm over them but even that made Bhima's face twist with pain.

Kautik said, 'With what could they have beaten you?'

'Cane, slaps, blows,' Bhima said in an off-hand tone.

But Kautik wasn't listening. She was muttering to herself, 'I don't know why you let yourself be kicked around. You could be good, eat-drink, go to school, have fun. But no. You must go and get thrashed for no reason.'

'I'll do it. I'll start going to school again, maay.'

Kautik's heart was touched. She smiled and said, 'You're shameless to say that.'

'I'll really go. I'll never behave badly again.'

'And you shouldn't too, child. Poor people have to keep to their place. If you behave like this, there's not a door you'll be let in at.'

Bhima said, 'Yes, maay. What you're saying is right. I agree.'

Kautik was again touched by his innocence. Smiling to herself, she said, 'Come along now. Let's eat, you and me together.'

Bhima got up instantly, as though nothing had happened. He took the water pitcher from his mother's hand and washed his hands, feet and face. Kautik stood by him, giving him light with the oil lamp. She was watching his every little move, sometimes indulgently and sometimes with suspicion. Kautik served food in a common plate and they ate off it together. Kautik continued to watch Bhima's face when he wasn't looking. She couldn't believe someone with such an innocent face could have done any wrong. Noticing how hungrily he was piling food into his mouth, she would murmur now and again, 'Easy, son, eat easy.'

Dinner over, she applied an opium-turmeric paste to his green-blue back. She told him to sleep on his stomach so the paste wouldn't get wiped off. She pulled a soft cloth gently over him to cover his back. He agreed with every word his mother said to him till he was overcome by sleep. She got up from his side only when his voice sank into the sounds of sleep.

For a few days after this, Bhima appeared to have returned to the old life with his parents. He fell in with their world of kitchen, verandah, plinth, Tivase and Shendurjana. He accompanied Nama and the other boys to and from school, resisting the temptation of buses, the bus terminus and tea shops.

One day, while the boys were gulping down their morning meal before rushing to school, Mahadev told Bhima to carry his bundle of clothes as far as the metal road. Bhima readily agreed. As Mahadev was about to leave, Kautik asked him, 'You'll meet me in the Shendurjana market, won't you?'

On the face of it, the question was unnecessary. Every Tuesday, a few hours after Mahadev had set up his shop in the garment row, Kautik would also come to the market for their weekly shopping. She'd show him the money she had earned during the week and ask him what provisions she should buy for the coming week. She always asked him for advice, though she knew exactly what she needed to buy, because she wanted to honour him as her husband. That's why she even sought him out in the market.

Since this had been their practice and yet she had asked him the question, Mahadev realized she had meant to ask him something else. And he was right. Kautik was asking him for extra money for Diwali which was coming soon. At first he tried to fob her off. The Koundnyapur fair was coming up in a fortnight. He wanted to put up a big stall there for which he'd need to raise extra money. He told Kautik his plan was to collect all his income from the smaller markets and buy as much merchandise as he could from Umravati for the fair. He tried his best to get Kautik to go along with the plan. He failed. Finally he had to give in, as always, to Kautik's argument. But he was wary now as he ordered Bhima to lift the bundle of clothes and they set off towards the metal road.

Kautik accompanied them to the point where the road from Talegaon comes in and the road to Shendurjana branches off. Here Mahadev took the bundle from Bhima and set off on the Shendurjana road. Bhima and Nama took the road to Tivase and were soon there, hitching lifts all the way. As they passed the bus terminus, Bhima waved his hand towards the nearby maidan, saying, 'Nama, looks like the tamasha again, bey.'

'Let it be. We'll stop by on our way home. We're late.'

But Bhima was already moving towards the maidan as though he couldn't help himself. Nama had no choice but to go along, his feet heavy, his mind disturbed by thoughts of school.

They reached the maidan. A lot of tent material had just arrived. Some had already been unloaded, while the rest was in the process of being unloaded. Uncoiling the ropes, as thick as boa constrictors, demanded the labour of several men. The enormous tent roll itself, called for the strength of as many men, to haul it off the goods truck onto the ground. Catching sight of a red-faced monkey, Bhima said, 'This isn't a tamasha, bey. It's a circus, I think.'

'It is.' Now Nama's curiosity was also aroused. 'Aren't there no horses and things in this circus?'

'Must be. They're still to come.'

'Yes, oh yes. And there'll be elephants too, eh Bhima?'

Just then, a young boy who was carrying iron tent-pegs on his shoulders, looked at Bhima, recognized him and called out, 'Hey Bhima!'

Forgetting Nama, Bhima strode towards Bashir, the young man. But even before he could get within talking distance of him, Bashir said, 'Where did you go die all these days, bastard?'

'You're asking me,' Bhima retorted. 'You're the one who was hiding your mug. You said you'd come running if they got me. They got me alright, but you ran away, bastard.'

'You think I'm the running kind? One of them got me too.'

'And let you go later?' Bhima asked in surprise.

'Sure,' Bashir bragged. 'When he got hold of me, I gave him such ones he'll never forget. I'm not like you, see? You get two slaps and you're crying like a woman.'

'Two slaps hell. They really gave it to me, sticks, chappals, kicks, blows, the bastards. Lucky my father's shop was right there. Or they'd have got me locked away.'

'You're just a scare-shit bastard. But let all that go. Are you coming to work in the circus?'

'Hell no. My father'll hammer me.'

'If you're so scared of him, best you wear bangles and blow on the kitchen fire. It takes luck to get work like this, you know.'

'What's the daily rate?'

'Full eight annas,' Bashir said, twirling an imaginary coin off his thumb, licking his lips, and continuing in a thick voice, 'plus two meals. Meat with fresh spices and wholewheat rotis. Get it?'

'When is payday?'

'Whenever you want it.'

'No, really?'

'Swear by Allah,' Bashir said. 'The circus stays here for ten days.'

'And then?'

'It moves to the fair in Koundnyapaur.'

'Can I go along?'

''Course.'

Bhima was silent, thinking. Nama saw this and said tearfully, 'Don't go, Bhima o.'

'What d'you say? You want me to ask the manager?' Bashir stopped to ask. 'And after the fair, the circus'll go to Madras. They'll take us, they said.'

'Really?'

'Do I ever fib to you?'

'Yes, ask.'

As soon as Bashir had gone off to ask the manager, Nama began pleading with his brother. 'Don't go please, Bhima. If you go, maay will kill herself. That day she was saying...'

Bashir came back grinning, said the manager wanted to see Bhima. Bhima instantly handed his books and slate over to Nama. 'Take them home.'

'But tatya'll beat you.'

At that Bhima turned on him suddenly, like a tomcat who's been teased for too long, and spat out, 'Now will you shut your mouth and beat it or you want something to help you?'

Thoroughly frightened, Nama gave up on his brother

and hurried to school. By the time he got there, school was over. The teacher had let the boys off early because they were breaking for the Diwali vacations. Sudhakar and Dom greeted him happily on the way saying, 'No school for ten days.'

So Nama returned home with them. He told Kautik what had happened with Bhima. Hearing the story, Kautik slapped her forehead with her palm in despair.

The Diwali vacation was on and Nama was playing on the plinth. Kautik and Sita sat in the dark of the kitchen, chatting away in loud whispers. About chores. About field work. About daily wage work. The old man sat sewing an ear-flap bonnet on the verandah. He had made himself comfortable on the cover of the old tin trunk and was tearing his eyes wide apart to see the gathers he was making on the bonnet. Just then, the thread broke. The old man put his hand under the machine top and drew out the bobbin. He noticed that there was no thread in the bobbin. Looking at the reel on top, he realized there wasn't much thread left on that either. The blue cylinder on which the thread was wound showed through quite clearly. The old man said casually, 'Nama, will you get a reel of thread for me from Ganpat's shop?' Nama said, 'Yes.' At that very moment, Kautik called out from the dark, 'Nama, look after Yasodi for a while, will you?'

The old man knew what that meant. He dragged himself up from his seat saying, 'Never mind. I'll get it myself,' and hurried away towards the shop in a huff.

The old man's action must have had some effect on Kautik. Because she tossed her head scornfully and said to Sita, 'Let him go. I can't help it if he's angry. Why should my child work for him? He's supposed to be their granddad, but don't ask if he's ever thought to give them even a little strip of garment to cover themselves.' Kautik stopped to draw breath. 'Why clothes? If he brings home something to eat from the market, he'll hide behind his trunk and eat it. He doesn't say then, Nama come and have some of this. So why should my boy do his work?'

'You're right. The old man's always been like that. Stubborn.'

'Let him be. If he's stubborn, he'd best know I'm a few times more of that.'

The old man entered the verandah then with his reel of thread. Nama asked innocently, 'Did you get your reel, abaji?'

'What's it to you if I did or no?'

'Hear that?' Kautik said to Sita in a voice only she could hear. Then they continued with their interrupted chat.

The old man Raghunath Tailor was about to sit down when he realized that the thread had slipped out of the needle. He'd normally have asked Nama to thread the needle for him, but now he asked Sita's Gunji to help him. She too had threaded his needle for him many times. By now, all the children around knew how to do it. The job done, Gunji skipped off with the paisa he gave her to buy sweets.

A while later, for some unknown reason, the old man shot up from the trunk. He threw open the cover and began rummaging through the scraps of cloth in it, till he reached the bottom. Then he slammed the cover shut and straightened up, muttering, 'I knew something like this would happen.'

He ran around then, looking under the cutting board, on the machine, down by its pedal, wherever ragged cuttings of cloth lay. At last, having looked everywhere, he couldn't stop himself saying aloud, 'Nama, so some meddling's happened, eh?'

'Where, abaji?'

'Nowhere,' the old man said, speaking to himself but loud enough to be heard. 'If there's been meddling, there it is. My mistake. I had to screw myself leaving the trunk open, didn't I?'

Following Kautik's signal from the kitchen, Nama asked the old man, 'But won't you tell what's happened?'

'Where did that bit of leftover cloth go from here?'

'How do I know?'

'Why would you? Whose son are you and who do you speak like and look like?'

'What, abaji?'

'Nothing.'

'Why not say it out,' Kautik now spoke directly to the old man from inside. 'You said something, so why say it was nothing?'

''Course I'll say it. You think I'm scared of you?'

Reacting to the old man's suddenly raised voice, Kautik first appealed to Sita, 'You decide, Sita. Did I even budge from here?'

Sita said truthfully, 'No, uncle. Kautik hasn't got up from here. I've been sitting here with her all this time.'

'You see,' Kautik said, emboldened with this proof of her innocence. 'Good it happened in front of you, Sita. If this isn't how it always is, you can call me a low-caste man's daughter. Who'd believe such a thing if I told them?' Then Kautik turned towards the verandah and called out in a bold voice, 'I don't know why, but he picks on me like this all the time, one way or another.'

The old man, who'd been silent till now, suddenly burst out in the typical Varhadi accent, 'Let it go, woman. What you wasting your no-good time for? We know you're the lord highness's daughter!'

This got Kautik mad. But it was Sita who spoke, not wanting them to quarrel in her presence perhaps, or just because, like all truth tellers, she had to say what she knew. 'No, uncle. I've been sitting here all this time.'

'Sita, don't you get into this, poor soul,' Kautik said, now raring to go at the old man and in no mood for intervention. Shouting, she said, 'This isn't the first time. Let him go on as much as he wants. He'll jabber and shut his mouth when it gets tired.'

That did it. As expected, the old man's smouldering temper flared. Sparks flew between the two. Kautik stepped out of the dark kitchen onto the verandah. Her hands danced, the veins in her neck stood out. Their raised voices grew and filled the air. Men and women going past the plinth glanced upwards in their direction, their feet hesitating but then moving on. There was nothing new in the fight. It was going the usual way.

Diwali came two days later, but with none of the excitement Kautik had felt the previous year. She did what needed to be done in a half-hearted way. She didn't stay up all night on the thirteenth day of the moon making Diwali snacks. Bhima wasn't around anyhow. But she didn't even ask Nama to grate the dried coconut for her. She didn't get up at dawn on the fourteenth day of the moon to heat water for everybody's baths. She merely circled Mahadev's and Nama's faces with the oil lamp, vermilion and rice salver as a token gesture. And as a gesture, she boiled just enough vermicelli to sweeten their mouths. She herself tucked a fresh sari under her arm and went out to the bath-stone well after the sun had risen. Even as she did all this, she kept sniffling and sighing, and the water kept running out of her eyes and nose. Every chance she got, she went at Mahadev's ears. 'Nama says we'll find Bhima in the circus. Will you take a look?'

The first few times she said this, Mahadev held his peace; but on the day of Lakshmi Pooja, he yelled at her, 'I'm not going anywhere. You go if you want to.'

Kautik let out a heavy sigh. Lakshmi Pooja came and went without her prayers. All she did, because she had to, was make some wholewheat flour and jaggery sweet and set it before Mahadev and Nama. When she began putting away what remained after they'd eaten, Mahadev had to ask, 'Don't you want to eat?'

'I will.'

'When?'

'I will when I need to. Don't go after me about it.'

'Eat or don't,' Mahadev said. 'Starve yourself for that boy.'

Kautik didn't reply. But she gave him a long fixed stare, which made him swallow all further argument.

That's how Diwali passed. Gradually, Kautik returned to normal. She stopped sighing. Tried to stop sniffling. One day, she won her fight against herself quite unexpectedly. She forgot her grief over Bhima in her excitement over Mahadev's business. When he returned from Umravati, it was with a larger, heavier bundle of goods than usual. He opened it proudly for his wife to see the contents. When she'd filled her eyes with looking at them, she asked him happily, 'And you got all this for forty rupees?'

'Forty rupees will buy smoke from an incense stick,' Mahadev lashed out at her, his ego wounded. 'Talk about something more than a hundred.'

'And where did so much money come from, o?'

'The rest of the goods are on credit.'

'Credit? How could they give you that?'

Mahadev's ego took another knock. He retorted, 'How? If a man doesn't have that much credit in the market, why should he call himself a businessman!'

For the first time in her life, Kautik looked at her husband with admiration. That look strengthened Mahadev's sense of his maleness. In a strong voice he asked her, as he folded and arranged his goods the way he wanted, 'So, you're coming to the fair?'

'Me?'

'You and Nama also.'

Kautik covered her grinning face with her sari and said, 'Dear God.'

'Oh yes. You know what fairs are. A smart businessman

never goes without a couple of helpers. You hear a chap say I'm going by myself, you know he's going to sink.'

'But what'll I do there d'you say?' Kautik asked, still smiling to herself.

'You don't have to do anything. I'll sell, you just sit there keeping an eye on the customers.'

'In the shop?'

'And then?'

'I never...'

'You never what? There's always a couple of men in every shop.'

'Am I a man?'

'Women come too. How can a single man do everything? Can he go shit or even eat in peace?'

'Nama can go with you.'

'And who'll cook and clean?'

'Eat in the eatery.'

'Oh that should work out fine. Sell goods worth a hundred, bring home seventy-five and get a taste of the wholesaler's chappals.' Mahadev's voice was full of irritation.

Kautik's pride reared its head now. She said sternly, 'You don't need to get hammered with anybody's chappals on my account. Just tell me when we're supposed to leave.'

'Tomorrow morning. We'll have to leave before daybreak.'

'I'll have to carry food for the road, I suppose.'

'Food for the road won't do. Carry a couple of big measures of flour and stuff and cooking things and plates and all.'

Then Mahadev remembered something else. 'Listen. Is the anarasa dough you made for Diwali still around?'

'Yes, it is,' she replied. 'But I've kept it for Bhima. I thought I'd make him some hot anarasas if he happened to turn up.'

'We're not going to wait around for that wastrel. Do whatever you have to with the dough and take it along. It'll come in useful when we're hungry.'

Kautik's whole family was on the road to Koundnyapur well before daybreak.

Mahadev carried the merchandise and Kautik the cooking stuff. Yasodi slept in the sari sling hanging across her back. Nama carried the water pitcher. In it, lay a coil of rope as thick as his finger. On his head, he balanced their lunch pack containing bhakris and pithla. It was with such assorted baggage that Kautik's household began trudging down the road.

Once in a while, they could hear bells and hooves closing up behind them. They would clamber on to the bank or step down into the ditch by the side of the road to give the vehicle way. They'd turn back to look at the approaching cart. The bullocks draped in back-cloths would clatter up snorting, then pass on. On the road again, Kautik and her family would be enveloped for a while in the dust cloud churned up by the cartwheels. They would hardly have walked the distance of another field or two when they'd hear the sound of another cart coming up.

Mahadev was getting progressively more tired as they walked. Even in those shivery cold days, the sweat would gather and drip off his chest and back. He'd lower his bundle and wipe it off his chest and stomach while Kautik and Nama rested. Sometimes Kautik would say to Mahadev, 'Why don't you let me carry the bundle and you take my stuff?'

Mahadev wouldn't hear of it. As soon as he'd rested enough, he'd continue walking. Soon the east began to lighten. Pre-dawn turned into dawn and dawn into morning. The morning too grew old, moving into afternoon. The sun, nowhere in sight when they had left the village, now hung directly over their heads. Mahadev's halts became more frequent. The time between them contracted. Soon he was resting within earshot of the last halt. Wiping his sweat at one such halt, he could not help asking, 'Why do you think my body's all trembling like this, o?'

'Is it trembling then?'

'Yes, it is.' Mahadev looked down at his arms and legs and said, 'Look how suddenly the hair's standing on end all over me.' And yet, when he'd rested enough, he hoisted his bundle on to his back just the same. That was the last stop. Soon they were within sight of the Wardha river. Crowds of men and women nestled in her curved embrace. Many more were still coming. Handcarts and bullock-carts arriving from all directions were being unloaded and unharnessed. Some tent stalls were already up. Other tents were in the process of being set up, pegs hammered in, ropes pulled hard to tauten the cloth.

Kautik's family wound their way through the clutter till they finally found the row where the readymade garment sellers had set up their stalls. Mahadev fixed his eyes on a gap between two stalls. It struck him as a fine place for business. When he lowered his bundle there, the next door shopkeeper said, 'Don't put up your shop there.'

'Why not?'

'It's someone else's place.'

'Whose?'

'Raghunath Tailor's. He's gone to get his stuff.'

Kautik and Mahadev exchanged glances. Kautik said nothing, so Mahadev began to unwind the jute rope around his bundle of goods, saying off-handedly to the shopkeeper, 'We'll sort it out when he comes.'

'Why be stubborn?' Kautik who had been quiet at first now spoke up. 'It's better to go now than have to go after he comes.'

'You don't understand.' Mahadev shrugged off his wife's suggestion. 'This is a good place. We'll make good sales.'

Mahadev continued with his work. The rope was untied. The base cloth laid out. Then he began laying out the clothes, one below the other like tiles on a roof. Kautik sat at the back of the shop, nursing Yasodi and watching Mahadev with a hard, frozen stare. Nama squatted at the side of the shop or scurried from side to side, helping his father lay out his goods. Soon, the whole shop was laid out the way Mahadev wanted. He stood staring at it with contented eyes. Before he'd had his fill of looking at it, the old man Raghunath came balancing a bundle on his head and stopped before the shop. His eyes dilated like a drunk's to the size of saucers and he asked Mahadev, 'Whom did you ask for putting up your shop here?'

'Ask? Why?'

'This place is mine.'

'Maybe. You put your name on it, did you?'

The old man flung his bundle to the ground. Then pawing the ground as though readying for attack, he said to Mahadev, 'You want to know if I put my name here, do you then?'

Mahadev stood up, sticking out his chest, 'Yes. Tell me.'

Kautik rushed to intervene at this point, wanting to save her husband from her father-in-law. 'Let it go please. Don't start a useless quarrel in a crowded fair. We can put up our shop somewhere else.'

She didn't wait for her husband's answer but began to gather up his goods. Soon he too joined her. They tied up the bundle and Mahadev moved on, his family trailing after him, till they found another site. After the shop was laid out there, Kautik asked Mahadev, 'Will you eat now?'

'Wait. Let me make the first sale.'

The first sale happened at four in the afternoon. Mahadev touched each pile of cloths in his shop with the sovereign head rupee coin that the customer had given him. He muttered something as he did so and cracked his knuckles. Then he said to his wife, 'I don't feel like eating at all. But I'll have something if you want me to.'

Nama filled the pitcher with water from the river. Then he and Mahadev sat down together to eat off a common plate.

Bhakris from the cloth bundle and pithla from the aluminium pan—Mahadev served himself both. Kautik sat in the shop with Yasodi at her breast. Whenever a customer stopped by the shop, Kautik's hand would automatically make sure that her sari covered her head and shoulders properly, while she instinctively lowered her eyes. The customer might take his time looking around, then ask for the price of some garment. Kautik would turn to her husband, holding up the piece the customer was asking about. Mahadev would stop chewing and tell her the price. 'A rupee and a half.'

When this had happened a few more times, he said, 'Get up from there now. I've finished eating.'

'So soon? How much bhakri did you eat?'

'A half or so maybe.'

'Only? Why?'

'Why? Because I can't eat more than I can.' Mahadev stepped into the shop saying, 'Get up from there. Let me serve the customer.'

Kautik got up and went to the back of the shop to have her meal. She ate whatever remained from what Mahadev and Nama had eaten. She pulled her sari more closely round her head so people wouldn't see her eat. Yasodi was asleep on her lap. Nama, who had nothing to do, sweet-talked his father into letting him go to see the fair.

Nama wandered around the fair for an hour or more. He saw the well of death, the mountain-like tent of the circus, the animal house at the back. He stood on the other side of the tin wall listening to the roaring, trumpeting and neighing of the animals. At one point, the urge to see the animals became so strong that he plucked up enough courage to peep through a crack in the wall. He saw nothing but got abused by someone inside. He swallowed the abuse and quietly returned to his father's shop, feeling forlorn. When he got back, he snuggled up to his mother's ear, pleading.

'Maay, will you give me money to see the circus?'

''Course I will,' she snapped. 'I'll just hand myself over to that circus man. Then you'll get to see the circus every day.'

Rebuffed, Nama trailed off to the shop and sat on his haunches beside it, his face small and pinched. He sat looking at the men and women passing by and helped his father and mother when they needed help.

As the day darkened to evening, Mahadev sent Nama off to buy candles. When night fell, he placed one candle at each end of the shop. But, by then, the shops on either side had lit their gas lamps. Some shops even had two. Mahadev's candles were wiped out of existence by their dazzle. Dark shadows devoured his shop. A customer who left the shop on Mahadev's left would go straight past his shop and stop at the next. The shops on either side couldn't hold the crowds that thronged them. Meanwhile, Mahadev sat smoking bidi upon bidi.

Kautik had set up three stones for the cooking fire and was busy making bhakris. Nama kept nodding off, sitting up, with his sister Yasodi asleep on his lap. Even in her sleep, her tiny lips continued to make sucking sounds. At midnight, Mahadev packed up his goods and tied them in a bundle.

Resting his head against the bundle, he lay down without dinner. When Kautik pressed him to eat, he said, 'I don't know why but I have no desire for food.'

Mahadev opened the shop the following morning while Kautik was brewing tea for everyone. Out of the blue,

Sadashiv Brewer turned up there, looking for them. Since they were fellow villagers, he asked if he could leave his stuff with them.

As they sat chatting, he said, 'Good I remembered. Where's your Bhima these days?'

'Who knows where that sister-mother-fucker is!'

'I thought I saw him in the circus.'

'Really?' Kautik asked. 'What was the wretch doing there?'

'What else? The usual. Lifting tables and things. Rolling in tiger cages. That sort of thing.'

'Didn't you tell him that his maay was here?'

'How could I tell him, sister?' Sadashiv asked, laughing at Kautik's ignorance. 'He was in the arena, I was in the audience.' Kautik thought about this and then said to Mahadev, 'Shall I go over and see?'

'What for?'

'See if I can meet him.'

'Sure. Go try.'

'Why?'

'He'll be in the tent. Who do you think's going to let you in?'

'Let them not,' Kautik said, her mind made up. 'They can't stop me coming back.'

'Do what you want.'

'I think I'll go.'

'Can I go with you, o maay?'

'And who'll mind the girl?'

'Why not take her along with you,' Mahadev said sarcastically.

Kautik did take Yasodi along and Nama as well. Pushing her way through the crowds, she arrived at the circus tent. Handing Yasodi over to Nama, she approached the iron gate of the circus and began to peer over it. Sick at heart, she began to walk along the front of the tent from one side to the other, back and forth. A half hour or so later, a voice called out from inside in Hindi, 'What d'you want?'

'Bhima,' she called back.

The man inside didn't catch what she said. Irritated, he asked her again, 'What d'you want?'

'Bhima, Bhima, the tailor's child, Bhima.'

He still didn't get her. 'I don't know him,' the man said angrily and moved away.

But Kautik would not go away. She stood where she was, wringing her hands. She began pacing again from this end of the tent fence to the other, like a caged tiger. Another hour passed and suddenly Kautik felt her hopes rise. She spotted a broad-chested young man, darker-skinned even than herself, who was ambling along beyond the gate from left to right. Kautik called out to him by whatever name came first to her lips just to draw his attention. The young man walked to the gate. He was wearing a white vest and his hair was held back by a green kerchief. He was carrying a bucket of soaked horse gram. Coming up to the gate, he too shouted in Hindi like the previous fellow, 'What's it?'

Once again Kautik pronounced the name Bhima in three or four different ways. Impatient with her attempts to make him understand, he shouted, 'Who? The coolie?'

Kautik pretended she understood and nodded. The young man went off. Again Kautik waited at the gate. A while later, Bhima himself showed up. He was dressed like the other young man in white vest and green kerchief. As soon as he noticed his maay, he whipped the kerchief off his head. Tying it round his wrist like a wristwatch, he came up to the gate and said roughly, 'What're you doing here?'

'You're asking me that, you shameless wretch!'

'Look here,' he began in the tone one uses for a child who needs restraining. 'No babbling here. If the boss hears you, he'll bundle you off.'

'You're scaring me with your boss, eh? Call him out here, let's see this boss of yours. Now are you coming back to the shop quietly or not?'

'Look, no yelling around here.'

'Oh? You've grown high and mighty, haven't you?'

'That's right. Now go away. Go.'

'I'm warning you.'

'I said go.'

'Wait I'll get him to come and...'

'Go. Go and get him. They'll welcome you into the tent, sure.' And Bhima swaggered off, disappearing inside the tent.

Kautik was beside herself with helpless rage. She hurled abuses and curses at Bhima's back till he disappeared. On her way to the shop with Nama and Yasodi, she continued to scatter her curses on the wind, muttering to herself that she'd get Mahadev to straighten Bhima out good and proper. However, when she got to the shop, one look at Mahadev's face and all her anger against Bhima vanished temporarily into thin hair. She just stood looking at him, sad and helpless.

He was still sitting in the shop, but his knees were pulled up erect against his chest, like a couple of sticks propping it up, with his chin resting on them. Kautik asked him hesitantly, 'Why? Why are you sitting like this, o?'

Mahadev began murmuring something to himself without lifting his head.

'Look at me please.'

It was only when she'd repeated the request a couple of times more, that he lifted his head painfully from his knees. Somehow it looked shrunken. His face had turned grey like an overripe mango. His eyes seemed to have retracted from their sockets and turned inwards. Tears floated along their rims. When Kautik saw his state, she quickly took his hand in hers and dropped it just as fast. 'And you've been sitting in the shop with this high fever in the body,' she asked in a tone of authority.

'Then where should I be sitting?' he asked, his voice as frayed as his body.

'Get in there,' Kautik said in a tough voice, waving towards the back of the shop. 'Cover yourself with a rug and keep down for sometime.'

'And the shop?'

'I'll look after it.'

'What do you understand about it?'

'I'll ask you what I don't. Or pack up for the day, so what.'

Mahadev gave way after a series of yesses and nos. He went to the back of the shop. Spreading a rug on the ground, he lay down and pulled another over his body and face, tucking it in tight around himself.

Kautik sat in the shop. Customers came, looked around. If they liked something, they asked for the price. Kautik would hold up the garment for Mahadev to see. He would uncover his face, take a look, call out the price and cover his face again.

At lamp-lighting time, Kautik packed the shop and tied all the stuff in a bundle. She placed the bundle at Mahadev's head. The other shops continued doing business till midnight in the light of their gas lamps. Kautik's family sat in the dark, Mahadev wrapped in his rug and Kautik at his feet. Every once in a while, she'd run her hands over his body. Then she'd ask in a small, piteous voice, her face pinched like a sparrow's, 'How do you feel now, o?'

'Shall I make you tea?'

'Do you need more covering?'

'Don't worry about the goods.'

'I've kept the money carefully.'

'Nama is still awake.'

'Yasodi's just fallen asleep.'

'Yes, we've eaten.'

'Yes, I cooked.'

When all the shops had closed and silence descended at last, Mahadev pulled himself up, laid his head against the bundle of goods and sobbed uncontrollably. Kautik dabbed at her own eyes and ran her hand over his back to give him courage. 'Please stop. Don't cry like that.'

Instead of stopping, Mahadev burst into even louder sobs. In between his sobs, he muttered, 'I'm getting all kinds of terrible thoughts in my mind.'

'What about?'

'About you, the goods, the loan...'

'Don't you worry about us. We're just fine.'

'That's not what I mean. I'm thinking, suppose the worst happens one of these days...'

'Look here,' Kautik said in a warning voice. 'You're not going to say inauspicious things at this inauspicious time.'

Then she too put her sari-end to her eyes.

After a small pause, Mahadev said, 'If I sleep through the fair, who'll sell the goods and who'll pay the credit to the supplier is what I'm asking.'

'It'll get paid,' Kautik said spiritedly. 'The fair's not over yet.'

'But who's to tell, by the time it ends, I...'

'Well, let it end. We're not selling vegetables that we should worry they'll rot with keeping.'

'But I told him I'll pay him soon as the fair got over. If he doesn't get the money in time, you think that man will let me even stand in his doorway next time?'

'He'll get it. The supplier's money will get to him in time.'

'How?'

'I'll take it to him,' Kautik said. 'I'll lay out the shop tomorrow morning.'

And she did too, exactly the way Mahadev had laid it out like tiles on a roof. Mahadev stayed wrapped up in this rug. Her heart broke to see him lying under the sizzling embers of the sun. She began to look around at the other tents, wondering and thinking to herself for a long time. Soon she simply had to go into the next-door tent and ask the owner, 'Brother, will you do me a favour please?'

'What?' he asked without shifting his attention from his customers.

'My man is not feeling well,' she began.

'Oh. So?'

'I was thinking if you could let him sleep in here till the sun goes down a bit?'

'Where do you see any place for him, lady?'

Kautik glowered at the man incredulously till her anger cooled. Then she stomped off back to her own shop. She pulled out a spare rug angrily and laid it over Mahadev, muttering, 'Lord Shadul, you're the only one. Kill us if you wish, save us if you wish.'

She sat down in the shop again. The customers came and went. To begin with, she'd ask Mahadev for the price of goods they liked. But when she realized he'd fallen asleep, she began to take her own decisions.

The first customer who came by after that held out a cap before her. The minute he heard the price she named, he quickly paid her the sum and hurried away with it. The next-door shopkeeper saw the transaction. With the knowing air of an expert, he asked her, 'How long have you been doing business, woman?'

'How long? This is my first time.'

'That's why,' he said, satisfied with himself.

'That's why what?'

'How much did you ask for that cap?'

'Three annas.'

'I'll give you five annas. Go walk through the whole fair. See if you can get me a cap like that for even that much.'

Kautik looked at her husband now. Consoled to see

him still sleeping, she wrapped all the goods in the shop in their bundle, tied the bundle securely with rope and sat beside him with Nama, Yasodi and the bundle by her side.

Mahadev's fever ended with the fair. They gathered together all their stuff and packed it. When they were all set, Kautik said, 'Wait. I'll go and try for the last time to see that wretch.'

'Why don't you give up on that sisterfucker? Let him die.'

Kautik wouldn't have that. But when she returned from the circus, she said brusquely to Mahadev, 'Come along. Pick up those cooking things.'

'What did the boy say?'

'He's run away.'

'When?'

'Three or four days ago,' she answered. 'Come on. Get up.'

'But can you carry the weight of that bundle all the way, o?'

'I'll have to, won't I? Or you think you'll carry it with that fever in your body?'

Mahadev fell to thinking. Meanwhile, she stopped to put her arms around the bundle saying, 'Think afterwards. Give me a hand first.' The bundle was hoisted on to her head and they were all walking again. As they passed Raghunath Tailor's shop, they noticed the empty gap and realized he must have already packed up and gone. They hadn't gone more than a couple of miles when they heard a cart coming up behind. They were about to clamber up the roadside bank when Sadashiv Brewer, sitting on the shaft of the cart, called out, 'Hey sister, want a ride in the cart?'

She got into the cart with all the baggage. She would have been trudging for six hours to get to Talegaon. Instead she was there in two, and not a drop of water in her stomach had moved.

She had hardly climbed up the plinth when the old man at the machine turned saucer-big eyes on Mahadev while saying to her, 'Woman, you don't like me saying things. Then why do you make me say them? When you went to the fair, did you lock the door?'

Mahadev glanced at his wife. She asked the old man, 'Who says I didn't?'

At this, the old man got up and rushed over to Sita's house. When he came back with her, he said, 'Ask her.'

'That's right, Kautik. When the old man got back, the door was open.'

'Well, that's too much I'll say.' Kautik put her hands on her hips and said, 'But you have the keys, don't you?'

'Yes.'

'Was Bhima here?'

'He was. But I didn't give him the keys. You had told me yourself not to.'

'When was he here?'

'Yesterday. Evening time.'

Kautik saw everything. She hurried indoors. She began to search through the pots in the pot stack, plunging her hand into each one. Each time it came up empty, she would slap it on her forehead. At one point, she shouted loud enough for those outside to hear, 'Dear mother, look at that. He's even eaten the anarasa dough, all of it, raw. He has to be a demon's child, what else!'

In the course of time, Nama wrote his fourth grade exam. The results were soon to be declared. But the teacher kept telling the boys every day that they would be announced the following day. Nama would feel dispirited then. All the eagerness with which he'd gone to school in the morning would be lost on the return journey. He'd walk home with sluggish feet. Kautik would ask him about the result even before he got in through the door, and the crestfallen Nama would murmur that it was still not out, his lips working to contain his disappointment. After a few days of this, Mahadev once said, 'The result's bound to be out some day. Why not come with me?'

'Where?'

'To the Shendurjana market.'

'What for?'

'Just like that. Someone for me to talk to. And you'll begin to understand the business too.'

'No please. I don't like it there.'

'How could you like it there? You can't romp around there like you can in the village,' Mahadev said, angrily lifting his bundle and hurrying down the plinth.

Kautik shouted at Nama then, through clenched teeth, 'Why do you say no if he wants you to go with him? Go after him, go.'

Nama could never argue with Kautik. He went after his father, stamping his feet angrily all the way. He caught up with him on the road. Mahadev noticed him but said nothing for a quite a while. Then he said, 'Nama, see if you can manage this bundle.'

Nama didn't answer.

'So is your tongue lost that you can't talk?'

'I'll try lifting it,' Nama murmured.

Mahadev hoisted the bundle onto Nama's head. Nama tried with great difficulty to balance it, but the strain made his neck tremble like the smallest pot on the very top of a pot stack.

Mahadev assured him it was only till he finished smoking his bidi. He lit a bidi then and continued to walk. When he finished smoking, he took the bundle off Nama's head. Nama's neck had gone stiff with the weight. He jerked it this way and that, up and down, till it slowly came back to normal.

When they got to the Shendurjana market, Mahadev laid out his shop in his usual style. He served his customers till the sun went down. Around sunset, a man who looked like a Marwari came and stood before Mahadev's shop. Two of his lower and two upper teeth were gold. Digging into them with a silver toothpick, he said, 'So Mr Tailor, have you made up your mind?'

'Oh God. I forgot again. I'll tell you for sure next Tuesday.'

'You'll have to tell me soon. Otherwise we'll make some other arrangement.'

'No, sahib, please.'

'Well, you heard me,' he said and moved away, bidding Mahadev goodbye with a 'Jai Ram!'

'Ram Ram,' answered Mahadev.

When the Marwari had gone, Nama asked his father, 'Tatyaji, what does he want you to decide?'

'He's been saying if we go stay in Mozri, he'll give me a machine.'

'The same thing you were telling maay about that day?'

'Yes.'

'When are we going then?'

'I'm ready to go now, son. But your maay's heart doesn't like it.'

Nama wasn't sure what to make of that. He didn't want to ask more questions either, scared that his father would shout at him. Soon it was dark. As they tidied up, Mahadev gave Nama a coin. 'Go get yourself something to eat,' he said.

'What shall I get?'

'Anything you like.'

'Sugar discs.'

'Hith! How many will you get of those for two annas. They'll only touch the lips while the stomach waits. Get puffed rice and roast gram. That's for us poor people.'

'What shall I get it in?'

'Get it in your cap.'

The following day, Nama woke up while it was still dark. Kautik was sprinkling dung water on her part of the plinth to plaster it. Her forearms and legs up to the knees were covered in the greenish water. Standing beyond her ambit, Nama said, 'Maay, wait. I want to touch your feet.'

'Nothing wrong with my feet.'

'Hey, poor soul, teacher said today we must pay respects to our parents.'

'Then go touch the man's feet first. Then bow before Lord Shadul.'

Nama went to the verandah. Mahadev lay snoring there. Nama touched his feet without waking him. He returned to Kautik from Lord Shadul's shrine and said, 'Will you stop working now at least?'

'Don't burden me with having to bless,' she said, without stopping her work. 'People get to eat what's in their fate. Nothing else works. Go to school now and no more talk.'

Nama entered the class with his schoolmates. He found the atmosphere completely altered. The boys weren't jumping and shouting as usual. Nobody had put a chair on the teacher's desk with the largest boy in the class, Shankrya, sitting in it and the rest of the class crowding around it. Shankrya wasn't doing a take-off on the headmaster, but sitting erect like everybody else in his own seat, like a statue of Gautam Buddha.

Sensing something unusual in the air, Nama asked Shankrya, 'Are they telling us who passed who failed today?'

'They are and all. Can't you stay shut, you son of a bitch,' Shankrya shouted. 'Else you'll get us kicked along with you.'

Sometime later, a flock of three or four teachers entered their classroom.

The toothless headmaster walked to the chair and sat in it. The class teacher spread the class register before him.

Turning back the frayed edge of his jacket sleeve, he put his palms on the table and peered into the register. So did the headmaster from behind his thick glasses. Then he called out, 'Nama Mahadev Tailor?'

The suddenness of the call sent Nama's tender heart thudding and his body began to tremble. Still he stood up by habit and responded with a 'Present, sir.'

The headmaster's face grew doubtful as he looked up and down. Even his voice sounded doubtful as he said, 'Are you Nama…?'

'Yes, sir.'

'Come here.'

Nama was terrified. His body was now trembling quite visibly. He walked up to the desk on feet that had grown light as a breeze. As he stood there, the class teacher's hand fell on his back with the softness of a flower. Soon the headmaster's hand replaced the teacher's. He said, 'Who helps you at home with your studies?'

'Nobody, sir.'

'Do your people own a field and all?'

'Where'd they get that from, sir?' It was the teacher who spoke instead of Nama. 'His parents are daily-wage workers.'

'Is that right?'

'Yes, sir.'

'This year, he didn't even have all the books he needed.'

'Why didn't you buy them?'

'In last year's drought, maay couldn't manage the money. And tatyaji said if you don't have books, don't go to school.'

When he heard this, the headmaster's admiration for

the boy surged up. He put his arm around him. He said to the other boys in the class, 'Did you hear that, you louts? He's no bigger than a twig but he's stood first in the class. That's what learning means.' The headmaster stopped suddenly. He was looking at Shankrya who was bending his forefinger backwards like he was shooting marbles. The headmaster roared, 'You pig. Eat this fellow's shit. You've been four years in the fourth.' Then he turned to Nama again and said, 'Well, want to go on with school?'

'I'll have to ask maay.'

'Ask. But go to the English teaching school. I'll try to get you a freeship.'

'But the books in the English school cost a lot, no?'

'Not too much. I'll give you what you want from my own salary. Will that do?'

'Really?'

'Yes. You have a father, don't you?'

'Yes.'

'Then tell him to meet me. Tell him Kasar teacher wants to see you urgently.'

'Yes, I will.'

As soon as the results of the village boys were announced, they left without waiting to hear their other classmates' results. Nama hurried home with them. That day, Nama and Sudhakar who had passed, decided to go home by the dirt track instead of waiting for the bus. Nama couldn't wait to get home as early as possible to tell his father and mother of his achievement. His feet moved as fast as they could through the mud.

When the village was still about four fields away, Nama

spied Bhima coming towards them. There was a clearly visible crescent of down below his nose now. As soon as he was near enough, Nama barred his way and said, 'Bhima, I passed my fourth, I did.'

'Good,' Bhima responded. 'Now move,' he said, brushing past him.

Nama felt hurt. He flung curses at Bhima's back and muttered more under his breath. But he'd hardly gone a dozen paces or so when he heard Bhima call, 'Come here, bey.'

Nama couldn't refuse, seeing the look in Bhima's eyes. He went towards him, stamping his feet sulkily. Bhima said, 'Do something for me.'

'What?'

'Keep this pack of cards with you for some time.'

'But these are ganjifa cards for gambling.'

'So, you son of an oaf, that's what they are.'

Then he drew something else out of his pocket. Putting a two-anna bit in Nama's hand, he said, 'Get yourself something to eat.'

Nama's anger cooled. Waving the brand new pack of cards at Bhima, he asked, 'Where shall I keep this?'

'In your satchel. And don't let the old woman see them.'

'Old woman? Which old woman?'

'Maay, you idiot. Don't you understand simple things? Go, run.'

'Was maay at home?'

'I don't know.'

'And tatya?'

Bhima flew into a rage. 'You think I keep a watch on those motherfuckers?'

Nama didn't understand, and seeing the general state Bhima was in, he didn't want to try. He simply turned about and continued on his way. As he passed through the village common, he saw a crowd of boys gathered around Yesonta like ants around jaggery. Yesonta's cap was pulled over his forehead. His hand slapped the beat of the song he was singing on his bare thigh. '*Bits of glass on a sharp stick/ Won't you come up to my attic*,' he sang. When Nama and the other boys came up, he plunged his hand in his pocket and brought up a fistful of change. 'Take that, fellows. Go eat your fill.'

'What for?'

'Celebrate,' one of the boys in the crowd said. 'Yesonta won a pile in cards.'

'How much?'

'Ten rupees.'

'From?'

'Nama's brother.'

'Shut up. My brother doesn't gamble,' Nama rushed to take Bhima's side. 'And where would he get so much money from?'

The other boys laughed. What more could Nama say? He went home without a word. He climbed the plinth and entered the verandah. The kitchen door was closed. Yasodi was asleep in the open verandah, on the floor, her thumb in her mouth as always. Beside her stood a clay dish containing a soggy hash of bhakri and gravy set out to dry. A stream of water had trickled out from underneath Yasodi, stopped short of the dish and dried up.

Nama went straight to Sita's house. As she gave him

the keys, she said, 'Your mother's kept some milk pudding in the stone bowl. She wants you to have it.'

'Just me?' he asked, overjoyed.

'No, Yasodi and you.'

Nama returned home on feet that were in tune with his joy. He unlocked the door and walked into the darkness of the kitchen, groping to find his way. Suddenly he tripped over something. It was the stone bowl, the one that had held the pudding, but empty now except for a little water as if somebody had washed his hands in it. Giving up on the pudding, Nama placed an upturned iron basin beneath the hanging sling. He reached up to lift the basket out of it. There wasn't a scrap of anything in it. He returned to the verandah wondering what to do. He waited for an hour for his maay to return, then another half an hour. Finally he picked up the clay dish from beside Yasodi, carried it indoors and finished off all the hash that was in it.

Kautik climbed up the plinth as the sun set. She flung down the sheaf of lentil stalks she was carrying on her head. Leaning against the wall of the verandah, she wiped the sweat off her face with her sari-end. The first words she uttered were, 'Did you eat?'

'Where was the bhakri?'

'Go look with my eyes.'

'There isn't any.'

'What? No bhakri?' Then she asked, 'And how did you like the pudding?'

'I didn't have any.'

Kautik was struck by a thought. Shaking Yasodi awake, she asked, 'Was Bhima here?'

Nama answered, 'Yes.'

'That's it. That son of a pig must have eaten everything. Never mind. I'll roast you some bhakris this minute.'

She sat down to roast bhakris. She kneaded the flour, Nama snapped the stalks off the chillies. Then he remembered and said, 'Maay, I passed.'

'Really?'

'Swear on you.'

Then Nama described to his maay everything that had happened in class. Kautik's eyes gleamed with pride as she listened. She had to ward off the evil eye. So she circled Nama's face with her dough-covered hands and cracked her knuckles at her temples. 'You must pass every year. Study well and become a big man.'

Taking this opportunity, Nama quickly said, 'Maay, headmaster said I should go to an English teaching school now.'

At that Kautik heaved a deep sigh. She said wistfully, 'Tell him we're not that lucky. It's hard enough doing what we're doing. An English school means lots of money...'

'Not lots. Kasar sir said he'll get me a freeship.'

'And what about your textbooks and notebooks?'

'Teacher will give me those too he was saying.'

'Really?'

'Swear on you.' Then Nama pleaded for all he was worth, 'You'll let me go to English school, won't you?'

'You really want to go on studying, no?'

'Yes, maay o. I want so much to learn English.'

'Let me think about it.'

'And Kasar teacher wants tatyaji to go meet him. You'll send him, no?'

'I will.'

When Mahadev got back home with his pack of goods, Kautik proudly gave him Nama's big news as she served him dinner. Mahadev listened to the story. His eyes filled with pride as he looked at Nama. But soon his tongue was rolling slyly in his cheek. And when the story ended, he stopped between two gulps of water to say, 'Well, whose son is he!'

Glancing at him from the corner of her eyes, Kautik said, 'Not only yours.'

''Course.'

''Course,' Kautik teased. 'And that older smartass? He's also only yours, isn't he?'

'Think of it, where is that sisterfucker?'

'Somewhere around in some ghoul-place. He was here a couple of days ago. Scraped all the pots clean.'

'I never get to set eyes on him, dead or alive, the sisterfucker.'

'That's how worried you are about him.'

'Oh yes! I should give up all my work and go worrying after him now.'

'Why? Let the stud run at large through the village.'

'Look here, don't bother me with your nig-nag when I'm eating.'

Kautik kept quiet, sensing the irritation in Mahadev's voice.

But as she continued to serve him, her face was flaming with anger. After dinner, Mahadev settled on the cot. Kautik sat making up a betel leaf for him. As she unrolled the betel-leaf pouch, Mahadev took the bidi out of his mouth and said, 'I just remembered. I met Natthuseth again this Tuesday.'

Kautik lowered her head. Without responding to him by a single word, she began cracking areca nut with the nut-cracker a little more forcefully than required.

Looking at her through narrowed eyes, Mahadev muttered, 'I said something.'

'Maybe you did.'

Mahadev pulled deep on his bidi. He took his right leg off the left and placed the left over the right for something to do. Then shaking both legs rapidly, he said, 'That's all you have to say?'

Mahadev's tone and expression riled Kautik. She fixed him with a stare and was about to say something dreadful when she heard a movement on the verandah that cooled her temper whether she liked it or not. The old man had walked in. He had set down his load and had bent to unlock his truck. The next moment he started up. Stomping off instantly to Sita's house, he dragged her and her husband over by the hand. Holding the oil lamp up over the bolt and chain of the trunk, he said loudly, 'Look at that lock. Do you see it?'

'It's open,' Sita said awkwardly.

'Give me two blows with your chappals if it isn't,' the old man said, raising his voice further. 'You two, husband-wife, are always taking her side. Now open your eyes and see her deeds. Or you'll say what terrible things the old man says.'

At that, Kautik pushed Mahadev aside and came to stand in the kitchen doorway. Resting one hand on the door jamb, she took in the scene on the verandah with dilated eyes. Standing with her hands on her lips, she made Sita very nervous. Uncomfortably trapped, Sita muttered something like 'What can we outsiders say...'

Kautik couldn't stay silent any longer. She said to the old man, 'You want to say something about someone, why don't you name the person straightaway?'

'Am I scared of your old father that I shouldn't name names,' the old man shouted, trembling with anger.

'I'm warning you, father-in-law. You'd best not bring my people into this.'

'Don't try and scare me with those eyes. One blow and I can make you forget how to make big eyes. Don't take me for Mahadev, see?'

'Why do you drag his name in for no reason?'

'Lord, what a devoted wife,' the old man mocked dancing his fingers before Kautik. 'If you're such a great wife, why did you bring him back here? Wasn't it you who took that stupid ox away to your mother's house? So why didn't you blinker him and put him to the threshing wheel, hanh?'

Before he could complete what he was saying, Mahadev threw Kautik's hand off the door jamb and pushed his way out. 'What's this scene you're making?' he asked the old man.

'So you've turned up to open your big mouth for your wife.'

'Look, look, look, you're saying more things than I'll take. Don't tell me later I didn't warn you.'

'You trying to threaten me? And I'm going to run from a woman's man like you?'

'Are you going to shut your mouth or...' Mahadev said, taking two steps towards him.

Kautik stopped him saying, 'Go in. Don't get into a useless fight.'

The old man too said the same thing but in a way that was aimed at insulting Mahadev's manhood. 'Yes, go. Go in. Put bangles on your wrists and sit by the cooking fire.'

'Are you going to shut up or not, you crooked face!'

'Shall I show you what a crooked face looks like?'

Shaking off his wife's hold, Mahadev said, 'Do that.'

'Watch out, Mahadya.'

'I'm watching. You just tell me.'

'Don't dare me.'

'I'm daring you, you old bag.'

The next moment, a pair of scissors flew off the machine top over Kautik's shoulder and hit Mahadev on the forehead, a little above the eyes. Mahadev instantly began to do sit-ups like a man possessed. He became impossible for Sita, Kautik and Sukhdev to control. Struggling with them, Mahadev shouted at the old man, 'If I don't kill this old bag now, don't call me Mahadev Tailor.'

The other three managed at last to push him indoors but he continued to shout, 'He can't escape me now, the arsefucker. I'll get him one of these days.'

Kautik wasn't silent either as she pushed Mahadev down on the cot. She was answering the old man on the verandah word for word, dismissing everything he said. Neither of them was willing to give up. Afraid that the quarrel that had seemed to be dying down might flare up again, Sita and Sukhdev stayed out on the verandah out of neighbourly duty. Sita was in the kitchen trying to calm Kautik down. Sukhdev was saying to the old man on the verandah, 'Bhima must have broken the lock. Why would she do it...'

The old man answered with real feeling, 'If it was a few rupees that'd just be a scratch. But twenty-five rupees is a wound. I denied myself and worked hard to put away that money. It wasn't ill-gotten that I should keep quiet now.'

Indoors, Kautik said, as she wiped the blood off Mahadev's forehead, 'He's after our life. As though it's us that's telling that wretch to...'

The wound Mahadev sustained with the blunt pair of scissors that the old man had flung at him wasn't even big enough to be called a wound. It was a barely visible cut on his eyebrow. The point of the scissors had taken off some hair leaving a bare patch the size of a tamarind seed. But that was excuse enough for Mahadev to stay home for the next fifteen days. As soon as Kautik went to the fields, he'd go off into the village, to spend time in Brewer's shop or sit with the village medicine man. By the end of fifteen days, the wound had healed completely with Kautik's treatment of turmeric and opium paste. But the skin was scarred and the bare patch still bare. Nor was hair ever going to grow on it, so it would always look like a streak of leucoderma. Kautik began to nag him now about his staying home. Finally, he beat the layers of dust off his bundle of goods and resumed visiting the markets.

Now, every time he returned from the market,

particularly from Shendurjana, he'd tell Kautik about meeting Natthuseth. She would lose her temper instantly and start arguing angrily with him. The minute she heard Natthuseth's name, her face would grow hard and Mahadev's hopes would come crashing down. He'd mutter to himself, but loud enough for her to hear, 'Man thinks to do one thing but God plans it differently. What can you do, Mahadya, if it's written in your fate that you'll trudge from one village to another all your life like a stray dog?'

Kautik put up with this for as long as she could. Then she decided to speak out the thoughts that had been smouldering in her mind all along. She began by saying, 'You talk as if you're going to be freed from jail. Man must think out what he wants to do. Nothing comes from hurry and scurry.'

Kautik would have said much more but Mahadev's dream for the future now found voice. 'You talk of hurry and scurry,' he said. 'But that Natthuseth has been after me these two months and every Tuesday I tell him I'll think about it and tell him the next week and you're talking of my hurry and...'

'Go on then. Do what you like.'

He wasn't happy with Kautik's curt consent. He said, 'Do you think I'd be doing something wrong? Don't you think I want some good to come to us?' Kautik said nothing to this. So he continued in a more enthusiastic voice, 'I thought if that Natthuseth gives me a machine, I can teach the two boys the trade. We'll make enough to fill our bellies, and then if we're careful and god's with us, we'll even have an acre or so of land in a couple of years. But that's a far-off thing. For now, there'll at least be comfort in our lives.'

Kautik said irritably, 'That's why I am telling you to do what you like. Ask a man where he eats? In a tea shop. Where he sleeps? In a motorbus. It's only us wretched women who have all the problems.'

'Hey, but there must be women there too, no?' Mahadev said, getting what Kautik was hinting at. 'Or do they all come to Talegaon to have their babies?' Then he said abruptly, 'Look, why don't you say straight off that you don't want to leave Talegaon?'

'Dear mother, listen to that. What kind of man...here's me talking straight...'

After this, neither of them said a word. Finally, Mahadev spoke as a last attempt. Grinding the butt of his bidi into the ground, he said, 'So you're saying you don't want to come, hunh?'

'Did I say that?' Kautik now wanted to make up. 'I only needed to know what you've done for a place to stay there.'

'Sethji said he'll arrange something.'

'Have you seen the place?'

'What's the need? A place is a place.'

'And the machine?'

'Haven't seen it.'

'That's good,' Kautik said tartly. 'So when do we go?' Then added, 'I'd say let's take the road tomorrow.'

Ignoring Kautik's sarcasm, Mahadev said, 'Get ready then.'

After weeks of tension between the two, Mahadev had finally won. He agreed to leave his village with wife and children for Natthuseth's, for the temptation of owning the old machine he'd been promised. They decided to leave on Friday, an auspicious day. Meanwhile, Kautik began to pack whatever household goods they possessed. She tied up everything in packets, from salt and oil to flour. While she worked in the house, she sent Nama off to Tivase at daybreak everyday. He hated making the long trip there and back in the sun for no reason. But he'd go all the same, sometimes in fear of his maay, sometimes tempted by the half-anna she gave him and sometimes for the joy of his friends' company if they were going that way. He'd look for Bhima wherever he thought he might find him. The minute Kautik saw him come up the plinth, she'd ask, 'Well, did you meet him today at least?'

'Did you even find out where exactly he's gone?'

'You should have asked in the tea shops and all.'

One day, Nama reported, 'A boy in a tea shop said Bhima went off to Umravati in a truck carrying oranges.'

On Friday, after Mahadev had had tea, the cart rolled up to the plinth. He, Kautik and Nama began to load their luggage onto it. Sukhdev, the cart man, stood in the cart arranging things properly. When all the stuff was loaded, he began to secure it with a hemp rope. Mahadev made a last trip into the house to check if they'd left anything behind, and returned with a large pot. As he crossed the verandah, he upturned the pot to empty it of the last drops of water. Sitting on the verandah watching him, the old man hissed, 'I'm telling you nicely now, don't touch that pot.'

'Why not?'

'Did it come from your earnings?'

'Did it come from yours then?'

'At least it was my father's.'

'I guess I don't have a father.'

'That's right. And I don't have a son. Now put that pot down quietly, understand?'

'And what if I don't?'

'I'll see how you don't…'

Kautik grabbed the pot from her husband's hand then and banged it down on the ground. She said to her father-in-law, 'No need to see anything. Here. Take it with you when you die.'

With that, she went quickly down the plinth. She set Yasodi on the pile of rugs in the cart and the cart began to roll. The cartman drove it and Mahadev walked beside it, chatting with him. He was carrying a bottle of cooking oil in one hand and a bottle of kerosene in the other, swinging them as he went. Kautik was still talking to the neighbouring women who had gathered around her. Sita stopped dabbing at her eyes and asked, 'When will you come back to Talegaon now?'

'Why should she come back here?' said Basanti from next door.

Kautik said with certainty, 'Why shouldn't I? This is my home village after all. Even a king won't do for you what your home village does. What do you say, Sita o?'

'That's the truth.'

'Sita, my sister, do one thing for me.'

'What?'

'If my Bhima comes, tell him that…' she paused, then

said, 'and if of an evening he comes hungry, give him something to eat. I'll go now. Basanti, I'm going. Rukhma, I'm off. Don't forget me, o...'

Kautik and Nama left their village behind. Mahadev was waiting for them under a neem tree. Though the twists and turns in the road hid the cart from view, the rattle of its wheels and sound of the bullock bells told of its being within call. Kautik had barely got to the neem tree when Mahadev said to her, 'Listen, can you carry these bottles for a while?'

'Dear Lord, now even the bottles are too heavy for you! Give.'

'They're not heavy,' he said as he walked on. 'It's my hands. I feel as if they've gone numb.'

'What?'

'Now how can I tell you what. Look, I was carrying those bottles, but I didn't feel I was carrying anything.'

'How long have you felt like this?'

'I felt a little like it last summer. I stopped feeling it when the rains came. I'm feeling it again now, after the heat set in.'

'Dear mother. Now this is something new, I'll say.'

'It is and all!' Then he asked helplessly, 'Why do I feel like this?'

'How can I tell? I never saw it nor heard it before.'

Meanwhile, Sukhdev had stopped his cart and was waiting for them. 'What's all this chatting, sister?' he shouted back at them. 'Why don't you get in the cart?'

She got into the cart. Within an hour after that, they were crossing the river and entering Mozri. Mahadev made inquiries and traced Natthuseth's house. They halted nearby in the shade of a neem tree while Sukhdev let go of the reins and sat on the shaft of the cart smoking a bidi. Everybody's eyes were fixed on Natthuseth's mansion and the spot where Mahadev had disappeared into it.

Sometime later, they saw him emerge and walk lightly towards the cart. Kautik asked him urgently even before he reached them, 'So, what does he say?'

Mahadev took a bidi and matchstick out of his pocket in a leisurely way; then said with similar lack of haste, 'They say Seth is not in the village.'

'Now what's this, dear mother,' Kautik exclaimed. Putting her hands on her lips, she said, 'Where's he gone do they say?'

'To Umravati.'

Kautik sank to the ground. A few minutes later, Sukhdev said to Mahadev, 'But he must've left word about your place and all.'

'They say no.'

Putting her palm to her forehead, Kautik asked, 'When will he come back?'

'In two or three days.'

Nobody spoke for a while after that. They didn't even look at each other. Then Sukhdev said in a resigned voice, 'All right. Get in the cart, sister.'

'What for?' Kautik asked, squinting up at Sukhdev without moving her hand from her forehead.

'Back to the village.' Then he turned to Mahadev, 'What d'you say?'

'What else,' Mahadev answered in an easy tone.

'You can go back like some flighty gadfly. I didn't want to leave in the first place...'

Kautik's voice showed she was still dazed from the shock.

Some more time passed in this state of numbness. Then Sukhdev felt compelled to ask, 'So what do we do now, Mahadev?'

Mahadev lit another bidi. Sukhdev repeated his question a couple of times more. Finally it was Kautik who answered. 'He won't say a thing now. I'll tell you. We're not going back.'

'Where will you stay here?'

'We'll find a place on somebody's verandah. Or we'll roast our bhakris and eat them under some tree for a few days. A dead man finds space. Why not the living?'

Sukhdev was shocked. He looked around. Then making up his mind, he said, 'You're sure you're not coming to Talegaon?'

'Yes.'

Then they set to unloading all the stuff from the cart. Standing on the shaft of the empty cart, Sukhdev said, 'I'll be off then, sister.'

'Wait. I'll make some tea.'

Sukhdev laughed. Turning the cart around, he said, 'At such a time? You want to kill me with shame?'

He had placed his hand on the bullocks' tails when Kautik got up hastily and said to him in a secret voice, 'Brother, don't tell anybody in the village what's happened to us, swear on my life.'

Sukhdev reassured Kautik and drove away. Kautik

returned to the shade of the tree. Mahadev settled down more comfortably and lit another bidi but without looking at Kautik. He didn't have the guts. Neither of them spoke, so Nama asked, 'Ma, where's our house?'

Kautik stared at Mahadev and waved a hand towards the Marwari's mansion, 'There it is. That mansion is ours. Soon we're going to buy land as well.'

Mahadev smiled to himself. Kautik tossed her head and said, 'I don't feel like laughing and all. This is why man shouldn't give up a half to run after a full.'

Mahadev grew solemn. He stared blankly at the smoke billowing out to his mouth. A while later, Kautik said, 'Don't sit there smoking now. Go beg a few feet of shade for us from someone till Sethji comes back.'

'Not me.'

Kautik clapped her palm to her forehead again. Mahadev sat staring up into the tree, at the still raw neem fruit. Kautik watched him with a mixture of anger and pity. After a long time, she got up with a deep sigh of resolve. Taking Nama with her for company, she approached an ironsmith sitting at his bellows. The man, about Mahadev's age, was flipping a glowing piece of iron over and over on his anvil. A grown-up girl was hammering it with a sledgehammer. She wore a printed kameez, patched in several places with scraps from an old dhoti. The underarms of both sleeves were drenched in sweat. She stopped hammering when Kautik and Nama approached. She wiped the sweat off her cheeks and forehead with her sleeve. Kautik stood cooling her feet under the shady eaves of their house. She asked the girl, 'Can you tell me, is there a tailor's house around here?'

'No,' answered a woman who emerged from indoors and spoke in Hindi. 'Where are you from?'

'We used to live in Talegaon.'

'What brings you here then?'

'Our deeds in the last birth, dear lord.' Kautik looked around searching for a place to sit. Noticing this, the woman said, 'Sit here in the shade.'

Kautik sat down. Fanning herself with her sari-end, she narrated her whole story because the ironsmith and his wife sounded really concerned. They both clicked their tongues in sympathy again and again as they listened. Then they began to discuss something in their own language. When they had reached a decision, the woman said, 'I'll empty out the other part of our verandah. You can stay there for as long as you want.'

Now Nama said he was thirsty. Kautik asked the girl with the sledgehammer to get him some water. But the ironsmith's wife said to Nama, 'We're Mussalmans, son. There's a Hindu house there. Go and…'

'Such things don't count for children,' Kautik said to the girl. 'Go and get the water, dear.'

When the girl had gone in, Kautik asked the woman about her. 'Your daughter-in-law, is she?'

'Daughter. Not married yet.'

When Nama had had his water, Kautik, he and Mahadev began to carry all their stuff from under the tree to the house, piling it up in the corner of the verandah that the ironsmiths had offered them. Bano put the sledgehammer down and came out to the verandah. It was strewn with all sorts of odds and ends—yoke-straps for cattle, curved pieces of a cartwheel, dried cow-dung pats, sticks and twigs. Bano collected them all and took them out to the backyard. She made a pile of them there, and below the pile, she scattered shreds of a castor plant that had just begun to bear fruit. Next, she undid the ropes tied to the tethering pegs by verandah and pulled up the pegs. She took the palm-frond broom from Kautik's hand and rapidly swept thorn pods, fruit stones, goats' hair and turd off the verandah, ending by washing it down with a bucketful of water.

Kautik set up a cooking fire with three stones and started her cooking. She didn't have enough utensils, so Bano got her some from their kitchen. Some of the iron things like the dough-kneading basin, griddle, flipper and vegetable cutter were brand new. By four in the afternoon, she had finished making a lunch of bhakri and pithla. After lunch, Kautik and Mahadev lay down for a nap. At dusk, four ewes and their kids rushed bleating to the verandah and stood in their normal tethering place. No amount of shooing would make them go away. Finally Bano grabbed them by the ears and dragged them off to their new tethering pegs in the yard and looped the ropes around their necks.

ထ

When Mahadev heard Natthuseth was back, he instantly went over to see him. When Natthuseth saw Mahadev, he bared his gold teeth by way of a smile. He told him to go inspect the machine. A servant went with him to show him where it was—in Natthuseth's cowshed. The cattle were out grazing. Their tethering ropes trailed lazily on the ground. The stench of dung and urine blew in puffs through the air. In one corner of the shed stood an immense stack of long, cut stalks of grain, fenced off by a wall of horizontal bamboo slats. Two slats made up the fence door. The servant pulled the ends of the slats out of their holes in the wall and ushered Mahadev in to stand beside the two-man tall stack of stalks. After he'd dragged out a couple of hundred bundles or more of stalks, Mahadev caught his first glimpse of the machine. With the servant's help, he began to pull at the machine, stuck deep in the remaining bundles of stalks. When at last it came loose, he slapped the dust off it with his dhoti. He blew hard into its mechanical parts, and then tried to turn the wheel. It was so rusted that it refused to budge. When Mahadev put all his strength to it, it made a clicking sound and moved. 'I guess that was the needle,' Mahadev muttered.

'Must've been.'

'That's why it…' He tried to turn the wheel again. It whirred for a while, then stopped once more. Mahadev used a little more force but it still remained stuck. He didn't dare push it any harder, so he rose and said, 'Let's go.'

'And the machine?'

'Let it be for now.'

'Why are you giving up?'

'There's nothing left of it,' Mahadev said, dusting his hands. 'The rust's eaten it all up.'

'Can't it be mended?'

'Why not? But the repairs will cost more than a new machine.'

Mahadev returned with the servant to Sethji's mansion.

When Natthuseth saw Mahadev approaching, he pulled his silver toothpick out of his gold teeth and said, 'So? Good machine, eh?'

'Yes.'

'Has to be. It's not even all of five years since I bought it.'

'Yes.'

'So when will you start work?'

'Soon.'

'That's right. Get started early. The bullock fair is coming. New clothes have to be made for all the servants.'

'All the servants?'

'What did you think? Home clothes meant just my clothes?'

'Not quite that.'

'Exactly. So tell me quickly, when will you start?'

Badly trapped, Mahadev said firmly, 'I'm not feeling very well. Let me feel a little better, then I'll start.'

Fifteen days went by after this. Mahadev had not touched his bundle of readymade clothes. Except for mealtimes, he spent all his time sitting on the cot hauled up next to Qasam's bellows. Qasam would chat with him while he worked on the piece of iron before him. One day, it rained and the bellows on the verandah couldn't be used. Mahadev and Qasam sat in Qasam's dark house, chatting like old friends. They'd met each other earlier in the Sallburdi fair. Qasam told Mahadev he had never failed going to the Big Mahadev fair in the last dozen years or so. He'd like to continue going every year, he said, for as long as he lived. 'If it is Lord Mahadev's will to allow me to do so,' he said with deep devotion.

Mahadev told Qasam that he had been to a fair only once—the one is Sallburdi—and that was out of anger against Kautik. When he heard of Qasam's plans of joining the Mahadev pilgrims and then going to the Big Mahadev fair, he said he would like to go with him. Such were the warm, sweet exchanges that happened between them as they sat together chatting.

While they sat lost in their world, Nama and Yasodi had come by several times, turn by turn, to call Mahadev home. He'd sent them back each time with a 'Yes, I'm coming' but he hadn't managed to wrench himself away from the cot and the devotion-filled talk they were having. Finally, Kautik lost her patience. She turned her head in Mahadev's direction and yelled out to him from where she sat. Mahadev could not ignore that voice. He got up fretting. He strode into his part of the house and slapped his goods bundle hard making the dust fly. Picking it up, he fumed at Kautik, 'Don't I know why you're yelling like that. I've noticed how you get a belly ache every Thursday.' He hoisted the pack on to his head and said, 'There. That's what you wanted.'

Kautik too yelled back. 'The bhakris are done. Eat a few mouthfuls and go.'

'You can sit and eat them all,' he said and disappeared in the direction of Shendurjana.

Kautik packed some bhakris in a cloth and gave them to Nama. 'Go run after him and give him those.'

'Yes.'

'And if he doesn't take them, go with him to Shendurjana. And if he does without making a fuss, ask him if he'll go see Kasar teacher.'

Nama ran for his life. Getting the lunch to his father wasn't so important. Asking him to see Kasar teacher was. It wasn't surprising then that he saw Mahadev earlier than anyone would've expected. He called out to him and Mahadev actually stopped. He even took the lunch packet quietly. After he'd heard Nama's all-important message, he sent back another to Kautik. 'Tell her she mustn't expect me back soon. I'll go to Umravati directly from the market for more goods.'

'Yes.'

Before he knew it, Nama had already walked a few fields talking to his father and even passed the bus terminus on the metal road. He bid goodbye to his father some way down the road and turned back. As he reached the bus terminus again, Bhima suddenly jumped off a goods carrier which had just come in and halted before a tea shop. 'Hey you, where's maay?' he demanded in bazaar Hindi, as usual.

'Back home in Mozri. Tatya's just left for Shendur...'

'I know.' Bhima turned to speak to someone in the goods truck and then said, 'Come on. Show me the house.'

When they cut across the same fields and arrived home,

they found Kautik, Bano and Sakina sitting on Kautik's verandah. Bano sat with her legs stretched out before her and her hair hanging loose. Sakina was picking through it for lice and nits. When she found one, she'd pass it to Bano to crush between her nails. Kautik had laid out some betel leaves on her thigh and was busy smearing them with lime and catechu.

Nama called from the yard, 'Maay o, Bhima's here.'

'When did you come?' Kautik asked Bhima as he came into the yard. Bhima's attention was not on his maay but fixed on Bano's breasts. His eyes were struggling to get into her kameez through its open neck. Though unaware of his eyes, Bano was trying, out of sheer habit, to make sure that the brief strip of cloth that served for top scarf was covering her youth adequately.

Sakina looked at Bhima with curious eyes and asked, 'Is that your older son, Kautik?'

Soon, she and Bano rose to go back to their own part of the house. Bhima's eyes wouldn't let go of Bano's body even now, though her back was turned. They clung like a drooling dog's to the swing below her waist. It was only after Bano had disappeared that he turned his attention to his mother.

'So how are you?'

'Who told you we were here?'

'Bhima gets to know everything,' he said in Hindi.

'Dear lord, you've become chatty! Where were you all these days?'

'Been travelling a lot. Umravati, Nagpur, Wardha.'

'And money?'

'What do I need money for?'

'Why? Are the bus and truck people your fathers? Or mine?' Kautik's tone now betrayed a hint of admiration.

'Must be yours. Husband of that old woman in Hinganghat.'

'Go on, you little monster. Don't you dare call my mother names. Come and eat.'

'We're not hungry.'

'Won't you eat a couple of mouthfuls with me?'

He took off his cap and spun it from where he sat to the top of the trunk. Then he began to grope in his pockets.

'Looking for your box of matches, hunh?' Kautik asked pointedly.

Bhima laughed and said, 'Not at all.' He sat beside his mother to eat out of her plate. Halfway through the meal, he said, 'Who was the Mussalman woman who was here?'

'That's Sakina. This is her verandah.'

'And the girl?'

'Her daughter.'

'Guess she's married.'

'Not yet.'

'She must have a father.'

'Then? Would she be fatherless?'

'And brothers?'

'None, poor soul.'

'Older one?'

'None older, none younger.'

Bhima ran his hand over his stomach and belched with satisfaction. He washed his hands and wiped them on his kerchief. As he did so, he gazed with great concentration at the flowers in its design.

'Now where's your next trip to?'

'See. You don't want me to stay with you, hunh?'

At this, Kautik raised her hand from her plate and scolded with mock anger, 'You want a slap now, do you?'

He held out his cheek quite shamelessly. 'There. Slap me. I've not had a taste of your hand for too many days.'

Later, Bhima looked around him as he sat on the verandah. He noticed Qasam who had just come out to start the furnace. Waving towards him, he asked Kautik, 'Tell me, maay. Is that the girl's father?'

'Yes. Why?'

Bhima didn't answer. But he moved towards Qasam's bellows as if drawn to them. Sakina, who was pulling the chain of the bellows, said to her husband, 'See, this is Kautik's older son.'

'Is that him?'

Bhima was quicker than Sakina to answer the question and he did so with great politeness. 'Yes, uncle.'

'Sit down then. You even speak our tongue.'

'Yes, uncle. Most of my friends are from your community.'

'Is that right?'

'Swear on God, uncle.' Bhima glanced at the upended string cot standing by with its many knots and strips of cloth replacing frayed portion of rope. Bhima pulled it down and spread himself on it at ease. His hand groped for and drew out a bundle of bidis and a box of matches from his pocket.

He held both out to Qasam and said, 'Here, uncle. Have a good puff.'

Both lit their bidis. Along with the smoke, their words too rose into the air and faded away. They smoked and chatted till evening and would have continued after dark had Kautik not called Bhima home for dinner. During dinner, he said to Kautik, 'Maay, I get the feeling I should work now.'

'You'll work?' Kautik could barely hide her joy. 'What kind of work will you do?'

'Whatever you say. If you tell me to graze cattle, I'll do even that. But I don't want to leave home now.'

'Swear on me?' Kautik couldn't believe her ears.

'Swear on you. This is where I want to be.'

'Then let him come back. He'll get back from Umravati in a few days. I'll ask him to fix you up somewhere.' Kautik's voice was full of trust.

It was dark. Nama was hungry. He asked his maay to serve him dinner. But she said, 'He might come back tonight. We'll wait. If he comes, we can all eat together. What do you say, Bhima?'

'Don't worry about me,' he said. Kautik picked up her small water pot and went to call Sakina. As usual, they left together for nature's call. She took Bhima's word and left Nama waiting for his dinner.

A little while after they'd gone, Bano came out of the house with an aluminium pan. She squatted on her haunches in the yard to scrub and wash it, her head bent low. As soon as Bhima sensed her movement, he changed his place from the rug to the top of the trunk from where he could stare at her. As he stared, he sang the popular film song '*Your eyes are like daggers that kill/ Don't let them meet another's eyes*.' He continued singing the song all the time that Bano was in the yard. It was only when she went indoors again that he changed his seat once more, from the trunk to the rug. And when he heard Kautik coming back, he stubbed out his bidi.

It was about nine-thirty at night when they heard Mahadev's voice. Bhima recognized it even from a distance. He pulled his knees up to his chest instantly, circled them with his arms and pushed his face down into them. Mahadev saw him immediately. As he put his pack down in its corner, he muttered, 'So this thing is still alive. I thought I must be…'

'All that can come later. Eat first,' Kautik said, standing between her husband and Bhima.

'Nothing will come later. Who cares anyway,' Mahadev said, taking the water tumbler from Kautik's hand and bending down to wash his hands.

Kautik served dinner. Everybody stared at their plates as they ate. Bhima finished first and got up to wash his hands. He went out, groping in his pocket. Mahadev finished last. He sat down on the rug and lit a bidi. Kautik rolled up a betel leaf for him and broached Bhima's subject. 'Do you think you can have a talk with him?'

'Never.'

'How can you say that?'

Mahadev gave her a sharp look. 'Now are you going to nag and complain?'

'Nothing of the kind.'

'Then what's this?' Mahadev demanded. 'That time you tried sending him to school...How many days did he go?'

'He'll behave now. He's grown up.'

'Nobody grows up. A dog's tail doesn't straighten out because you put it through a tube.'

Kautik kept quiet for a while. Mahadev continued to talk. Once he had let off all the steam, she said, 'Why not try this once?'

'And if he doesn't do as he's told?'

'If he doesn't, it doesn't change our fate. He's the one who'll have to eat cow dung for his bad deeds.'

Mahadev was about to speak but they heard Bhima's cough in the dark as he came back and entered the verandah with lowered head. Mahadev looked up at his face, but Bhima wouldn't meet his eye. At last Mahadev lay down and pulled the rug over his face. Bhima continued sitting where he was for a long time after that. Then he too lay down to sleep.

After tea the next morning, Mahadev lit a bidi. Looking out somewhere into space, he asked, 'Where were you all these days, eh?'

'In Umravati,' Bhima answered with great alacrity.

'Doing what?'

Bhima looked down. Kautik shouted at him for his own good, 'Is your mouth stitched up not to speak, you corpse!'

'I was doing coolie work.'

'What else?'

Bhima didn't speak. When Kautik threatened him, he said with great difficulty, 'Nothing else.'

'Are you telling the truth?'

Bhima was silent. Mahadev said, 'You weren't doing head massage?'

'What head massage?' Kautik asked.

'Ask him.'

'I wasn't.'

'Watch out. Watch out. You're telling more lies,' Mahadev shouted. 'Shall I ask Kasar teacher? Didn't you run away when you saw him on Wardha station, leaving your customer's massage half-done?'

'Yes.'

'How long will you go on like this? You think our caste people will keep you in the caste if they see you doing low barber work?' Bhima shook his head. Mahadev said, 'Who will marry you then? You left school. Fine. You weren't going to become a barrister anyway. But what about daily wages? Or are you going to slap oil on people's heads all your life?'

'No.'

'Don't just shake your head like an ox, you sisterfucker! Just tell us once for all what's in your mind.' Mahadev paused then said, 'Decide. You going to go to the markets with me or learn tailor's work?'

'Whatever you say.'

'Then go to Sheshrao Tailor to learn on his machine.'

'In Tivase?'

'Yes.'

'I'll have to go on foot, I suppose.'

'No. I'll buy you a car.'

Kautik stepped in hastily with, 'So when will you start?'

'Any time you say.'

'Go from tomorrow. And take Nama with you too.'

Nama started and asked, 'Where to?'

Mahadev rolled his tongue in his cheek and said, 'Where to? Sheshrao's machine.'

Nama's cheeks puffed out in a sulk. Kautik said, 'Don't you want to learn English?'

'Yes, yes.' He looked at his father and said happily, 'Oh. So you went to see Kasar teacher. That's what it was.'

The next day, Mahadev accompanied Bhima and Nama to Tivase because it was their first day. He settled Nama in the English school and Bhima with Sheshrao. From then on, the two began their daily trips between Mozri and Tivase. The distance was double that between Talegaon and Tivase that Nama used to walk earlier. But he was so eager to learn English that he didn't feel the distance at all. He was older too. Two small mounds like an eleven- or twelve-year-old girl's breasts had grown on his chest. An accidental knock against them made him draw his breath in with pain.

Along with these physical changes, his voice too was changing. As the days went by, his body shed its tenderness, turning coarse and tough. Moreover, except for the four fields he had to cross on the dirt track up to the bus terminus, the rest of the distance between Mozri and Tivase was covered by the metal road which made walking easier. So Nama had nothing to fear. As for Bhima, he didn't know what fear was. He was the great terror personified, ready to terrorize fear itself.

When school broke for the bullock festival, Nama spent all his days at home. One day, when he was sitting on Sakina's verandah, playing with his baby sister, Kautik hurried home from work unexpectedly. 'Son, go in and spread a rug on the floor,' she said to Nama.

Qasam asked, 'Why, what's the matter?'

Kautik winced and said, 'How can I tell you? Please ask my sister to step over if she's free.'

Supporting her stomach with her hands, she went indoors. She lay down on the rug tossing and turning. 'Son, go quickly and see if Sakina aunty is coming,' she said frantically.

'Why? What's the matter?' Sakina asked as she entered. 'Didn't you go picking chillies?'

'I did go, dear mother, but this stomach wouldn't let me be.' Kautik was grimacing with pain.

'Why, o? How're you doing?'

'How can I tell, poor soul?' So saying, Kautik bit hard on her tongue.

'Shall I call Anji?'

'Maybe you should.'

'You think you're ready?'

'I can't even say I am.'

Sakina put a finger to her mouth and exclaimed, 'Dear mother! Can't you tell that much? It's not your first time!'

'That's not what I mean.'

'Have you completed your days?'

'Long ago.'

'So why didn't it come?'

'How can I tell, dear lord?'

'You must have counted wrong.'

'No, dear soul!' Kautik stopped short. She caught her tongue between her teeth. She tried to turn over, supporting her stomach with her hands. Now Sakina took her hands off her hips and said, 'Nama, be a good boy and run to Anji's. Tell her my name.'

Anji the Mang woman came. She upturned her metal bowl, banged it on the ground in the yard and went to Kautik's rug. Sakina put a coconut-shell bowl in Nama's hand as she created a private area for Kautik. 'Run to the shop and get a paisa worth of castor oil. Go.'

Nama rushed off. Anji asked, 'You've completed your days, I suppose?'

'Why isn't it coming then?' Sakina asked.

'Listen to that!' Anji said. 'Is that in anybody's hands, do you think? Some babies just will not come down in time. Didn't Vacchi, the Patil's wife, take a full twelve months?'

Bano, who had also come in, blurted out, 'Twelve?'

'And then? What has this one seen till now, eh Sakinabi?'

'But that time Vacchi's baby came dead, didn't it?'

'Is giving or taking life in man's hand, you tell me...'

An hour or so later, Kautik seemed to return to normal. She straightened out her sari and shoved some twigs into the fire. She brewed a huge panful of jaggery tea. Anji drank it in her own bowl. Bano went to their house to fetch cups and saucers. She returned, saying to Sakina, 'Have your tea and come home quickly. Abba says the Patel wants his sower blade delivered by this evening.'

Sakina returned to her work after some time. She began to pull the chain of the bellows. Bano took hold of the sledgehammer and Qasam began working on a piece of red-hot iron. Kautik made bhakris for the evening and did the rest of her chores, moaning all the time. Later, Bhima swaggered home from Tivase. He asked about dinner. Gathering that it was not quite cooked, he dragged the cot into the yard so that part of it was in Kautik's half and part in Qasam's. He got Nama to fetch a rug. He spread it on the cot, and sat on it, his feet dangling over the side. His eyes shifted from the road outside to the bellows and then back again to the road. Once in a while, he recognized a passer-by and called out, 'Is that Ajabya now?'

'Yes.'

'Come along in. Don't you want a smoke?'

'Not now. I have to milk the boss's buffalo.'

'Do that later. Why bother so much about the boss' buffalo?'

A couple of other fellows too went by. One stopped and said, ''Course I'll come in.'

'Where's Shamrao?'

'He'll be here. He was having dinner.'

'And Nago?'

'He'll come too. He and I just got back from Davra.' He smiled secretly and said, glancing at the bellows, 'Are you going to take out a bidi or just get us pregnant with inquiries?'

Bhima too glanced at the bellows. Keeping his voice as low as he could, he said, 'Do you get pregnant with just inquiries? Are you Mozri fellows so delicate?'

'Look here, don't you bad mouth us Mozri chaps, see?' he said looking at the bellows. 'Otherwise, later you'll say you weren't warned. Come on. Out with the box of matches.'

'Do I ever keep matchsticks?'

'Then there's the furnace.'

'The furnace,' mused Bhima. 'But it's looking extra hot today.'

'Too hot for you?'

'Not at all.' And Bhima walked over to the furnace. He lit one bidi at it. Then, lighting another, he said hesitantly, 'Here, uncle.'

'I don't smoke bidis,' Qasam said without looking at him.

'But that day...'

'That was that day.'

Returning to the cot, Bhima said, 'No problem. No problem.'

The moment he sat down, Goma whispered in his ear, 'The furnace is really blazing today, eh?'

'I said so, didn't I?' Bhima answered in a voice low enough for only Goma to hear. 'But Bhima's the kind of man who'll not rest till he's lit his bidi, no matter how hot the furnace. Here, bastard, take a puff before the bidi goes out.'

By now almost all of Bhima's friends had gathered. Their idle chatter rose and dissipated in bidi smoke. Shamrao said, 'Hey Bhima, at least tell us a story or something.'

'I'll tell you something else.'

'Something else then.'

'Talk is only words,' Bhima recited, blowing smoke into

the sky. 'Words are for birds. The pretty one winked, and her youth was in ruins.'

'Well done, Bhima! Bravo!' His excited friends slapped his back and his thighs. Shamrao glanced at the bellows and couldn't resist saying, 'At this rate, you're going to ruin our women, you bastard.'

Bhima turned to look at his own doorway. 'Easy. The old woman's at home.'

For a moment, voices were lowered. Even then one of them said, 'Bhima, go on. Tell us at least one story. You know so many.'

'Which one d'you want to hear?'

'The one you told us that day.'

'About the Mussalman woman?'

Two or three excited voices said, 'Yes, yes,' together.

'Listen. There was once a Mussalman woman.'

'Hunh.'

'She had a daughter.'

'To be married?'

'The girl was married.'

'To someone in the village, hunh?'

'Yes. Once she came crying home to her ma.'

'How sad!'

'And then?'

'Then? They began to talk. The mother asked the daughter:

Why do you cry, dear?
Mother-in-law beat me.
Why did she beat you, dear?

I broke the pot.
How did it break, dear?
When I squatted to wash it, it slipped from my hand.

Qasam threw his tongs down on the ground and shouted, 'Get a pitcher of water and pour it on this coal.'

Sakina said fearfully, 'But the sower blade must be given tomorrow.'

'To hell with sower blades. Just do what I say.'

∽

It was night. Sakina and Kautik had gone out for nature's call as usual. Nama and Bhima sat on the verandah waiting for Kautik to return. Qasam, who came just then, ignored Bhima who was right in front of him and asked Nama, 'Hasn't your father returned from Shendurjana yet?'

'No, why?'

'When he comes, tell him there's bhajan singing at Devrao's.'

'Can I come?'

'No. It's another village's do. We don't want boys and girls hanging around there. Send your father.' And Qasam went on his way.

Tired of waiting for his mother, Nama turned his attention to the game his sister was playing. Yasodi held one end of a strip of cloth. She'd tied a toy clay pot to the other end. She stood with one foot resting on the frame of the cot with the cloth strip lowered over the side, the way village women do when they draw water from the well. The moment she noticed Nama looking at her, she said in the voice and tone of her mother, 'Nama, I've put your bath water on the fire.'

He too entered into the game, saying, 'What? Still drawing water?'

'Yes and what? I've just got back from the fields.'

'Whose?'

'Natthuseth's.'

'What did you go for?'

'Picking chillies. What else?'

'Work over?'

'We only started yesterday. Is it going to be over so soon?'

Yasodi spoke with her eyes fixed gravely on the clay pot.

She was too cute for Nama to keep away. He just had to grab her and smother her with kisses. As a result, the cloth strip slipped out of her hand. Struggling to free herself from his hold, she shouted, 'Now see, my rope and waterpot have fallen in the well.'

It was quite late and Kautik had still not returned. Fed up, Nama went over to Sakina's. He wondered whether Kautik was sitting with her. There was no sign of Bano anywhere. He found Sakina and Kautik deep in conversation. Sakina was saying to Kautik, 'D'you think I feel good to say such things, being her own mother? But it's as they say. Tell the world of your pride. Tell nobody of your shame. That's our story. Even to think of getting Bano married, mustn't I have at least two hundred rupees at my waist?'

'You must too.'

'But whatever we bring in, we eat off the plate. So you

tell me. Where's people like us to get so much money from?'

'That's true too.'

Sakina looked around to make sure Bano wasn't anywhere within earshot. Then, lowering her voice to a delicate whisper, she said, 'That's why we try to cool this young blood by putting it to work on the hammer. Left idle, it'll grow hot. We're poor people after all. If something happens that shouldn't, where'll we go to hide our faces?'

'That's all very well. But how long will you go on like this?'

'For as long as Allah wills,' Sakina sighed. But then she said hopefully, 'If Allah brings it into his heart, the girl's fate might brighten one day.'

'I suppose so. Even the state of a garbage dump changes, so why not ours? We are human beings after all.'

They continued chatting till Kautik heard Mahadev's voice calling her from their side of the house. He sounded furious, so he must have called her a couple of times before. She snapped at Nama then, telling him he should have stayed home and told her as soon as Mahadev returned. She picked up her water pitcher from Sakina's threshold and hurried home. When she got there, she realized that he wasn't angry so much because of her absence, but because of his male pride that was tied up in his bundle that day. Untying the bundle, Kautik saw that he had brought back all the provisions required for the traditional meal for the bullock festival. Kautik took the packets out one by one, feeling each one first to guess what and how much there was in it before opening it. When she opened the large packet of wheat, she couldn't help asking, 'How much is that, o?'

'A full big measure. Why?'

'Will that do for us now?'

'Why? Did you want a whole binful,' he asked. 'A full measure was enough even for a festival like Diwali and now...'

'If there's enough for chapatis, is that enough?' Kautik asked, her eyes on the future. 'Won't I need to make sweet semolina and such things when I have the baby?'

'Is that happening now?'

'No,' Kautik said, her voice sharp with sarcasm. 'Dig the well when you're thirsty.'

In the normal course, Kautik and Mahadev would have stretched this argument further. But Kautik decided to end it there. After dinner, Mahadev went to Devrao's for the bhajan singing in good spirits, got angrier with every step he took on the way back home as he listened to Qasam. By the time he got home, he could barely contain his rage. It was only because Bhima was asleep and Kautik cajoled him that he kept quiet for the night.

The next morning, when Kautik had put his bath water on the fire and set the jaggery tea to brew on the hob, Mahadev sat before the very mouth of the fire to warm himself against the cold. A bidi smouldered in his hand. Bhima sat lightly, barely touching ground, his back against the adjacent wall.

Mahadev bent his head to draw heavily on his bidi, then looking up, asked yet again, 'What did I ask?'

'But I said nothing.'

'Was Qasam lying then?'

Bhima couldn't answer. Kautik said, 'Let it go. He must not have said it. One of the others must have said it. Now don't quarrel on a festival day.'

'But I'm asking why this sisterfucker should gather those boys around him here?'

'He won't another time.' After Kautik answered her husband, she asked Bhima for assurance. 'So, will you sit with those scoundrels in Sakina's yard again?'

'Why blame them? Don't we know what this sisterfucker is like? Weren't those boys living here before he came or have they just dropped down?'

Without heeding Mahadev, Kautik said to Bhima, 'So? Are you going to keep collecting those boys here?'

'No.'

'He says he won't. Let it be for now.'

Mahadev continued to mutter. 'You're saying let it go now, but you'll remember your gods when he takes advantage of you.' She saw that he was going to carry on muttering, so she sent Bhima off to get mango leaves for the auspicious flower-and-leaf garland for the door. Mahadev sat muttering for a while and then fell silent.

Later, Kautik began preparing the festive meal with Nama's help. Twice as she ground the cooked chickpea and jaggery stuffing on the grinding stone, she stopped and threw herself on the floor in agony. She went out for a bit, returned, and struggled to complete the cooking. She managed somehow to finish making the puranpolis. She made the accompaniments with great difficulty. She served her family. By the time she could have her own lunch, the village bullocks and calves were already on their way to the village common, decked out in gorgeous backcloths and jingling brand new bells. On this day, they were to be worshipped and paraded in great style.

After lunch, Mahadev took Nama and Yasodi, who was wearing a new dress to see the cattle parade. Though the jacket Mahadev wore was still the old one, Kautik had scrubbed it clean with soap. But his cap was new, selected from his own goods, and Nama wore a new pair of shorts.

Everybody was at the parade. Natthuseth's bullocks, standing in a row, were a special sight. They wore velvet backcloths and silver ornaments glinted on their foreheads. Even Natthuseth's servants, all twenty or thirty of them, who stood holding the bullocks' reins, looked pleased with themselves in clothes made like uniforms from the same bolt of fabric. Everything they wore was brand new—shirts, jackets, dhotis, shoulder cloths and pink turbans. Other people in the show were dressed much more simply in comparison.

After the parade broke up, the bullocks came by people's doors in pairs. When they came by her door, Kautik stopped them, washed their hooves, put vermilion and rice on their foreheads, did aarti and then put a coin into the hands of their keepers. Those who didn't know her, accepted the coins for what they were worth, but those who did, said, 'What's this, aunty! You give only once a year, even then you're so stingy!'

Kautik would first try to persuade them to accept what she'd given. But some refused to be persuaded. Then she'd change the coin from an anna to two and send them on their way. The same bullocks would then stop at Sakina's door. Sakina would not worship them. But she did give money, depending on how well she knew the keepers.

At the crack of dawn the next day, without even getting out of bed, Mahadev began shouting loud enough for the neighbours to hear, 'Take away flies and mosquitoes, oh goddess Maarvatt...'

Bhima was shouting, 'Take away coughs, colds, diseases, oh god Budgya...'

Kautik woke Nama to shout, 'Take away the enemy and the foe, oh Maarvatt...'

Theirs was not the only home from where these calls were heard. That morning, every male member of every household in Mozri was shouting out the same pleas.

At dawn that day, little village boys held their own parade of toy bullocks. When it was morning, the parade broke up and the boys scattered all over the village, clutching their wooden and clay bullocks, asking for money at every door. Kautik gave all of them a paisa each. One pair of brothers carried only one clay bullock between them. One held the head half and the other the tail half. Teasing them about this, Kautik gave them only one paisa between them but she had hardly turned back to go indoors when a quarrel broke out between them over the paisa. It grew so heated that Kautik feared the two parts of the bullock would soon be four. So she went out again and gave them another paisa. That made peace between them.

As the day progressed, Bhima, still sitting at home forlorn, said to Kautik in a small voice, 'Maay, can you give me eight annas?'

'Don't play little boy with me,' she snapped. But soon enough, she softened and said, 'What d'you want it for?'

'I need it.'

'Don't I know what for? You want to go gamble in the village and what!'

'Not to gamble,' Bhima pleaded piteously. 'Swear by you.'

'Wretch! Don't swear by me,'

Kautik tugged at the cloth purse at her waist. Bhima saw this and sang out, 'Giving, giving, maay's giving me money.'

When he had the money in hand, he said, 'Maay, you're so nice, o!' The next minute, he was out of the house, prancing away like a calf.

A while later, Mahadev came home. As he picked up his bundle, he said, 'So you gave the young fellow money, did you?'

'Why?'

'Because he's on the common playing ganjifa cards.'

'Let him if he is. Just for today. The whole village is playing cards today.'

'I see,' Mahadev said, but let it pass. Lifting the bundle to his shoulder, he said, 'Don't expect me back for the next four or five days. It's the feast—good for sales. I'll visit all the markets in a row and see my luck.'

'All right.'

'And send Bhima to Tivase at least tomorrow morning. Or he'll spend all day playing cards.'

That night, there was bhajan singing on the platform round the tree by the Hanuman temple. A group of fifteen or sixteen people, including Qasam, were gathered there. Before the singing began, the ektara player strummed on his string. The tambourine player held the tough leather of his drum to the fire. He stroked the skin over and over with his hands warmed at the fire. Then, slapping the drum, he shouted, 'Right, Brother Qasam. Let's start with you.'

Qasam, hungry for acknowledgement, felt deeply happy. Stroking his beard, he began, 'Let me sing for ever your blessed name.' When two stanzas still remained to be sung, Nama called his attention to Bano standing by the platform. Putting down his cymbals, he went to Bano. Returning to his seat, he said, 'Nama, she's calling you.'

Most reluctantly, Nama put down his cymbals, got up and climbed down to where Bano stood. 'What is it?' he asked.

'Your maay wants you home. She has pains in the stomach.'

'Isn't Bhima there?' Nama asked, walking back with her.

'You think I'll look out for that wretch,' Bano snapped in anger.

When Nama got home, his maay was rolling on the rug in agony. She tossed and turned, moaning, 'Dear mother, what's to become of me?'

Sakina sat beside her with a drawn face, trying to console her. Once in a while, she'd peer out into the dark, straining to hear. When she heard Nama coming, she told Kautik, who instantly turned on her side to face him.

'Thank god you're here. Go fetch that wretch back from wherever he is.'

When she heard Nama ask, 'Where will he be?' she lost her temper. But Sakina told him he'd be either at Ajaba's or Shamrao's place.

'I'm scared to go alone.'

'Bano will go with you.'

'No, I won't.'

Sakina said angrily to Bano, 'Why? Why won't you go with Nama?'

Bending her head and rubbing the dirt off her neck, all Bano would say was, 'I won't go so I won't.'

Sakina turned to Nama, stroked his face, called him sweet names, told him the people in the temple were wide awake and so were Natthuseth's guards, so he had nothing to fear. Finally Nama agreed to go. He stamped out of the house, his cheeks puffed up in a sulk. He went to Narayan's place where he found Bhima too. They sat crowded around a lantern. Going up to the group, Nama said, 'Bhima, maay wants you home.'

'Can't come now.'

'Maay is carrying on terribly.'

Bhima didn't answer. He threw down his cards. 'Come on,' he challenged the others.

Raking in the money lying in front of the others, Bhima yelled, 'Will you go now?'

Nama was scared. But he waited a little while longer. Then he said in a final way, 'So you're not coming?'

Bhima flung down another heap of coins, turned and raised his hand. 'You want me to tell you some other way I'm not coming,' he shouted.

Back home, Nama told Kautik everything that Bhima had said. Kautik moaned, 'Dear mother, who'll go now in the middle of the night?'

'I'll go,' Bano said suddenly. 'Tell me what to get.'

'Oh please,' Kautik said gratefully. 'Go take a rupee from the lowest pot there, go.'

Bano ferreted around in all the pots and said, 'There's nothing here.'

'It's tied in a red cloth. See.'

'Nothing here. See yourself.'

Kautik reached for the red cloth. She looked through it anxiously, crumpling it to make sure. Slapping her forehead in despair, she muttered, 'Now what am I to do with this monster? Where can I go begging this time of night? The wretch has made life a misery.'

Sakina stopped Kautik. She sent Bano to fetch a rupee from her house. Putting it in Nama's hand, Kautik gave him the list of things she wanted—dried ginger powder, pepper, mace. She made him and Bano repeat the list. She told them to get Anji the Mang midwife on the way to the shop or back. Bano picked up the lantern and she and Nama set off to get all the stuff. When they returned, Kautik was happy to see they had got everything. In better spirits now, she asked Nama to go to Vacchi the Patil's wife and say your maay needs a torn old sari.

'I'm afraid of the dog maay,' he said.

'Get going this minute, wretch,' Kautik shouted, her voice sharp with pain. 'You're sitting on my chest all of you, saying, when's this one going to die, when will we eat her funeral rice-and-curd.'

'Stop talking now, Kautik. Just lie down easy,' Sakina said. Then she turned to Nama, 'Go, child, sleep now. There's an empty cot by the bellows. Go.'

Nama went to the bellows. Yasodi was already asleep on the cot, her thumb in her mouth as usual. Nama lay down beside her.

He woke up in the morning to Kautik's agonized screams. He ran to their house and peeped in fearfully. Sakina caressed his face and said, 'Go out there and play, my son.'

Repressing her sobs, Kautik asked, 'Who is it?'

When Sakina told her, she let her sobs burst out saying, 'Let the poor child come in. Let me have at least my Nama with me.'

Screwing up his nose at the bad smell in the room, Nama stepped in with a thudding heart. As soon as she saw him, Kautik held her hands out to him and began to wail. Caressing his back and face, she said, 'You came to see your little brother, didn't you, son? But what little brother can I show you now, my love?'

She held Nama tight to her and sobbed aloud. When he heard her, Nama too began to cry. Shevanti said, 'Have you gone mad, sister? If you carry on like this, who's to take care of that poor soul, eh? Now calm down. What's happened has happened.'

At noon, Nago came from Tivase with the cloth. Shevanti heated water. Mankarna massaged the baby with ghee and bathed him. Subadri handed him over to Kautik. Kautik filled her eyes with the sight of him as she wound the cloth around him. As she passed the baby to Bhima, she couldn't help shouting bitterly, 'Take him, you devil. He died out of anger against you. Hold him properly now at least.'

As Bhima lowered his head and began walking across the yard followed by a few other people, Kautik broke into a wail.

'What will I say now when the man of the house returns?'

&

The next day, Bhima tore his playing cards into shreds and threw them into the cooking fire. He handed over the eight or ten rupees he had in his pocket to Kautik and got ready to go with Nama to Tivase. Kautik saw all this and said, 'Of course, you're off now, wretch. Scared of being thrashed with his chappals when he gets back from the market!' She paused and then said, 'But don't go for a couple days more since you've not gone for this long. Go after the third day rites of the dead.'

On the third day, Kautik gave Bhima two metal bowls. She put cow urine in one and milk in the other. Bhima carried them to the crematorium. He smoothed down a patch of soil. He plucked the leaves of two trees that came to hand and twisted them together into a cone tacked by a thorn from the thorn bush. He put the cow urine and milk together in the leaf cone, set it down, lit an incense stick beside it, folded his hands together and returned home. Kautik burst into sobs again when he returned as she had done when he'd gone with the bowls of cow urine and milk.

After that, Bhima and Nama began once again to shuttle daily between Mozri and Tivase. Bhima was trying hard to learn tailoring from Sheshrao. Nama was doing just fine in his studies. He noted down every word the teacher uttered. At home, he wouldn't miss a chance to speak English to whoever came his way. One day, Bano asked him, 'Did the school finish early today?' Nama answered in great style in English, 'Yes.'

'Why?'

To which the answer was in a mixed tongue. The first word 'how' was in English and the next two 'do I know?' in Marathi.

Kautik started speaking to him once with, 'What I'm saying is…' To which his answer was, 'Why don't you say what you want to say,' in which only the word 'what' was in English.

Once he said to Yasodi 'You are my sister.' This time, all the words were English.

Nama loved every moment of school. The teacher would hold him up as a model before the dunces in his class for putting his heart and mind into his studies. Things went smoothly for Nama for a couple of months. Then obstacles rose tall before him, one after another.

One day, Kautik, stroking Yasodi's body and cheeks, which had grown more and more pinched over the last three days, said to Nama, 'Go call Sakina, son.'

He answered, 'I'm going to school.' But then he saw the look on his maay's face and in her eyes, and went to fetch Sakina. As soon as Kautik saw Sakina, she said in a small voice, 'No, Sakina, the girl hasn't taken a morsel of food for three days now.'

'Why, what's wrong? Is it a fever or something?'

'No fever as I can see.'

'Then why are you so worried?' Sakina tried to ease Kautik's heart. 'It's nothing to make a sparrow-face about. She's a child, no? There's always little ups and downs.' She paused, then asked, 'Not coming cotton-picking?'

'How can I afford not to come, sister?' Kautik said, calm and cold. 'God's made sure of that much. You'll eat only if you work, wretch, or starve to death!'

'Any news of Bhima's father?'

'None, worse luck. He went during the bullock festival, and no sign of him still. He said he'd be back in a few days,' Kautik said, wiping her eyes with her sari-end. 'When I think of him, all sorts of thoughts run in and out of my mind.'

'Was there some hot talk between you, husband and wife, before he left?'

'Not a word, no.' Kautik was beginning to sound tearful. 'Sometimes I'm afraid some young thugs might have beaten him up on the way. Sometimes, I even think he could be killed...' She broke off on a sob and covered her mouth with her sari to choke back the words. Her body was trembling.

Sakina consoled her. 'Now shut, my sister. Don't bring rubbish to your mind. He'll be back soon. Why will he leave his children and go off?'

But words still tumbled out from behind Kautik's sari. 'Look how God's going after us all the time. Only He knows what's in His mind.'

After more such talk, Sakina managed to get Kautik

back under control. Then they discussed whether to leave Yasodi to Bano's care or ask Nama to stay back from school. Bhima butted in then, saying, 'I'll look after Yasodi.'

'Why? Don't you have to be at the machine?'

'I won't go today.'

'But why not?'

'A chap gets fed up sometimes,' he answered in the tone and manner of his father.

The two began to argue. Nama saw his opportunity. He took vague permission from his mother and slipped out, taking the road to Tivase. Kautik made Bhima promise that he would keep a strict eye on Yasodi, clean her up if required and then set off with Sakina for the field. Bano stayed back because the furnace had to be plastered that day.

When his mother had gone, Bhima left the sleeping Yasodi behind and went for a loaf in the village. When he returned home, it was with Ajaba, Shamrao and the rest. He pushed the still sleeping Yasodi into a corner and spread a rug in the empty space. Four bottoms attached themselves to the four corners of the rug and soon heaps of cards and coins began piling in the centre. Bhima staked the one rupee he had and won six or seven rupees off it to begin with.

In the afternoon, Bano came out to the furnace carrying a basket of cow-dung and a pitcher of water. She started kneading mud into the dung like dough. From that moment, Bhima's attention wandered from the game. It was more fun to talk now. His voice grew really loud because of something that happened with Shamrao. He had left the game to step out for a while. When he returned, he accidentally knocked against the door. This dislodged the stone wedged under the door to hold it and the door flew shut. Seeing his chance, Bhima shouted out a song:

Air is the only contact between us, so,
Open the window,
Let the breeze blow.

When the door was thrown wide open, Shamrao said softly, looking at the furnace, 'My queen is still on top?'

Ajaba said, 'So Bhima what happened to that Rasool Miya's wife?'

'Where were we when I stopped telling the story?'

'Don't you remember even that?' Shamrao asked, slapping Bhima on the back. 'Where's your attention anyhow?'

'Rasool was sent to jail,' Ajaba gave Bhima his cue. Then he demanded his winnings. 'Come on. Give me my four annas first.' Bhima carelessly shoved a few coins from the heap before him in Ajaba's direction and took up the story.

'A few days passed.'

'How few?'

'A year and a bit.'

'Oh? And then?'

'Well then, one day Rasool Miya's wife's spinning wheel broke.'

'Give me four annas,' Shamrao said. 'And then?'

'That was the end of the wife's means of earning her food and drink.'

'That's the way it was, hunh?' Ajaba said. 'Give, that's eight annas.'

'After that, the wife wrote her husband a card.'

'Is that a letter?'

'Right. And do you know what she wrote?'

'No. Give me eight annas. What?'

'The scoundrel is one up on the king, the foot of the throne's given way…'

'Go on. Why have you stopped?' Narayan said. 'I hope you have money? Or I'll stop dealing right now.'

'Of course I have. Go on. Deal.'

'Good. So then?'

'…And the queen has run away.'

Everybody turned to look at the bellows. Ajaba said, 'So she's finally escaped!'

'No. Nobody escapes the king,' Bhima retorted. 'He says, how long can my tender mango hide behind its leaves?'

Their idle chatter continued till dark. By then Bhima had turned his pockets inside out. Afraid his maay would soon be back, he sent his chums away. He himself dusted the rug and returned it to its place.

That evening, Kautik returned from the fields as early as she could, worried about the girl. She emptied out bean pods, some from a cloth bundle and some from her tucked up sari, and asked Bhima at the same time for news of Yasodi.

'How's the girl been?' she said, her face small with worry.

'She's been sleeping.'

'Didn't she wake up at all?'

'She did.'

'Did she have curd-rice?'

'No. She vomited. And shat once.'

Kautik was bewildered. She went to Yasodi who lay wrapped up in a rug. Stroking her body, she asked, 'My little one, how do you feel, o?'

'Will you eat something?'

'Shall I make sweet semolina?'

'Will you have milk?'

'Have a drop. I'll put jaggery in it.'

To all these questions Yasodi snapped out only one answer.

'I don't want anything.'

'That won't do,' Kautik said, her eyes fixed on Yasodi's face while her hands stroke her body. 'Tell me how you're feeling, dear?'

Yasodi didn't tell her anything. She didn't say a word. That morning, she had not had any fever, but now, you could feel the hot waves coming off her body even from a distance.

Kautik's eyes filled with tears again. As always, she needed Sakina to lighten her burden, to speak out her fears to. She sent Nama to call her. Both worried about Yasodi's rising temperature. Sakina suggested some herbal medicines she knew of. Kautik didn't have the right leaves to make smoke. So Sakina got some from her house. The dried leaves were crumbled into powder and sprinkled into the mild heat of a cow-dung cake fire. Yasodi's fevered body, bare and naked, was heated even further over the fire. She was made to breathe the smoke in through her nose and mouth. It made her sneeze again and again. She spluttered and choked and didn't have enough breath left in her even to cry or complain. Still Kautik and Sakina went on with the treatment till they were satisfied. Then they wrapped her in a rug. Nama was made to sit beside her to make sure she didn't throw off her wrapping and to wipe her dry if she sweated. The two women were still not satisfied, but they returned to their chores because they had to. As she left Kautik's house, Sakina reassured her, 'Don't you be scared now, Kautik. Trust in Allah. If she worsens, send Nama to me.' Then she went back to her house.

Kautik's body was leaden with worry and fatigue. She did her work lifelessly. She lit the fire, stuffed the bean-pods in a pan and set it on the fire. She threw in a fistful of salt and then went about her other work. One moment she was at the fire, next at Yasodi's side, then on the verandah and then in the yard. As she moved about, she sighed. Dinner time came.

The bean pods in the pan, blackish green and grey to start with, were now the colour of tea leaves. She threw little heaps of them before Nama and Bhima. They were steaming hot, but the boys began to peel and eat them instantly.

Sighing long and deep, Kautik turned away from her immediate worry and said, 'Bhima, tell Sheshrao to keep an eye out for your father when he goes to Umravati.'

At first Bhima didn't answer. But when Kautik repeated the same thing, he said, 'I'm not going back to his machine.'

'Why not?'

'Because I've said so once.'

'You must have shown him one of your tricks.'

'Who says?'

'Then why don't you go?'

'I don't like to.'

Kautik slapped her forehead and said sarcastically, 'Then come pick cotton with me.'

'Really I will.'

'Have you no shame of yourself or of people?'

He stopped her, saying, 'Listen, you. He doesn't teach me a thing. He hasn't taught me even buttons and button-holes in all these days. It's just go there, get that...that kind of rubbish all day.'

Kautik was watching him incredulously as he spoke. He continued, 'So I said I'm better off cotton picking. It'll make me some money at least.'

'You've grown too smart now, haven't you?'

'Leave it then,' Bhima flung down an empty pod. 'I'm talking sense but you won't have it.'

'Because I know what's happened. You've been up to tricks.'

'Which arsefucker says so?'

'We'll soon know.'

The next morning as she packed her food and Nama had packed his, she asked Bhima again, 'So you're not going to the machine?'

'Unhuh.'

'Then will you at least keep an eye on the girl if you're sitting at home?'

'Yes. Yes,' he said, pleased. 'Didn't I do that yesterday? Even cleaned her vomit and shit.'

'We all have to do these things, son.' Kautik didn't ask for more. Taking advantage of her mood, Bhima at once said, 'Maay, give me eight annas.'

'You'll not get such pamperings from me.'

'I beg of you.'

'Get away. Stop fooling around or I'll crack your jaw.'

Bhima held out his cheek. 'Here. Hit me. I've not got it from you for years,' he said, laughing.

'I'm not laughing,' she said, gathering together her cotton-picking cloths. 'I don't even have a broken cowrie shell to knock against my teeth.'

'Not even a broken cowrie, eh? Want me to show you?'

'All right, show me where,' she said after a pause.

Bhima went laughing then to the pot stack. As he lifted down the two top pots, Kautik pounced on him. They pulled and pushed, but she was no match for him. In the end, he managed to snatch the coins from the bottom-most pot. Kautik grasped the fist in which he was holding them with both her hands. She mustered all her strength to prise it open. But it was no use. Freeing his hand, Bhima ran into the yard.

He stood there, wary but laughing, loudly counting, he shouted out to her, 'If you'd given me eight annas quietly, would your rupee-and-a-half have got away?'

Kautik was furious. She lunged at him thinking he was off his guard. But he wasn't. He ran off like the wind. She stood where she was cursing the air, 'You rotten corpse, may the food you eat poison you.'

She raved and ranted but finally quietened down. She asked Nama, 'Aren't you going to school today?'

Nama's heart missed a beat. He mustered all his courage to say, 'Of course I am, maay. It's my half-year test today.'

'Go then. I'll stay with the girl.'

'You'll drop your wages?'

'What can I do then,' she said. 'Can you trust that ghoul? I can't leave the little one in pain and go to the fields.'

Relieved, Nama was about to set off for school when she said, 'Go to Sheshrao's machine and say to him, when you go to Umravati…'

'…look out for tatyaji.' Nama completed his mother's sentence.

'And also ask him if Bhima's at the machine.'

'But he's here.'

'Just ask him that and see what he says,' she said. 'And if he tells you some tale about Bhima and asks you where he is, what will you say?'

'What?'

'Say he's disappeared.'

Nama agreed to do what his maay said and went to Tivase. He wasn't even at Sheshrao's shop before Sheshrao called out to him, 'Hey boy, where's that father of yours?'

'I was going to…'

'And that Bhima?'

'My brother?' Then, remembering the line about Bhima, he said, 'He's disappeared.'

'You're big cheats all of you...' Sheshrao began before he could stop himself. 'Good I didn't come to Mozri.'

'Did you want to come?'

'Your brother has brought me to it. What else can I do?'

'Why? What's happened?'

'Your brother sold off a customer's order.' Then Sheshrao muttered to himself, 'Let me just set eyes on him. Then he'll see what Sheshrao Tailor can do.'

Seeing Sheshrao's state, Nama didn't dare tell him about his father. But he was even more scared of his maay. So he started giving Sheshrao her message. He'd hardly finished when Sheshrao knotted the thread in his needle with an angry jerk and said, 'Yes, sure I'll look out for him. As if I have no other work. With all the favours you folks have done me.'

Nama stored everything Sheshrao said in his mind. These days his maay would stop whoever was going down Umravati way to tell them about Mahadev. When Nama got back home, she had stopped a cartman carrying cotton. 'I know there's not much chance you'll see him in such a big city. But you never know. If you just happen to, say to him Yasodi is burning with fever.'

The cartman said yes for something to say. Then he moved on. Coming to herself, she asked Nama what had happened at Sheshrao's. Nama told her word for word what had happened. Kautik fumed and fretted till dinnertime.

That night, she cooked nothing. She set some stale bhakri before Nama. Seeing the empty basin, Nama said, 'What will you and Bhima eat, maay o?'

'I'm not eating or anything,' Kautik said angrily. 'And I won't be feeding that fellow from now. Let's just see how he manages…'

Nama ate his half bhakri and chilly powder quietly. Just then Sakina came over as usual to help Kautik look after Yasodi. Both sat beside the girl. Seeing the girl's dull face in the light of the lamp, Kautik kept dabbing at her tired eyes with her sari. All night Sakina kept saying to her, 'Don't cry, my dear one. These things happen. They do.'

In the morning, Kautik woke Nama, calling out to him in a weak voice. When he opened his eyes, he saw Sakina and Kautik sitting on the side of Yasodi's cot exactly as they had been the previous night. Sakina's eyes too looked tired now. Her bloodshot eyeballs seemed to protrude a little. The rug on Yasodi's stomach heaved up and down at a rapid rate. Kautik said to Nama in a barely audible voice, 'Son, see if that monster is alive or dead.'

'Didn't he come home last night?'

Kautik flew into a rage at Nama's natural question. 'You deathhead, why would I ask if he had?'

Nama set off quietly to look for Bhima. He came back saying, 'He's on the common. Under the peepul tree.'

'What's he doing?'

'I don't know. There's lots of fellows there—Shyamrao, Ajaba.'

Kautik left Sakina with Yasodi and took Nama with her to the common. Bhima was sitting under the peepul tree playing cards. He was squatting on his haunches, holding down a pile of currency notes under one foot. He didn't shift even a fraction when Kautik approached him.

He only stuffed the notes from under his foot into his pocket. His expression was stern, arrogant, as of a person lost in his own heady world. Coming up to him, Kautik said, 'You wretch, what's going on?'

Shyamrao stopped halfway through dealing out the cards, glancing first at Kautik, then at Bhima. Seeing his confusion, Bhima said to him sternly, 'Go on. Deal. And start playing.'

Trembling with rage and insult, Kautik said, 'Now you're wanting me to show you what's dealing and playing?'

'Look here,' he said, suddenly turning on her. 'Just go back quietly the way you came or don't say I didn't warn you.'

Kautik was stunned by Bhima's unexpected attack. She moved away to keep her self-respect but as she turned to go, she said, 'Just you wait, wretch. Let your father come home. If I don't get him to tear you into finger-sized bits and scatter them, my name isn't Kautik. What's taken away your senses, boy?' Next moment, she was on her way home.

Finally, Nama was forced to miss school and stay home that afternoon. Yasodi had brought everybody to a standstill. Kautik was home in any case, but even Sakina couldn't bring herself to go cotton picking. She sent Bano in her place instead, so she wouldn't lose all her wages, while she herself sat with Kautik by Yasodi's side. She went home only at meal time and that too because Bano and Qasam insisted. She returned with lentil curry and a bhakri-and-a-half for Nama. Kautik hadn't cooked and hadn't eaten. Every now and then, she passed a hand over Yasodi's body, caressing her and calling out to her in a tearful voice. Not only did Yasodi not answer but by nightfall she wasn't even opening her eyes. By now, Kautik's sari couldn't dam the flow of tears. They found a way around it and dripped down like a leaking roof. Sobs rose constantly to her throat. Even Sakina, who had always been such a support, was utterly helpless. Not a word of courage passed her lips. Everybody was waiting for the inevitable to happen. They knew in themselves what they couldn't bear to say. Half a bhakri had filled Nama, his appetite taken away by grief over his maay and Yasodi.

It was lamp-lighting time. The air was filled with the sounds of villagers and cattle returning from the forest. Women, bent under the weight of cotton, passed by the door.

Just then, they heard Qasam shout out to Sakina in a way they had never heard before. 'Where are you, wretched woman? Are you dead and buried out there?'

At first Sakina thought Qasam was shouting at Bano. But when he shouted again in the same way, she got up from Yasodi's cot muttering, 'What's come over this man today, shouting like that for no reason?'

'He must have come home tired from work. There might be no bhakri at home,' Kautik suggested.

'So what? He never shouts like that.' Stepping into their part of the house, she said, 'Has someone attacked you that you're shouting like that?'

'Does this one have to be shown how attacks happen?' Qasam was even angrier. 'Half her life's over and she hasn't got a cowrie's worth of brains.'

'But what's the matter? Can't you tell me?' Sakina said, offended.

'Go in and find out,' he said, pointing to the door with a trembling hand and rushing in after her. This was followed by muffled sounds of squabbling.

At dinner time, Kautik got Nama to make a boiled mix of rice and lentils. Then, as she scraped a deerhorn on the rubbing stone to make a paste for Yasodi's medicine, she suddenly remembered something and sent Nama to Sakina's. Nama was already calling out, 'Aunty, aunty...' as he ran through Sakina's yard towards the bellows, when Qasam, who was lying on his cot, sat up and said, 'Here fellow, where are you going?'

'Maay wants aunty to...'

Before Nama could complete the sentence, Qasam held up his hand saying, 'Get out. Go.'

Nama was amused. He laughed and made a move to go on. Qasam roared again, 'Didn't you hear what I said?'

This time Nama noticed the terrible look on Qasam's face and felt afraid. He went back home and told his maay what had happened. She too said, 'He must have been joking or something.'

'He wasn't and all. If he was, wouldn't Bano have been laughing from inside?'

Kautik saw his point. Growing thoughtful, she rose from her place and went out herself. When he saw her in the yard, Qasam sat up again on his cot. Before Kautik could say anything, he said, 'Kautik, I'm telling you plain and simple. You'd better look for another house.'

'Why? What's the matter?'

'Didn't I say you'd better look for another place? That's enough.'

Kautik glanced once at his door and once at her own. Then, without moving from her place, she put her hands on her hips and said, 'But why can't you tell me what's wrong?'

'Go in and ask your sister.'

Kautik went in. She saw Bano sitting in a dark corner. Her legs were drawn up, her head was in her knees and she was heaving with sobs. Sakina sat before the cooking fire patting bhakris in the light of an oil lamp. Her eyes were wet, her nose was running. She wiped it now and then on her knees. Neither she nor Bano moved or even lifted their eyes to acknowledge Kautik's presence. Kautik waited. She looked at the girl and the mother in turn and finally asked Sakina, 'Sister, what happened?'

Nobody moved. Kautik sat down near Sakina and said, 'What am I asking?'

Still the same. Then Kautik moved over to Bano's side. She laid her hand on her back, then stroked her head. That set Bano off sobbing again, her whole body trembling. Kautik wiped the girl's eyes with her sari, whispering, 'Hush, hush.'

That's when she noticed Bano's exposed chest. She quickly asked, 'How did you tear your shirt?'

That was it. Bano couldn't suppress her tears any longer. They burst out in violent sobs and wailing. Kautik sighed and moved over to Sakina's side, her mind made up. Sitting very close to her, wiping her own eyes, she asked as one who had a right to know, 'Now why aren't you telling me what happened?'

'Why force us to speak of our ill luck?'

'Whatever it is, you have to tell me. Aren't I a sister to you?'

Sakina sighed. She dried her eyes. But she said nothing.

'Aren't you going to tell me?' Kautik demanded. 'If you don't, it'll kill me.'

Sakina still didn't say a word. She only kneaded the ball of dough with greater force.

Kautik said, 'I'm asking you on Yasodi's life.'

'You're terrible, swearing by that poor sick soul.'

'Then tell me straight and simple what happened.'

Sakina said helplessly, 'Why do you make me say it, my sister? Bhima meddled with Bano.'

When she heard this, Kautik was like a scorpion that's seen a lizard. Her body went completely limp. Hitting her forehead with her palm again and again, she said, 'When was that?'

'A while ago. In the evening. When the girl was coming home with the cotton.'

Bano burst into a wail again. Kautik sat muttering to herself, 'What can I do with this rotten corpse? Shits where he eats, the wretch. The dog-mange has brought me to drinking poison. Was this why the monster gave up running from place to place and stopped here?' She paused, then continued in deep shame, 'Now let him step into my house. Either he lives or I live. If I can't thrash him, I'll go to the police officer right now and tell them to lock up the corpse. That's right. So what if he's my flesh?'

Such were the things Kautik said to herself. She wept her own tears and dried her own eyes. Nobody said hush to her. Nobody said anything to her. After a long time, she rose and went home without saying, 'I'm going sister,' over and over again as she always did, and without having Sakina say, 'Go, my sister,' back to her. She went home and sat by Yasodi's cot. She told Nama to have the khichdi and cover what was left in the pot after he'd had enough. Though she sat by Yasodi, she was no longer stroking her body as before. She wasn't trying to make her talk nor was she wiping her sweat. She simply sat with her chin on her knees and her eyes staring at the ground in front of her. There was no life in her except in the blinking of her eyelids. Everything was still. When Nama had finished eating and reminded her of Yasodi's medicine, she flew into a rage, saying, 'Throw that medicine out. Let the wretch die—let it happen today instead of tomorrow.' And she continued the way she had been.

Nama spread his rug quietly, a little away from her, and lay down. He was just about to fall asleep when she seemed to wake up and said, 'Don't go to sleep, son. Give me a hand here.'

So saying, she hurried to the trunk. She began to empty it of all the foodstuffs. The earthen pot of jaggery came out and was emptied into an old sari of hers. The tin of turmeric likewise. Things that couldn't be tied up in the sari bundle were wrapped in paper packets. Stuff that couldn't go into either was flung onto the floor. Next the pots and the pans were divided into two lots, her own and Sakina's. She carried all her stuff into the yard where

Nama was told to arrange it in a pile. She spread a rug beside this mess and dumped the sleeping Yasodi on it. She covered her with a sari folded over eight times to keep her from the cold. She made Nama sit beside her while she went back indoors and stood the empty cot up on its side. She cast a glance over the house in the light of the oil lamp and stepped out with the lamp. She upturned a grain measure beside Yasodi and stood the lamp on it, but the wind pounced on it and blew off the flame. Kautik struck a matchstick and lit it again, but again it was blown off. She picked up a cane winnower that lay nearby and shaded the lamp with it, but the oil-lamp flame was blown off once again. Then Kautik gave up hope of light. She left Nama to look after Yasodi in the dark, saying, 'Stay there, my dear. I'll be back in a while.'

She hurried to Sakina's part of the house. She woke her up and led her by the hand to her own. She struck a few matches to light the utensils in the house and said, 'There you are, Sakina my one. Look after your house.'

Stunned, Sakina said, 'And where are you going?'

'I'll stay in the yard till daybreak; then I'll go to Talegaon.'

'Dear God! This has to be the limit. Did I even tell you to empty the house today itself?'

'You haven't said it, but shouldn't I have sense? I'm not the woman to covet the beams of the house where I eat.'

'Look here, Kautik, don't you do something thoughtless. Let the girl feel better then you can go where you want.'

'Let the wretch die. She'll die tomorrow so why not now?

'See what kind of mother this woman is,' Sakina said angrily. 'But will you heed what I'm saying even a little?'

Kautik wasn't listening. She wasn't even looking at Sakina.

Sakina said, 'What am I saying?'

'Whatever it is, take your stuff away.'

'Let the stuff be.' Then it struck Sakina to ask, 'And where's the boy?'

'In the yard. Where else will the corpse go?'

'In the yard. Have you gone mad, Kautik?' Sakina walked swiftly into the yard. She tried to pierce the dark with eyes torn wide and asked in a guessed direction, 'Where are you, Nama, my dear?'

The moment she heard Nama's voice, she turned that way.

But Kautik barred her way saying, 'Let him be. He's all right.'

'Go away. Move,' Sakina said pleading. 'I'm asking you on my life.'

'Maybe.' And Kautik continued to bar Sakina's way, refusing to let her take even one step forward.

Sakina stood for a moment, thinking. Then she said with threat in her voice, 'So this isn't the way you'll listen,' and went back to her house.

Kautik said to her back, 'All your stuff is in the house. Now if something goes missing, you can do what you like.'

She lay down beside Yasodi then and said to Nama, 'Lay yourself down if you want to, son.'

But Sakina was soon back, pushing her husband before her. She held up her lantern and saw Kautik lying curled up like a mother cat, with Nama and Yasodi nestling against her.

Snatching the rug off Kautik, Qasam said, 'What kind of low-down scene do you think you're making?'

'It's not a scene,' Kautik muttered without lifting her arm off her eyes.

'Good. Then get up and go in.' Then Qasam muttered to himself, 'A man says things when he's mad. Do you take them so badly?'

'Why badly? It's my coin that's fake. Why should I let good souls like you suffer on its account? I must suffer for my sins.'

'Shut up about sins and things. Get inside first.' Then Qasam said to his wife, 'Go set up the cot. I'll bring Yasodi in. Let's see how Kautik stops me from doing that.'

Qasam loosened Yasodi's wraps. Ignoring Kautik's tantrums, he put her against his shoulder and carried her in. As he lowered her to the cot, he said to his wife in a stern voice, 'Now go out and bring all that stuff in.'

Sakina went out and began collecting the kitchen stuff together. She said to Nama, 'Can you bring in those pans, my son.'

'Can I take them, maay?'

Kautik didn't answer. Qasam said to him, 'Why are you asking her? I'd like to see what she'll do. You get those pans in.'

And so all the utensils and clay pots and rugs and rags were brought back into the house. Then Qasam and Sakina led Kautik in and set her beside Yasodi. Settling down on the cot herself, Sakina said, 'And did you apply the child's poultice today?'

'No poultice, no nothing.'

'Did you make the paste at least?'

'I did.'

'So where is it?'

'I chucked it away.'

'You're really smart, aren't you?' Then she said to Nama, 'Son, where's that deerhorn?'

Nama brought Sakina the piece of deerhorn. She began to rub it to a paste on the rubbing stone. Satisfied, she said to her husband, 'Go. You can go and sleep now.'

After that day, Kautik never set eyes on Bhima's face again. So hateful had the mere thought of him become to her, that she'd fly into a rage if Nama or Yasodi as much as mentioned his name. 'Don't you dare talk to me about him,' she had warned them on more than one occasion. Soon they too forgot him. In the next couple of weeks, Yasodi, who had wilted during her illness, began to pick up strength, eat and walk about till she was quite well again. Thus Kautik's two biggest troubles were over. Perhaps that is why the three separate directions in which her heart had pulled and ached, now became concentrated on a single worry—Mahadev's disappearance. Sometimes a person who has faced many trials without flinching, suddenly feels defeated by something that seems not so difficult to overcome. That's how it was with Kautik now. She began to pine away by the day. She couldn't work as hard as she used to. Even when the work was light, she'd lag behind the other women. If the field they were working in ran beside the road, she was always the last in the line. She'd hardly have picked the cotton off a few plants before she'd straighten up and cast her eyes down the road as far as they could see. After a long time spent looking, she'd sigh. Sometimes she'd sniffle. And when she couldn't bear it any longer, she'd dab at her eyes. Sakina, who was almost always with her, would ask, 'Why are you wiping your eyes, dear one?'

'Caught a bit of dust.'

Sakina knew from experience what that meant. Not wishing to cause more pain, she would keep quiet. But Kautik would soon realize that she had lost the chance to feel the tender touch of sympathy and would begin to talk of her own accord in a heavy voice, 'Why ask Sakina, my one? You know how long it is since the man left the village and went away.'

Sakina no longer dared to give Kautik courage as she used to in the old days. She would remain silent and Kautik would pour out her grief in a torrent. 'All my thoughts are with the man. There are times when I think maybe he met some holy man on the way and decided to follow him. Or someone tempted him with a machine and he's gone off after it. Or I fear young thugs have done something terrible to him on the way...' She couldn't continue after that. She'd put her sari-edge to her eyes and stand trembling.

'Don't think such evil things. Don't harm your own with the thoughts of your mind.'

'I don't harm him in my mind, poor soul,' Kautik said. 'But it is as they say—the mind thinks worse than even the enemy does. That's my state.'

This was how they talked often and at length, in the fields and at home. Kautik would stop in the middle of some household chore and press her finger to her eyebrow. 'My eyelid's fluttering,' she'd murmur to herself. Then at times she would ask Yasodi or some other innocent child, 'Do you think we'll have a visitor?' If Yasodi said no, she'd get annoyed and say, 'When will you say yes, you pest!' and if she said yes, Kautik would exult, 'I'll fill your mouth with sugar.' In reality, Yasodi never got to see a single grain of sugar. Once when a crow sat on the roof cawing and Nama casually shooed it away, Kautik flew at him in a rage, for the crow was a sign of a visitor. 'You wretch, why don't you let it yell if it wants to. It's not swallowing your father's fortune, is it?'

That wasn't all. Kautik only had to hear of some fellow from the village travelling out, never mind which way, and she'd go stand at his door. 'Since you're going Nagpur-way, keep an eye out for the man of my house. Even if he's not coming back, you just have to tell me he's in such and such a place.' The man would nod and go his way. Kautik's eyes would then be focused on his instead of Mahadev's return.

The moment she heard he was back, she'd be at his door again, inquiring. 'Tell me. Did you see him?'

'No.'

'I don't suppose you went to the tailor's shops.'

'Er...I did. But I didn't see Mahadev.'

'Maybe in a temple?'

'Why a temple?'

'That's true too,' Kautik would say helplessly.

Once in a while, someone returning from a journey would tell her, 'Didn't see Mahadev. But I spotted Bhima.'

Kautik would ask, only by way of returning the man's courtesy, 'And what was he doing?'

'Shaving and massaging.'

'Let the corpse die.'

Once Shevanti's husband who had returned from Umravati told Kautik, 'I saw Bhima there.'

'But Patwari master was saying he saw him in Wardha. What was he doing in Umravati?'

'He was dancing as a tiger in the Mohurrum procession.'

'Are you sure it was Bhima?'

'Of course. I didn't recognize him but he saw me and greeted me.'

'Did he ask after any of us?'

'He did. If Yasodi was alive.'

That's how the days passed. The daily grind was crushing Kautik in body and spirit.

Then, one day, when she was least expecting it, Kautik heard the news. It was around dusk. She was trudging down the road in the company of the other farm workers, carrying headloads of cut lentil stalks, when she heard the rumble of a cart coming up behind. The entire row of women moved over to the bank on the side of the road to make way for it. The Marwari's clerk riding in the cart recognized Kautik and asked his servant to stop. 'Isn't that Kautik, the tailor woman?'

'Yes?'

'Any news of Mahadev?'

'No, worse luck.'

'What'll you give me if I tell you?'

Kautik flung her headload down when she heard this. The clerk was older to her and to be respected. So she smiled and said, 'I'll give you my girl.'

'But Yasodi calls me lisper.'

'How you get on with each other is your business,' Kautik retorted, laughing with the other women, but hurried on to ask, 'Where did you see him?'

'In Umravati.'

'Whereabouts?'

'At the tower clock. He was sitting on the parapet.'

'And where is this what-d'you-call it clock?'

'It's right there. In New Colony. Ask anybody and they'll tell you.'

'I'll send Namya to you as soon as I get home. Write it down for him, will you?'

'I will.' So saying, the clerk ordered the cartman to drive on.

Kautik's feet found new strength. A while ago, she'd been last in the line of women. As she neared home, she was half a field ahead of Shevanti, first in the line. It was with the same energy that she patted and baked bhakris from two large measures of flour and cooked some crushed split-bean cakes to go with them. They ate their fill. She packed the rest of the food for the journey. She counted the money in the pot stack. It wasn't enough. So she went, even at that hour, to the house of the man whose lentils she was threshing and coaxed him to give her what was owing to her that day itself, not wait for pay day the following Tuesday. She borrowed a couple more rupees from Sakina for safety and then lay down to rest, waiting for the day to break.

She folded up her rug as the morning star rose. She put the bundle of bhakris on Nama's head and called out to the sleeping Sakina to look after Yasodi while she was away. Sakina asked, 'When will you come back?'

'By the evening if I can. Or tomorrow afternoon,' she answered hurriedly and set off for Umravati.

They had hardly got off the bus at Umravati when Kautik asked the very first person they saw the way to the tower clock.

He told them how to get there with signs and landmarks. A little way down the road, she asked another man where the clock tower was. 'Further down this way,' he answered.

After they'd walked a good distance, she asked yet another person for directions. He said, 'This isn't where the clock tower is.'

'Where then?'

'Back there, in New Colony.'

Before she turned back, Kautik asked another person. His directions tallied with the first man's. She walked a long way down that road but then had to turn back again. Finally, it was afternoon by the time she arrived at the clock tower.

Looking up at the tall stone tower soaring above, Nama said, 'But maay, we went this way so many times.'

'Yes, son. But how to know this was the same thing we were looking for?'

Mother and son then entered an enormous walled area that went by the name of clock tower. They stepped in through the irongate and stood baffled. The place was not at all how they'd imagined it would be. It was a mountain of a structure that left them feeling totally confused. A doubt entered Kautik's mind, which was heaving turbulently like the sea in a storm. How could my husband, who wasn't worth even one stone of this building, have dared to enter it? She even wondered whether the clerk could have played a prank on her, though she knew he wasn't one for doing such things. But since she was there, she picked up enough courage to enter the building.

Kautik stopped every passer-by she could, to ask if he'd seen a man called Mahadev from such-and-such town. But the people in that place knew nobody but themselves. Then she noticed some idle people laughing in the verandahs of the Brahmavidya Mandir and the Girls' School and on the famous Hanuman parapet of the clock tower. They were an assortment of people, from retired government clerks to beggars, who sat under the same roof but kept their distance from each other to mark out their own space. There were other faces that bore a resemblance to Mahadev's, who rested quietly on their beddings. The flame of hope, which had been dying in Kautik, flickered to life when she saw those people.

She and Nama walked slowly along the side of the verandahs, carefully inspecting every face. Suddenly her hope sprang large and clear like the full moon. There was Mahadev, sitting calmly, leaning against a cement pillar, smoking a bidi. His beard had grown long, and his clothes, the same ones in which he had left home, were in tatters. Unwashed and uncared for, they had changed colour completely.

Seeing Kautik, Mahadev tried to hide his face. Such was the fear he felt at the sight of her, that if he'd seen a way out, he'd surely have run away. Perhaps it was his expression that made Kautik wonder whether it was Mahadev at all. Suppose it turned out to be someone else? The doubt made her stop where she was. But she sent Nama to speak to him, while she herself stayed back within earshot. When Nama was near enough, Mahadev pretended he had just seen him. 'What are you doing here, Nama?' he asked.

'Maay's also here.'

'What for?'

'Why would I come?' Kautik said, now moving up to Mahadev. 'Who am I to you that I should be coming here?'

Mahadev said, 'But why have you come here?'

'You can ask me that? How did you come and sit here leaving your wife and children behind?'

'My fate brought me here.'

'Dear god,' Kautik said, looking around to see if she could be overheard. 'And what big danger were you facing?'

'Don't I know what it was,' Mahadev said angrily. 'I'm here because ...'

'Yes, why?' Kautik looked at him closely, her eyes pleading. 'Where's your bundle and all?'

'Offered it up to Lord Mahadev.'

'Why?'

'Never mind. Don't dig up those things now.'

'And why this disguise?'

'Lord Mahadev's will.'

'Don't Mahadev me at every word. Just tell me simple and straight what happened.'

'When a man feels hopeless, he calls on God.'

'But what happened to make you feel so hopeless is what I'm asking.'

'What happened? What didn't happen? I know and Mahadev knows.'

That's how it went on for a while. Then Kautik sat down beside him. Nama had already done so. Some passers-by folded their hands and smiled at Mahadev as they glanced at Kautik and Nama's unfamiliar faces with curiosity. A little while later, Kautik asked him in a confidential voice, 'Please tell me. Where is the bundle?'

'Why make me say it, poor soul? Thieves stole it.'

'Dear mother, and where was that?'

'In the valley near Pimpalzhira,' he said. 'And do you think there was one or two thieves? Oh no. There were eight of them.'

'Dear mother,' she exclaimed. 'And what did they do?'

'What? Two held me, two snatched the bundle and the rest picked my pockets.'

Kautik stared at him. Mahadev continued, 'I said to them take the bundle but don't touch my pockets.'

'Then?'

'Then what? One of them pulled out a knife and held it to my throat.'

'Why did you let them do that? You should have given the money.'

'Do you know, woman, how much money there was?'

'How much?'

'Two hundred ten rupees.' Mahadev began to mutter to himself. 'Man thinks one thing and something else terrible happens. I had thought I'd pay off the wholesaler his one hundred fifty rupees after the Nare market was done. And with the remaining money, go to Tivase and buy Sheshrao's old machine.'

'Forget these things. So much is already lost. Your life's saved. That's more than good.'

'What use is that life!' Mahadev exploded. 'Goods lost. Money lost. Business reputation lost.'

'Bigger people lose these things. But they don't abandon their wives and children for that.' She pressed on in the same breath, 'So when will you come back to the village?'

'You want me back so the wholesaler can thrash me with his chappals? He wants his money and nothing else, doesn't he?'

'Who'll thrash you with chappals? He wants money, nothing else, right?'

'Dear lord. So we have our own field to pay off the debt.'

'Who wants fields? We have our lives. That's field enough. We'll repay the wretched money. Eat dry bhakri with nothing to go with it, work harder...what else?' Then, without pausing she said, 'Come back with us in the morning.'

'What will you make me do there?'

'What else but what people do to fill their bellies?'

'Forget people. I can't go out to slog in the fields any longer.'

'You can't get by saying you can't.'

'If I can't, I can't,' Mahadev said in disgust. 'This nagging is why I came and died here. But you turned up here too.'

'So I did. Now come home quietly. Nobody's going to nag you.' Kautik paused. Then began to ask again, 'What time…?'

'But woman,' Mahadev pleaded with all his heart. 'I don't know what you'll make me do when you take me back there.'

'We'll see about that when we get there. Come.'

Mahadev fell silent. Perhaps it was only to grope in his pockets. Kautik quickly asked, 'What're you looking for?'

'A bidi.'

'Shall I send for it?'

'If I can find a paisa, I'll send Nama.'

At that, Kautik triumphantly opened the cloth purse at her waist, took out a four anna coin and put it in Nama's hand. Looking at it with greedy eyes, Mahadev said, 'If there's a few more paise to spare, send for matches if you can.'

Instead of a couple of paise worth of bidis and one box of matches, Kautik happily told Nama to get a whole bundle of twenty-five bidis and two boxes of matches. Nama didn't know where to find the shop so Mahadev gave him the landmarks. Nama etched them into his memory and was about to go when Mahadev asked him, 'So do you want to see Bhima?'

'Where's that ghoul?' Kautik asked with deep contempt but some curiosity. 'Is he around here?'

'Yes.'

'What does he do?'

'Nama'll tell you when he gets back.'

'Why can't you?'

'Cuts hair.'

'What?'

'Am I lying then? You can go see in that saloon if you want to take a look.'

'Me? I'm not going to set eyes on him again my whole life.'

'Why now? You should hoist him over your head and dance. That'll give him more strength to show the soles of his chappals to his father.'

'Which father?'

'He has another,' Mahadev muttered furiously. 'That's what your own flesh is all about.'

'What do you mean?'

'Why make me talk about it?' But then told her all. When she heard the story, Kautik said, 'Nama, you will not go to that ghoul. Buy the bidis and matches and come right back. He is dead to us now and we to him'

Nama came out of the clock tower compound onto the road through a semi-circular iron stile meant for people to come and go, not the big gate through which they had entered. He was on his way to the bidi shop when he noticed a crowd outside a tea shop. He poked his head through the crowd out of sheer curiosity and saw Bhima. He was standing by the cash counter. The man at the counter, with a thick upturned moustache, was holding him by the hair. But Bhima was not a bit put off. He was saying to the man in a menacing tone, 'Look here, boss. I'll speak straight. If you care for your honour, let go of my hair.' As always, he spoke in Hindi.

Then a Marwari stepped out of the crowd and spoke to the tea shop owner in their common tongue. A few exchanges later, the owner backed off, taking care to do it in a way that wouldn't cause him loss of face. He let go of Bhima's hair. Bhima smoothed it down, blew on his puffed out chest and descended the steps of the tea shop. He turned off down the road after giving the crowd a contemptuous look. Seeing him this way by chance, Nama called out to him impulsively. Bhima spun around and said, 'What are you doing here?'

Nama told him. Bhima was only half-listening only because he had to. Then he said, 'Will you have something to eat?'

'What?'

'A snack, you son of a bitch.'

Nama tried to refuse but something about Bhima's appearance made him follow him into the tea shop.

Bhima ordered three or four dishes together—jalebis, chivda, ladoos. He shoved the plates towards Nama who asked him, 'Won't you eat?'

'No.'

'Can I take something for maay then?'

'Eat straight if you can. Don't show me fancy airs.'

Nama didn't quite get what Bhima meant, but he understood the anger on his face. So he fell to eating without another word. Meanwhile Bhima was asking him, 'Listen. When I came away, did that son of a so-and-so Qasam say anything?'

'No, nothing.'

'Nothing at all?'

'Unhunh.'

'About Bano and all?'

'Oh about that…' Nama remembered now. He wanted to get down to the bottom of that story. 'What happened that day, Bhima?'

'Don't meddle. You want to eat, eat quiet and take the road.'

Nama became aware once more of this new Bhima whom he didn't know. He continued to eat in silence. He felt quite full at the end of those four plates of snacks. There was no place in his stomach even for the tea Bhima had ordered. Bhima took a sip from it and held the cup up. Turning to the cash counter, he shouted, 'Boss, you call this tea?'

'Why? What's wrong?'

'Try it and see.'

'But what's wrong?'

'I'm not saying anything. You drink it or make the chap who made it drink it…you think our money's free? No sugar, no tea leaves.'

'Did you want it strong?' the owner asked, trying his best to keep his voice mild for the sake of his business. 'Then you could have…'

'Ask your man if I said so or no.'

The concerned man piped up then to save his skin. 'What d'you mean? When did you ask me to make it strong?'

'What! I didn't ask?'

Anticipating a battle of words, the owner intervened. He told Bhima to throw away the tea saying he'd get him another cup. But Bhima didn't want it now! He was in a hurry.

Outside, he asked Nama as he walked up to a betel-leaf stall, 'D'you eat betel leaf?'

'No.'

'Why not?'

'It makes your ears dark.'

'No such fucking thing happens,' he said impatiently. 'Now go. Move.'

'Where are you going?'

'To hell,' Bhima said. Then he walked off, rubbing lime with his forefinger into the crushed tobacco leaves in his palm and swinging to his own beat, as though he was quite alone in the whole world.

By the time Nama returned to the clock tower with the bidis and matches, Kautik had managed to get around Mahadev. He didn't sound so determined now not to go back. The plan kept swinging one way then the other between the two of them. At one point, he said, 'What you're saying is all true. But what'll you make me do back in the village?'

'But I'm saying we'll decide that when we get back. We'll find some good soul to loan us fifty rupees or so at interest and buy goods.'

Mahadev looked closely at her face. Then, rolling his tongue in his cheek he said, 'You've got some money put away, no wonder…'

'I may or I may not. But you must come back first. We'll talk about all this there. People can get by in the village any which way with mud for walls and straw for sleep.'

She paused, then said, 'Get ready now. Get a shave first and then...'

'What bus can we get at this hour?'

They decided to return the following day. Kautik gave Mahadev money to get a shave. She washed his clothes at the tap after nightfall. It was midnight before they dried. Meanwhile Mahadev squatted in the dark of the verandah wrapped in a torn piece of Kautik's sari. He was shivering with cold. His clothes were still only half dry when he got into them. The three of them spent the rest of the night on the ice-cold floor of the verandah, something that several of those now sleeping there must have done for years.

This manoeuvre of Kautik's came back to plague her within a week's time. Every day as she finished her cooking and stood in the yard ready to go out to work, he would ask, 'So, what am I saying?' And she would say, speaking out of the deep pain of her heart, 'I swear by you. I don't have a cracked cowrie to knock on the teeth. Didn't I give it to you without you asking when I had it? And how would I have any? After you went, there was just me left to toil and feed four mouths.'

Then Mahadev would lose his temper and say, 'So I jumped from the flames into the fire, didn't I?'

'Dear Lord. What fire do you see here?'

'There is and what,' Mahadev would answer. 'You said we'd see when we got back to the village. And I said why not. Let me go back to the woman and the children and do some work instead of staying here.'

'So who stops you? Go to the fields.'

'Rot. I can't manage that now.'

'Who's forcing you then? You can sit around. I'm not saying anything to you.'

'So that's how it is...you'll live as mine, and eat what I give.'

When the exchange reached this stage, Kautik kept quiet, only looking at Mahadev with disbelief, anger or pity. The deadlock would be broken by a companion's call to work. Kautik would then come to herself, collect her bundle of bhakris and set off.

As the house emptied, Mahadev would become acutely aware of his loneliness. This feeling was intensified by his weakness and the way it had cut him off from the world. The grief of it would churn up his stomach, rise to his lips and spill over into the environment. Lying on his rug, blowing clouds of bidi smoke into the air, he'd ramble,

Why be proud of body and wealth...
There's mud in the eye, don't you see?
He built himself a palace and then...
Went to the jungle to sleep.

At other times, he'd stare at the roof and mutter, 'Mother of hope, father of despair, sister of the present, future's friend.'

There were times when Mahadev would sit for hours by the bellows, smoking bidis and muttering such things to Qasam, while pulling the chain of the bellows with one hand as if to pay for the space he occupied. He'd have no sense of time till Kautik returned in the evening and called out to him. Then he'd come back to himself. But he wouldn't move till she called two or three times. Then he'd get up and go indoors. He'd answer questions about what he'd eaten with, 'I wasn't hungry.'

'Eat now.'

'I'm still not hungry.'

Sometimes he'd say, 'I ate.'

'Where?'

'At Sakharam Bhende's house.'

'Why? What was on at his place?'

'Nothing. He was eating. He said to me, eat. So I ate.'

'You're a good one. Somebody says to eat to be polite and you eat.'

'What's wrong in that?'

'Do you know what the village people are saying?'

'What?'

'They are saying Kautik's husband's become a sit-around.'

'So let them. It's nothing to do with them.'

Mahadev would overturn all ideas of shame and conscience with such remarks. He'd deliberately behave more and more strangely. It seemed to happen without his knowledge.

In a way, he had been with Kautik when he was away and now that he was with her, he was really absent. She wanted him to be with her. If not for her, at least for the children. She wanted him to be like other fathers for their sake. She spoke of this desire to the village elders again and again and made them try to put sense into him. But all her efforts went waste. They were now like the bullock cart in which one wilfull animal has stopped pulling its weight. She was bent under a double burden. It wasn't just earning for the family, but everything else as well. The whole responsibility now rested on her, and her natural grit wouldn't let her escape the burden.

It was Saturday. Mahadev had gone as usual to the Maruti temple to belt out his devotional songs. Nama and Yasodi had finished eating and were lolling on the cot. She had waited a long time for Mahadev to come back before finally serving herself. She couldn't have had more than four mouthfuls when she heard a familiar voice around Sakina's house asking after Mahadev. She stopped chewing, listened, then asked Nama to go out and see who it was. But he was too slow for her impatient spirit, and she was in the doorway herself, lamp in hand before he could get there. The mouthful of food still unchewed, her food messed hand held behind her back, she raised the lamp and tried to pierce the pitch dark night with her eyes to make out who it was. But the person saw her first and asked, 'Isn't that sister?' she recognized the voice now.

It was Sukhdev.

'Dear Lord, it's many ages since you came to the home of us poor folk. Come in, won't you?'

'Where's Brother Mahadev?' He asked in a hurry.

'Won't you come in first? Why do you stand out there and ask?' Kautik asked him laughingly. 'You're not scared of me to come in, are you?'

But Sukhdev didn't laugh; he became grave. He took off his slippers in the yard. As he washed his hands, Kautik said, 'Take off your outdoor things. 'I'll serve you dinner.'

'I don't want to eat,' he said even more grimly as he sat on Nama's cot. 'Tell me where brother's gone.'

'He's gone to Umravati with his second wife.'

'Don't joke, sister. Tell me quickly where Mahadev is.'

Now Kautik's face also grew cold. 'Why? On what great work are you here?'

'Something. Finish eating.'

Kautik became thoughtful. Rolling the food around in her mouth, she asked, 'I hope all is well with the old man?'

'Didn't I say eat first?'

Kautik sighed. She removed the remaining quarter bhakri with the lump of lentils from her clay dish and put it on the ground. Pouring water on her hands she said, 'Now tell me.'

'Have you finished eating already?'

'Yes. Now tell me quickly.'

'The old man is all but gone.'

'Has he been ill?'

'Yes. The sickness has been wearing him down these six or seven months.'

'And you tell us at the last moment?'

'No, sister. He was in the same state on Tuesday. I'd sent Janrao out to you then. But you were in Umravati.'

'But I got back the next day.'

'But the old man came around that time. I asked him if he wanted me to send for Mahadev. He said don't let him step into my sight while there's breath left in me.'

Kautik let out a heavy sigh when she heard this. Then she woke up Nama and packed him off to fetch Mahadev. Nama returned saying, 'Tatyaji says he's not coming.'

'Did you give him the right message?'

'Yes. So he said, let him die if he has to. How does it affect my fate?'

Kautik slapped her forehead with her palm. Then she went to the Maruti temple herself and came back abusing Mahadev's inhumanity all the way. When she reached home, she said bitterly to Sukhdev, 'Let us go, brother. I'll go with you.'

'But what's the use of your coming?'

'What use would he be? Things that have to be done have to be done.'

She began to get ready. She asked Sakina for her lantern. Told her to keep a watch over the sleeping Yasodi. She took Nama along and set off down the road to Talegaon. Sukhdev had the lantern and both she and he strode fast, leaving Nama away behind. He scampered as fast as he could, holding up his stomach as if to keep his dinner in. Sukhdev and Kautik talked as they walked. About Mahadev's growing irresponsibility, old Raghunath Tailor's illness, his stubborn nature. Kautik was doing the talking. Sukhdev only said yes and no most times.

As they climbed the plinth, a thin voice from the crowd which had gathered around the old man's house said, with untimely enthusiasm, 'He's here. The old man's son's come.'

'No. He couldn't, dear soul. It's only me, Kautik,' she said. 'How's the old man?'

Nobody answered. Kautik broke through the women's group and went straight in. She bent to lift the cloth off the old man's face. Sita said, 'What's there to see? The old man's food-and-drink days are over.'

Then Kautik's lament flowed out in many streams. Beating her chest, she said, 'The old man was stubborn, o. He stuck to his mind, o. He vowed not to see our faces till the end of his days, o. Now who will fight with me, o? Who will drive me out of my house, o?'

So Kautik lamented over every memory of the old man's life as she remembered it. She dug her fingers into her flowing hair and wailed. She beat her chest and slapped her palm again and again on her forehead. Neighbours did their duty by consoling her saying, 'Cry any amount, but the old man won't come to fight with you.'

'That may be so. But a person feels it. Even a neighbour's eyes fill with tears, and she is his daughter-in-law, poor soul.'

'Nama, don't cry, there. Go sleep on my verandah.'

Meanwhile, Kautik's lament continued. 'He didn't let me take the big water pot, o. Said buy one with your own money, o.'

This went on till day broke. By morning, Kautik had finished her weeping. The tears had spent themselves. Only words remained. Now she was narrating the rest of the old man's memories in a dry voice and the tone of a storyteller. She continued in this vein till it was time for the cattle to be taken out to graze. Then Sukhdev brought her back to reality. 'Sister, shouldn't we make preparations for the funeral?'

'That's right, brother,' she said, repressing a sob. 'Of course we must.'

'Can you step out a minute?'

Kautik followed him wordlessly to the edge of the plinth.

He said, 'Sister, d'you have money for the cloth and all?'

'No, nothing, my brother.' Trying once again to suppress a sob, she said, 'The Lord has left me with an empty hand for the old man. Was I his foe in the last birth I want to know.'

Before she could complete what she was saying, Sukhdev whispered something in her ear. What he said made her shake her head sideways in a determined no. Sukhdev said in a tearful voice, 'Then what can we do?'

'Use whatever you have now. Later I'll...'

'If I had any, why would I ask you to open the old man's trunk, poor soul?'

Kautik thought, then asked, 'How much will we need?'

'Maybe fifteen rupees or so. That's counting the chopping of wood.'

'Fifteen,' she thought. Climbing down the plinth, she said, 'Wait, I'll be back.'

Kautik walked rapidly to Ganpat Brewer's house. The moment she saw him in his shop, she said, 'Brother, you've got to help me.'

'What?'

'Give me twenty rupees or so.'

'Ask for anything else but that, sister.'

'Don't say no. I am asking you on my children's lives.'

'That may be so, sister, but...'

She didn't allow him to finish what he was saying. 'You're asking yourself how Kautik the tailor woman's going to pay back your money. But don't. I'll keep the old man's house as security for the money.'

'The house?' Suddenly Ganpat's eyes shifted from his weighing scales to Kautik. 'Where's the house, sister?'

'Meaning?'

'You don't know?' he said. 'Of course. How would you? You came in the night.' He paused and then went on as if with great difficulty, 'I heard that Bakhadya bought it.'

'Who told you?'

'Just a rumour floating around,' he said. 'The old man had to eat, so he sold it off.'

'Well,' Kautik said easily. 'If he did, he did. He bought it with his labour. But you've got to give me the money. We will do any work that's going but we won't keep your money.'

'Sister,' Ganpat shrugged, his eyes returning to his scales. 'How can I tell you? Only yesterday in Umravati, Sadashiv...'

'You can keep the old man's sewing machine if that's any use, but don't say no.'

Now Ganpat's resolve shook. He got up, rubbing a palm against a wrist and saying in a heavy voice, 'Well, let me see in the house if there's any...'

'Yes, yes. Please see. Quick, brother.'

Returning from his search, Ganpat said with a false smile, 'Sister, by the old man's luck there was only this ten rupees in my trunk. See what you can manage with this.'

Pouncing on the note, Kautik said, 'Give it, poor soul. Better this than nothing. I'll manage with this somehow.' She turned to go.

So he said impatiently, 'And when will you bring the machine across?'

'Will I have to bring it here?'

'And then?' But he added generously, 'You can bring it when you can...after the old man's third-day rites or so.'

Kautik agreed and returned home. As she climbed the plinth, she asked Sukhdev, 'Brother, has Janya not come from Mozri?'

'No.'

'Then will you do something?'

She handed the money over to him and sent him to Tivase to get the funeral things. A few others accompanied him. Kautik sat down by the old man. Holding her head with one hand, she began whisking the flies off the old man's body with the loose end of her sari. As she talked to people who came to condole with her, she kept glancing alternately at the roads from Mozri and Tivase. A long time later, Janya returned from Mozri. Even he was climbing the plinth, Kautik asked him, 'Where is he?'

'He hasn't come.'

'What? Didn't you meet him?'

'I did,' he answered. 'But Uncle Mahadev said let him be dead if he's dead. I'm not coming.'

'Did you hear that, sister!' Kautik's second hand shot up and slapped her forehead. She said to Sita, 'Tell me, what's a woman to do now?'

Sita didn't say a word. A while later, Basanti's husband said, 'So-ooo, if he won't come, he won't. The old man won't stay for him now, will he? Somebody will carry him for sure.'

'Maybe, Brother Waman. But what's the use of having a son of your own flesh?'

'It may not be God's will that the son's touch should fall on the old man. What can anybody do about that?' Pausing a while, he said, 'Or they were enemies in their last birth, poor souls!'

Kautik wasn't saying anything, only listening. And while she listened, she kept her eyes on the road from Tivase. Sukhdev and the others returned on time. As soon as he came, Sukhdev looked around for Mahadev. When he heard Mahadev hadn't come, he pushed his feet furiously into his slippers, saying, 'Let me see how he won't come.'

Kautik responded with equal anger, 'Nobody's wasting time going back there again.'

'But who'll carry the fire?'

'Some poor soul will,' she answered. 'Yes, and what? A king may die, his kingdom doesn't; a husband may die, his house doesn't. People manage.'

Sukhdev's anger subsided. He and the others got down to preparations. The water on the fire in the yard was hot. The old man's body was washed. Grass was scattered on the bier that had been prepared, and the old man was laid out on it. They pulled the shroud over his body, smeared vermillion on his face and put a made-up betel leaf in his mouth.

When four men stood by the four corners of the bier, Sukhdev called out, 'Sister, who'll carry the fire?'

'Make Nama carry it.'

'He's only a child.'

'But who else is there of the old man's family?' someone asked, reminding the gathering of the custom.

'That's true.'

'Give it to him then.'

'Where is he?'

'Must be with Sita's children playing on the verandah.'

'Call him.'

'Call him.'

Nama came and stood far away from the bier, his eyes on his maay. Kautik said then, 'Go on son, pick up the pot.'

'I feel scared, o,' he said, moving backwards.

'Nothing to fear. He's your grandpa, boy.'

He moved further back, saying with decision, 'Never. I won't. I feel scared.' And he climbed down the plinth.

Kautik clenched her teeth and strode to the pot, thundering. 'You watch if he doesn't gobble you, you corpse. Like pit, like soil, like wheat, like bread. How could you turn out good?' Hoisting the pot in a single move, she said to the bier-bearers, 'Go on. Lift. Yes, and what? No one of his own and thrown into the jungle.'

Kautik was at Sita's house on the third day. Sita was heating water on her water boiler. Kautik was on the verandah dictating a letter to Nama. When it was done, she tried to remember her brother's address, calling it out to Nama as she remembered it. When the address was written, she sent Nama with the letter to find someone in the village going to Tivase and request him to post it there. Carrying the letter, Nama headed for Sudhakar's house. Meanwhile, the water was done. Sita led Kautik to the bathing stone. She began to wash her hair and bathe her body. A sob had risen to Kautik's throat as she stepped on the stone and Sita's consoling words had made her swallow it. But her suppressed tears ran out in the form of words and her stale grief became a litany of the old man's qualities, good and bad, which she made herself recall.

A long while later, she began talking about the house, when Sita said to her with complete confidence, 'Your brother knows as sure as anything that the old man mortgaged the house to Bakhadya, not sold it.'

'Then why did Ganpat say that to me? Surely there must have been some talk in the village.'

'Look, Bakhadya knows his own sins and Ganpat knows his. But I know this. He put his thumb-print on the mortgage paper in front of my eyes.'

'Brother Sukhdev? You were there?'

'Wasn't I?'

Just then Sakina turned up there. Sliding Yasodi off her back, she pointed Kautik out to her and said, 'See there. That's your maay, isn't it?'

Yasodi ran towards her maay like a wound-up doll. Sakina sat down in the yard and said indulgently, 'Your daughter made it difficult for us to eat or sleep. Look after her now.'

The two began to talk. They told each other of Mahadev's irresponsible behaviour. The old man's death and what followed was described. After Listening to Kautik with great sympathy, Sakina made a move to return to Mozri. Kautik tried to make her stay on till the thirteenth-day rites. Sakina said, 'I would have stayed, nothing much to it. But your sister's husband is going to the Mahadev fair, see? The big fair.'

'So?' Kautik asked, smiling. 'You'll meet him when he gets back, won't you?'

Sakina tossed her head at this and said, 'That's not it, poor soul. The girl will be alone.'

'Let her be. You stay. It'll make me feel good if you stay.'

Sakina's doubts about the plan weren't too serious. So finally, she stayed.

The thirteenth day dawned. Kautik's eyes were fixed as expected on all four village roads turn by turn. When she heard someone call, her ears would prick up like a dog's and then flop, disappointed. When they couldn't wait any longer, she said to Nama, 'Tell me. Did you write the correct address on the letter?'

'I wrote what you told me.'

'Then why hasn't he come yet?'

'Who?' Sita asked. 'Nama's father?'

'Don't even mention him. We can do without him. If he wanted to come at all, he would have come that day. Catch him coming now. Now he knows it'll be a question of money.'

Kautik paused and said, 'I was looking out for my brother.'

'He'll come.'

'Never,' she said, furious. 'He'll come directly now for my thirteenth day.'

'Don't say that. Maybe he didn't get the letter.'

'Funny thing not to get the letter. See if he doesn't get a money order on the same address, and what?'

Just then, Bakhadya's accountant came up the plinth. He called out from the yard, 'Is Kautik the tailor woman in?'

Kautik answered with great dignity, 'Who is it? Come in.'

'I'm not coming in and all that,' he said stiffly from the yard. 'I came to ask when Mahadev's coming.'

'How can I say anything about that…'

'Oh!' His voice was edged with a threat. 'Then listen to this. When you go back to Mozri now, vacate the house.'

Knowing full well what he meant, Kautik still asked, 'Why?'

'What do you mean why? We want to put a lock on the house.'

Kautik said nothing, nor did the accountant wait for her to speak. He went down the plinth, his leather chappals crunching and creaking as he went.

That evening, Kautik put all her things together for the return to Mozri. She tied and put out a bundle of leftover food and foodstuffs that she had bought for the thirteenth-day lunch. She got Nama to carry the bundle on his head while she stepped out and put a strong lock on the door.

'What's this? If that son-of-a-pig screams, then?' Sakina said.

'I'll see what to do when he does.'

Kautik dropped the key casually into her bag.

When the women got to Mozri, Kautik entered and settled down in Sakina's part of the house first. As she slid Yasodi off her back, she said to Nama, 'Run off, son. If his lordship is on the verandah of the Maruti temple or that Bodya mendicant's place, get the house key from him.'

To this, Bano said, 'But Nama's father has gone.'

'Where?'

'To the Big Mahadev fair.'

'And when was that?'

'Friday night. My father and him, they went together.'

Kautik hit her forehead with her palm. 'Take that, sister. That's what you call a man. Tell me, does he worry about anybody?'

'So what if he's gone. He'll be back in a month or so.'

THREE

Kautik didn't worry about her husband while the fair was on. His strange behaviour before he went to the fair had gradually prepared her for such things. In fact, what he'd done was almost reasonable compared to what she'd expected him to do. There was something else that reassured her. If a wayward animal goes with the whole herd to the jungle, the owner doesn't worry too much though it might break away. But when it goes off by itself, then it's time to worry. Kautik didn't worry because other villagers had also gone to the fair. Most importantly, Qasam was with him. He would hardly let him go astray. Kautik guessed shrewdly that he must be feeling so guilty about taking him along at all, that he'd do everything to bring him back to the village. So she returned to her life, working day and night, if not for herself, at least for Nama and Yasodi.

A month-and-a-half passed. Then Kautik's anxiety was back like a lost animal, licking at her heels. She kept throwing looks at Qasam's bellows now as she went about her work. It wasn't enough for her to see the cold furnace.

She had to go in and ask Bano for news of her father. If Bano and Sakina were not ready with their bhakris to go to the fields with her, she would hurry ahead, telling them, 'If he comes meanwhile, look after him.' And if they were working on some other field, she'd say, 'If he does come, be good souls and send me word on the Marwari's field for today.'

One day, Kautik and Sakina were working in separate fields. Sakina was in a field adjacent to the road. Looking up from her work, she saw a mendicant in a saffron robe, coming along the side of the road towards her. She noticed the pilgrim's shoulder cloth with pockets at both ends hung across his shoulders. When he came nearer, she recognized the mendicant from the village. Sakina climbed up the embankment, saying, 'Holy man, is the Big Mahadev pilgrimage over?'

'Why else would I be coming home, eh?' He was looking for a gap in the hedge through which to enter the field. 'Sakinabi, go on. Get your betel-leaf pouch out,' he said, pushing his way through thorn bushes to get in.

'Then why hasn't the man of my house come back?'

'Didn't I say bring out your betel leaves,' he said, laughing. 'Qasam has gone to Umravati.'

'To Umravati?'

'Yes. To find a husband for your girl.'

'Really?' Hiding the joy on her face, she looked around for a place to sit down. Pulling out the pouch hanging at her waist and pushing it towards him, she said, 'Why are you teasing me?'

'I swear on your life.' Then, as he decorated the betel leaf with all the ingredients one by one, he told her the whole story. Qasam had met an old acquaintance at the fair. They chatted. One thing led to another, till Qasam discovered his friend had a son of marriageable age. He too had spoken of Bano. Then, on his way back from the fair, he had gone to Umravati to see their house.

Excited at the news and blushing at the same time, Sakina moved the sari-end covering her face and asked, 'What does the boy do?'

'He drives a tonga.'

'Is it his?'

'No. It's somebody else's.'

'So what. As long as the boy is earning.' After a pause, Sakina said, 'So when is he coming back?'

'On Friday.'

'Next?'

'Yes. Brother Qasam has asked you to be ready. If there's a problem about money, he says to tell you to sell a goat in the Tuesday market, at half price if necessary but be ready.'

'All right.' And now she remembered Kautik. 'And Nama's father must also be with him, I suppose.'

'No. Not really.'

'Why? Didn't he go with him?'

'In a way,' the mendicant said between pauses. 'But forget it. Let Qasam tell you what he wants to about Mahadev.'

Sakina didn't ask him more questions. Perhaps she was so full of her own happiness that she didn't press the mendicant.

Sakina didn't tell Kautik her vague share of the news that night at least. She too was of the same mind as the mendicant. Let Qasam tell her what had to be told.

She found, however, that she couldn't control the time and the manner of telling. When she went to Kautik's yard to pick her up for the field, she could see by Kautik's excited hustle and bustle that she had heard of the mendicant's return from the fair. She was pleading with Nama to go over and get news. He was saying, 'My result's coming out today. I'll be late to school.'

Kautik lost her temper at this and was thinking of going herself. That's when Sakina fearfully told her that Mahadev was not with Qasam, giving her as few details as possible. When Kautik heard this, she said to Yasodi, 'Girl, don't pack my lunch in the basket.'

'Are you going to serve all day then?'

'What can I do in this situation? The man's gone and made another problem.' She walked off towards the field, swinging an empty lunch basket.

Returning home full of laughter at his result, Nama somehow repressed his surging joy till the evening. He was waiting for the moment his maay would come home and he would give her the news. As soon as she stepped in through the door, he said, 'Maay, I've passed.'

'Good.'

'I'm in the sixth now.'

'Hunh.' Then Kautik asked him, 'When did Sakina say?'

'When what?'

'Qasam. When will he come back?'

'Friday.' Then Nama said, 'And you know what, maay? I got four hundred and seventy marks out of five hundred!'

'What's the day today?'

'Tuesday. And you know what...'

Kautik screamed at Yasodi. 'If you're hungry, eat me, why don't you? As if I wander around with the bhakris. Can't you serve yourself?'

'But there's no dal.'

'So, what can I do? Take chillies and salt. Or you couldn't find even that in the house?'

'And maay, two boys in my class, older than me, failed...'

'Let them. What do we have to do with others? We can't wash our own; why go to wash other people's?'

'Who're you talking to, maay?'

'Whom can I talk to? I talk to myself. Who else do I have, mother or aunt, who'll sit here listening to me and say, "Hush dear. Don't weep like that."' Saying that, she went straight to her rug.

'Aren't you eating, maay?'

'No.'

'You didn't even take your lunch.'

'Listen to that! So much worry for me. If you want to eat, eat quietly. And if you don't, go to bed. Don't make me scream.'

Kautik's agitation didn't settle all through the night. As she lay awake, her disturbed mind ran amok. But by morning, it had returned to its path. The more she thought, the more her never-dying hope clung to the coming Friday, releasing her from the chaos of her doubts and fears. That's why, when she rose in the morning, she got down to work with renewed energy. She had her breakfast and as she left for the field with her lunch basket, she reminded Nama, 'Listen. When you heard you passed, did you go show your face to that Kasar teacher?'

'Yes. I went to the school yesterday,' he answered, excitedly. 'But the school was closed.'

'Then why didn't you go to his house?'

'I'll go today.'

'Yes. And bow and touch his feet properly when you do your namaskar. Don't do it from a distance.'

'I won't.'

When his maay went to the field, Nama set off for Tivase, excited by the thought of meeting the one person whose praise would be real—Kasar teacher. He went to the school but he saw no sign of the teacher there, so he went on to his house. Arriving there, he hovered outside, waiting to see some sign of occupation. When he saw no such sign at all, he made inquiries and then returned to Mozri with heavy steps. Back home, he threw himself on his rug and stayed there till his maay came home. Seeing him like that, Kautik immediately asked him, 'What's it? Something paining?'

'No,' he said angrily, his voice imitating Mahadev's. 'No paining, and no nothing.'

'Then why haven't you eaten?'

'Wasn't hungry.'

'Then come, we'll eat now.'

'Not now either.'

'When will you eat then?'

'I'll eat when I need to.'

'Now what disease has got you?' Kautik demanded. 'Take it in turns, all of you.'

With that, Kautik unfolded her rug briskly and lay down. Now Nama's dumb grief deepened. He was bitterly disappointed that his maay hadn't coaxed him into revealing his pain and there was no point in talking about it of his own accord. So he hid his face in his rug and began to snivel. When his snivelling became too loud to ignore, Kautik flung the rug off her face and, sitting bolt upright, shouted, 'Now are you going to tell me what's wrong or you want me to thrash you?'

Along with the question, she flung some suitable expletives at him.

Nama too lost his temper now. 'Am I saying anything to you? Carrying on like some illiterate woman!'

'So who were you talking to?'

'To my fate, that's who.'

'Dear Lord!' Kautik exclaimed, mocking Nama's sudden adult tone. 'What's this big calamity that's struck you?'

'Who cares?'

Now at last, Kautik was Kautik. 'Are you going to tell me without a fuss or you want me to kick your backside in?'

Nama too became Nama. 'I didn't meet Kasar teacher, maay.'

'So why couldn't you tell me straight,' she said, cooling down. 'Where'd he gone?'

'He's been transferred.'

'Let him be.'

'Let him be?' Nama said, voicing his anxiety, 'And who'll give me money this year for my school books?'

Kautik didn't answer.

A while later, Nama began to mutter to himself, half genuinely fearful, and half theatrical, 'Dear God, now school is over for me, Lord.'

Nama's anxiety churned up Kautik's soul, but she wouldn't change her ways for that and barked at him, 'Do you need the money this minute, you tongueless idiot?'

'Not this minute. But one day I will.'

'So you'll get it. Don't eat my head now. Lay down quiet.'

'There is bhakri for dinner, no?' Nama said, hiding the joy in his voice.

Kautik didn't answer.

Kautik waited fearfully for Friday. She counted the days as it approached, and she became more and more nervous. Her nervousness grew more intense as she returned home from the field on Friday. She practically ran all the way till Qasam's bellows came into view. Then her feet turned to lead.

The old cot was set up beside the bellows. On it, sat a man who looked older than Qasam and a youth who must have been Bhima's age. He was wearing a fez cap and stealing looks beyond the piece of old jute cloth that hung over Sakina's doorway for the first time, listening for movement within. Qasam and the older man were engrossed in chatting. Qasam was talking loudly and sounded happy.

Made even more uneasy by all this, Kautik didn't stop by at the bellows as she normally would, but went straight on to her part of the house. She was on the point of spreading her rug when Bano came in through the back door carrying an aluminium pan. She had covered her body and face with an old black burkha. She asked in a low voice to borrow flour, saying, 'Hurry, aunty' when Kautik took a little while to move. Getting up heavily, Kautik smiled all the same as she said, 'Don't be in such a hurry already, poor soul! You're still young...'

The blushing Bano promptly put down the pan and fled back home.

'Here. Take this,' Kautik called after her.

'I'm not going to take it now,' she said and disappeared.

There was no help for it but to put the flour in the pan and carry it to Sakina's back door herself. 'And where's Bano?' she asked looking around.

'What's this, Kautik? You've been teasing the poor child,' Sakina said and smiled indulgently at Bano's shyness.

After a little more light-hearted chatter, Kautik decided it would be best to get Mahadev's song of sorrow over with now rather than later. Leading towards the subject, she asked, 'So, when are your guests leaving?'

'Only after the engagement.'

Kautik didn't speak.

'Why?'

'What can you do even if I do tell you?' she said, adding after a pause, 'Has brother said anything to you?'

'About Nama's father?'

'Yes.'

'No.'

'Could you ask him now?'

'Now?' Sakina was shocked. 'You know what my man is like. You think he's going to tell me now?' She thought a moment and said, 'You've waited for so many days. Wait just a couple of days more.'

'What else can I do?' Kautik continued talking desultorily for a few minutes longer and then returned home.

On Friday, Bano's engagement was celebrated and Qasam's guests left for Umravati. Qasam went up to the main road to see them off, and returned home chewing contentedly on his betel leaf. He started for a moment when he noticed Kautik's open door. He'd have hidden his face if he could, he was so fearful of telling Kautik about Mahadev. But he knew there was a limit to how long he could avoid telling her and so readily entered her house when she called out to him, albeit muttering heavily, 'What do you want to say, poor soul, tell me.' Then he sat looking up at the ceiling.

Pushing her betel-leaf pouch towards him, she said softly, 'At least now will you tell me?'

Qasam heard, but he didn't lower his eyes. When Kautik asked him the same question again, he only shifted his position, and began shaking his leg. When Kautik pressed him twice more, he said, 'But how do I tell you even if I want to? I don't understand it at all.'

'Just tell me whatever it is. There's no escaping what's written in your destiny.'

'That's true and all.'

'So then tell me.'

'Mahadev has leprosy.'

'Hith! You're talking rubbish, brother.' Her heart had been pierced but her voice was dry as she dismissed what he said.

'What can I say now? Would I make such a terrible joke? You can go ask the mendicant if you want to.'

Now Kautik's dark-skinned face went greenish grey. Her lips began to twist in odd ways. Her eyes seemed to pull back from their sockets and their place was filled by tears. She sat for a long time without removing her sari-end from her eyes, and without saying a word. Qasam, squirming with guilt, made as if to go. Speaking in a voice as heavy as Kautik's, he said, 'I think I'll...'

Out of nothing more than common courtesy, Kautik murmured, 'Why should such a thing happen so suddenly?'

'Not suddenly,' Qasam said, feeling somewhat easier now. 'Mahadev was saying his fingers and toes had felt numb these last two years.'

'That's right,' Kautik said. 'The time we came here he told me in passing that his fingers had lost feeling.'

'So that's how...'

'Where's he now?'

'He went off with the sahibs.'

'Which sahibs?' Kautik looked directly at Qasam now.

Qasam relaxed a little more. He began to tell Kautik the whole story in the voice of a man who had accepted the guilt of having taken Mahadev with him in the first place. His head was bowed and the words came as if he had learnt them by heart.

When the pilgrims' procession to the Great Mahadev temple had started, Mahadev too had set off like the others with the pilgrims' shoulder cloth hanging across his shoulders. The first lap of the distance went off well. But as the sun grew hot and the pace increased, Mahadev's fingers and toes began to bleed. He ignored even that and continued to walk, struggling to keep up with the others. Later the blood from his toes began to flow. Toes and heels sprang cracks. The blood-soaked mud and sand from off the road began to enter the wounds. That made the wounds fester. So Mahadev tied rags around his feet. They'd come loose as he walked. He'd take them off, dust them and wrap them around the wounds again. He'd have to stop after short distances to do this. He'd sit in the shade as he tried to wrap and knot the rags with his numb fingers. When he could no longer manage, Qasam did it for him. He and the mendicant kept telling him, 'Mahadev, don't come with us. We still have a long way to go.'

But he wouldn't hear of it. Not even when they offered to make a collection to buy him a bus ticket back to Mozri.

They finally decided not to walk at the other pilgrims' speed but at Mahadev's pace out of village loyalty. In this way, they somehow managed to reach the Big Mahadev.

When the pilgrims turned back, the limping, bandaged Mahadev found himself in the middle of a group of missionaries. One of them spoke both English and Marathi well. Another spoke an English-accented Marathi while the third only spoke English. When they spotted Mahadev, they undid his bandages and examined his wounds. They discussed what they saw amongst themselves in English. They exchanged opinions, always waiting for the one who spoke only English to give his, which he did in a sombre voice. After a long time of such mutual consultation, the Marathi speaker told Mahadev that he had contracted leprosy.

Mahadev felt faint when he heard this. His eyes rolled in a strange way. Then the same man said to him, 'If you come to our clinic, we could organize something for you.'

'Food?'

'Yes, yes. And everything else. But you'll have to follow our rules.'

'I will. When will you take me?'

'You can come now. We're in tents right now. Stay there till the fair is over. Then we'll all go together.'

'All right.'

'If you want to meet someone, do it, then come back.'

'I have no kith nor kin here. But I'll give a message to my village friends.'

'All right.'

Before Mahadev left them, the man noted down his name, address and other details and asked him to say how long he'd take to return.

Qasam finished his story, which he had told in his usual style with the usual gestures. When he stopped, Kautik said in a voice people use to speak about the dead, 'But couldn't you have…'

'How much we tried to talk him out of it. How hard we

tried to make him understand,' Qasam said. 'But Mahadev wouldn't allow anything we said to pass into his ears. I said to him, what will your wife and children do if you abandon them like an ascetic?'

'What did he say to that?'

'He said, when were my wife and children dependent on me that they can't do without me now?'

Kautik sighed. She sat looking at the ceiling for a long time. She didn't bother any longer to wipe her eyes. She let the tears run where they would. Qasam had to say something, so he muttered, 'I'm feeling so bad I don't know what to say. It would have been better if I hadn't taken him with me.'

Kautik said, 'How can you blame yourself for that? He said he wanted to go with you so he went with you.' Saying so, she absolved Qasam of blame as he had hoped she would. Since she said nothing more, he removed himself from there.

Even after he'd gone, Kautik remained lost. She sat rooted to the spot, staring fixedly into space. Then she suddenly pulled her children close to her. Hugging them tight, she began to sob uncontrollably. Nama kept asking her, 'What's wrong, maay? Why are you crying?' But she wouldn't answer. She continued to sob as she ran her caressing hands over their faces and bodies.

From the next day on, Kautik's behaviour changed. She stopped eating properly, stopped dropping in on Sakina or insisting on her coming over for a chat. When Sakina spoke to her, she'd make curt replies. She scolded the children for no reason. If Nama didn't quite understand what she wanted in one telling, she'd shout at him loud enough for the whole village to come running. She'd pounce on him and beat him with whatever came to hand for the most trivial of mistakes. She didn't even go out to work the first few days. Worried for her, Sakina, hand over mouth, had said to her, 'How can you go on like this, poor soul? If you give up work for that man, what will you eat and all?'

'Eating's worth nothing,' she muttered as if to herself. 'When the life of the one for whom all the fuss is turns out to be just broken beams, who should a person toil and suffer for?'

'That's no way to talk. If a woman like you says such things, who will the children look to for support?'

A few more turns of similar conversation finally forced Kautik to put away her burden of gloom and say, 'That's one bind that the Lord God has put me into. If I didn't have this duty, I too would have picked up my cloth and stick and disappeared like my man.'

'That's sensible talk now,' said Sakina, relieved. 'It's true something dreadful's happened to the man. But suppose he'd died, you wouldn't have gone to heaven after him.'

'Is it in our hands to go to heaven? If such things were possible, why would we go through all the hardships down here?'

'See? You can talk sense,' Sakina said in the tone one uses to coax a child to behave. 'So come, let's go. Pack your lunch and all.'

Just then, Kashinath the postman came to Kautik's

door. He called out, 'Mahadev Wallad Raghunath Tailor!' and spun a postcard in through the door. Picking it up, Nama called out, 'Ma, ma, there's a letter from uncle, see.'

'Pack my lunch, girl.'

'Shall I read it?'

'Read it if you want to.'

'Oh! Read it if I want to, not if I don't, eh,' Nama said, hurt at Kautik's lack of eagerness to hear his reading skills. 'You're a good one.'

'Listen you monsters, who put chillies into the turmeric pot?'

'You did yourself last night,' Nama reminded her. 'So, shall I read the letter?'

'Then read it fast, you corpse. Have my tears burnt out?'

'*Brother Mahadev*,' Nama began to read. '*Your letter reached us. We were shocked by your father's death. I was to come to your place on the thirteenth day. I was all ready to leave. But I fell ill at the wrong time and couldn't come. Please do not be angry. My blessings to Nama and Bhima.*'

Nama looked at his mother's face when he finished reading. It showed no effect of the letter. So he said, 'Were you listening?'

'I am listening. Read it.'

'Read what? My head,' he said and looked at her, expecting her to get angry.

Kautik's face was neither angry nor calm. It was the way it always was these days. Hard like stone. Yasodi butted in just then to show her the salt in her fist. 'Shall I put so much in the dal?'

'Can't you hear? I told you to read.'

Sakina, unable to suppress her laughter at this, said, 'Oh, Kautik. Who are you talking to and what are you saying? Come. Take that lunch basket and let's go to work.'

'Yes. Glad you reminded me.'

Picking up her lunch, she set off for the field with Sakina. She'd just crossed the village boundary when she turned back again, returning home. Sakina went with her. She spotted Nama from afar, playing tipcat, and called out to him, 'I've left my basket behind. Get it, will you?'

Grabbing the basket from Nama, she turned back towards the field but instantly turned round again. 'Look, my tobacco box is in the verandah, go get it, there...'

At this, Sakina said, 'But the box is in your sari pleats.'

Peering into her tucked-up pleats as she walked, Kautik said, 'Oh yes. There it is. Come.'

They'd only gone a short distance when Sakina said, 'Kautik, I'm telling you for your good. Stop thinking about Mahadev now. If you go on like this, Allah alone knows what'll happen.'

It was with this kind of constant persuasion that Kautik gradually began taking an interest in life again.

One day, Nama sat sulking at home exactly like the day he'd heard of Kasar teacher's transfer. From the day school had reopened, Nama had been making his daily journeys from Mozri to Tivase and back to attend school. School work had begun in earnest. The other children had been eagerly buying new textbooks and notebooks for the new curriculum.

Soon everybody had bought their books. Only Nama would sit in the class without any. Every Wednesday, the teacher would look at him and say, 'Well, I hope you've got your books now at least.'

Nama would hang his head and say, 'No, sir. Mother says she'll buy them next Tuesday.'

This had gone on for two-and-a-half months with Nama always pointing forward to the following Tuesday, which seemed never to dawn. As a result of this and also perhaps because of the contempt that some arrogant teachers reserve for poor students, the teacher had flared up one Wednesday, 'Didn't I say if you don't bring your books this Wednesday, I won't let you sit in the class?'

'Yes, sir.'

'So then?'

'Can't afford to buy books, sir.'

'Then why treat yourself to school? Sit at home,' the teacher shouted. 'You can't go on like this forever.'

'I'll study without books, sir!'

'You think you're Agarkar or someone,' the teacher mocked. 'Just remember one thing. If you don't have your books and a dozen notebooks with you by next Wednesday, I won't let you step into the class.'

As good as his word, the teacher had sent him out of the class that day. Nama had begged and pleaded but to no avail.

So he had returned home and now sat in a sulk waiting for his maay to return from the fields. When she came home, he told her the whole story and said to her in a wounded voice, 'How will I go to school now, maay?'

'No how,' she said easily. 'Go to the fields with me. Son, your luck is punctured on all four sides. What can you do about that and what can I do?' Kautik continued to talk in this vein, half to herself, half to him. Taking advantage of a pause in her muttering, Nama said in anguish, 'But I want so much to go on with school.'

'You may want and want and want something but that Shadulbuwa must want it! Where can I run, all alone, wearing out my bones? You should understand these things without being told. You're not a child anymore!'

Nama fell silent because his maay had given him credit for being grown-up. Kautik went on, 'For this one year, we could sell off every pot and pan to buy your books. What do we sell every year after that? And look at the times. If you buy millets at seven this week, they're ten in next week's market. It's not like school's over in a year, when maybe we could eat husk and live under the stars.'

Nama was still silent. Once again, as she left for work, Kautik reminded him of his being a big boy, saying, 'See, son, you've got to think about it. You're not a child anymore.'

As Kautik left, Nama said to her, with deep pain, 'Then at least…'

'What?'

'Find me some place where I can learn tailoring.'

Kautik became thoughtful. 'Tailoring?'

'Yes,' Nama said, adding quickly, 'Put me on to somebody's machine for a few months. Then I can start helping you out with money.'

'What will you learn in a few months, dear Lord! Not even eyeholes and hemming.'

'Try me out. See if I don't.' Nama spoke with self-confidence. 'If I don't start taking in simple jobs in seven or eight months, stop calling me Nama.'

Kautik fell into thought again. Nama's sincerity had brought tears to her eyes. Hiding them, she said, 'All right. I'll look around. But you must come to the fields with me until then at least.'

After that, Nama began to accompany Kautik to the fields every day without grumbling or complaining. He worked hard because of the eagerness to learn new things that lay coiled around his heart. Or perhaps he did it to keep his maay happy. But soon he was working even better than her. He always led the group of women in weeding. It was the same with picking chillies. It was he who called his maay when it was time to leave for the fields. And it was he who put together their gathering baskets and cloths and packed their lunch. This routine continued for nearly two months. Then came the day when they went to the Shendurjana market and Nama reminded Kautik of what she'd wanted to be reminded of. 'Maay, you were going to see Sheshrao today, weren't you?'

'Yes, son. Good you reminded me,' she said, turning towards Sheshrao's shop. Reaching the cloth alley, she stopped before the shop. Sheshrao spied her through the crowd and said, 'Dear Lord, you're coming after many moons.'

'I've come when I need a favour,' she said smiling as she settled at the back of his shop. 'You'll do it, won't you?'

'If I can, I will. Tell me.'

'I am asking you to teach my Nama sewing.'

'Tell me anything else but that, sister,' he said his hands over his ears. 'That's one thing I won't do.'

'Why not?' Kautik asked, opening her crestfallen face into a smile.

'I just swore from Bhima's time not to take on any boy for teaching sewing.'

'But Nama's not like that, brother.'

'He might or might not be. But I won't get into that business again.'

'Look at it this way, brother,' she said, trying to coax him. 'If one of yours turned out like Bhima, what would you do?'

'I'd slice him head to toe into two. Don't think I'm joking, sister,' Sheshrao said with finality. 'I'm telling you how it is.'

Now Kautik fell silent, looking around for something to say. In all this time, Sheshrao hadn't lifted his head once to look at the mother and son and their now small, pinched faces. So he missed the signals that passed between them telling each other it was best to leave. As they turned away, Kautik said by way of farewell, 'So, you don't feel any pity for my Nama, brother?'

'No. No use getting angry later if I bury my anger now.'

Kautik and Nama set off on their way. They began to buy what they needed. As they finished, Kautik took Nama's advice and returned to Sheshrao's shop. Calling him out of the shop, she said, 'What if I leave the old man's machine with you?'

Now Sheshrao began to think. He thought about how much extra work he could take in with one more machine and how much that would add to his monthly income. Taking care not to show his enthusiasm too plainly, he said, 'Why don't you send Nama to his uncle's?'

'My kith and kin are all finished. You are the kith and the kin of this wretched widow-like woman. Now you decide. Will you take my Nama as your son and give him the means to earn his living or let him roam the town like a stud?' She paused, then said, 'Now tell me. When can I start sending him to you?'

'You mean you'll send him right off?'

'Yes,' Kautik answered shrewdly. 'Son, start coming to uncle's shop every morning from tomorrow.'

'Not from the morning,' he said, thinking hard. 'When will you bring the machine over?'

'Maybe next week.'

'Then do one thing. Let this week go. I'm thinking of going to Umravati. I'll send you a message when I get back.'

Kautik muttered as she walked down the road, 'I know you won't.'

And that's just what happened. Four weeks had passed and there was still no word from Sheshrao. While Kautik waited for the message to come, she got Nama to calculate how much money they'd get in return for the stock of grain they had. Every Tuesday, she'd say some such things, 'Tell me, we must be having about two-and-a-half kudavs of jowar stored up, don't you think?'

'Rubbish. Didn't you sell a bit that Tuesday when you bought material for Yasodi's long skirt,' he'd remind her. 'And then Krishna...'

'You're right. So how much do we have do you think?'

'Eight paylis, I guess.'

'And what would that fetch at ten annas?'

'Eight tens eighty,' he'd tell her. 'That makes five rupees.'

'And four paylis?'

'Two-and-a-half rupees.'

'How much do we need now to make ten?'

'Two-and-a-half rupees more, poor soul,' Nama would say, anguished.

Kautik would allay his fear by saying in an off-hand manner, 'Is that all?'

'Yes and all,' he would say. 'So we won't manage to get the machine back this week either, isn't that so, maay?'

'It's all right if we can't. Don't you worry,' she'd say, trying to give him courage. 'We'll make it up next week or the next.'

'I suppose we will,' he'd say, not believing her. 'But if it gets later and later, that Sheshrao shouldn't change his mind.'

'He won't. And if we get enough work this week, we'll be sure to manage next week.'

'There'll be enough work and all. But you don't put in your strength like you used to. You're always lagging behind even on the easy stuff.'

'I try and try all I can, dear Lord, to put in my strength. But what can I do? I can't work as much as I could. I don't know what's wrong.'

'It must be that shivering fever you had.'

'When?'

'When they told us about tatyaji, and you fell ill with shivering fever.'

'Yes. But what's that got to do with this now? That was two-three months ago.'

'Can't tell.'

The talk about retrieving the machine always ended around here, and then mother and son would wait for the following week to come. They would wait and something would happen unexpectedly to prevent them from making up the amount required for the machine. There mightn't be work all the days of the week or some other problem would present itself for which the solution was selling grain from their store. So two weeks became four and four became six before they had enough money for the machine. Kautik set off with Nama and the money for Talegaon to meet Ganpat Brewer. 'Good, I remembered. Since we are here, we'll go take a look at the house too.'

'Let's.'

They climbed the plinth. The front door of the house was locked, but not with the lock Kautik had put on it when she left. This was a brass lock of fancy style and at least a hundred seer weight. Kautik took a hold of it and pulled. The lock didn't make even a small click in response. Kautik peeped in through the crack in the door. There was a huge bale of cotton wool inside, cotton weighing scales and weights. Removing her eyes from the crack and stepping back, Kautik said to herself, 'So that's how it is, eh?'

'That must be Bakhadya's cotton in there, mustn't it, ma?'

'Who else's then?'

'And where is our lock?'

'He must have broken it, the ghoul, what else?'

'And our cooking pots and things?'

'Must be in there. Or he might have taken them to his house, I suppose!'

As they talked, Kautik was making for Sita's house. When they got there, she said abruptly, 'Sita, where's brother?'

Both husband and wife came out on the verandah.

Sukhdev said with a smile, 'Come in, sister. It's a long time since you were here. Please sit.'

'I won't sit and all. I had to ask you something.'

'Yes?'

'You'll tell me the truth?'

'What?' Both husband and wife looked puzzled.

'I want to know whether Bakhadya took this house on mortgage or bought it?'

'Mortgage.'

'You're sure of that?'

'What will I get from telling lies?'

'Was the mortgage agreement read out to you?'

'Not just once, let me tell you, but twice,' Sita said boldly. 'I heard it myself.'

'Sure?'

'What more can we say?'

Kautik was convinced they were telling the truth. So she turned around and said abruptly, 'Then come with me.'

'Where?'

'To Bakhadya's mansion.'

Now the husband and wife looked nervous. Sita said for something to say, 'What for?'

'To say before Bakhadya what you just told me. Then it's between him and me, I'll teach him.' Kautik was beside herself with anger. 'Why, what's there to think about?'

'Look, sister, it's like this. He's a big man. We need to go to him a dozen times a day for one thing or another.'

'But if you're telling the truth, why can't you go with me? No thief, no fear.'

'Everything you say is true, sister,' Sukhdev said, annoyance edging his voice. 'But I'm a poor man with wife and children. If he holds a grudge against me, he'll make it impossible for me to live in the village.' He paused, then said, 'Can I live like you, carrying my house on my back like a scorpion from village to village? Tell me.'

Furious to hear this, Kautik told Nama to get going. Sukhdev tried to make amends by saying, 'Sister, at least have some betel leaf and tobacco before you go.'

'I've given up betel leaf and tobacco,' she said and angrily strode down the plinth, pushing Nama before her. As she walked, she muttered imprecations. Not against Sukhdev, but against herself and her fate.

Soon she was in Bakhadya's mansion. It was Tuesday, so the accountant sat in the verandah doling out the week's wages. Arguments raged between him and the cotton pickers. Looking up from the angry exchanges, the accountant said to Kautik, 'Who's that? Kautik the tailor woman, isn't it? It's many days since you've been this way.'

Kautik said from where she stood, 'Deewanji, what have you decided about my house?'

'What's that?' Bakhadya's home-kept son-in-law looked out from the inner room and said in surprise. 'How can you ask? As if you don't know.'

'For how many rupees is my house mortgaged to you?'

'Mortgage? Are you sleeping or dreaming?' He turned to the accountant. 'Deewanji, take out that document.'

Deewanji got down to work. Bakhadya's son-in-law said to Kautik, 'You think I'd cheat you for your measly three or four hundred rupees? Four times that much worth of my crops get pinched by thieves and robbers, understand?' The accountant handed over the document to him. He made as if to throw it at Kautik. 'See. Open your eyes wide and see what's written in this.'

'Let me have that paper.'

He withdrew the paper, saying, 'You'll not get it.'

'Why not?'

'Why not? It's my wish.'

'I can read. I'll read it to maay,' Nama said.

'Aren't you smart?' he mocked Nama and held the paper out to the accountant. 'Read that out aloud.'

The accountant finished reading. Kautik said, 'I don't believe that paper.'

'You don't believe it then go to the law-court,' he said curtly, 'and bear the consequences.'

'If we had the strength to go to the law-court, why would we take all this trouble?' Kautik was boiling with rage within but was trying hard to keep her voice cool. 'I'll leave it to your honesty. Hold a cow's tail and announce before all these people that the paper tells the truth.'

His face contorted, the son-in-law flung the paper down before the accountant and said, 'You're the big Lady Truthful, aren't you? Nobody has ever dared me to hold a cow's tail and swear or doubted my honesty. And now suddenly it's Lady Truthful herself!'

Bakhadya's face was more eloquent than his speech. Kautik was infuriated, not so much by what he said but by his facial expressions and gestures. She fixed him with a raging eye and said threateningly, 'I'm warning you. There's no call for Lady Truthful and all. Don't say later that I didn't warn you.'

'Get out. Out of the mansion first.'

'You think I'll stay, you corpse?' Kautik marched to the stile gate and stopped. She squatted there and brought her fists down over and over again on the threshold, breaking all the bangles on them. Clenching her teeth, she began shouting curses in time with the beat of her wrists. 'May your food be poisoned, you ghoul. May ruin be your lot. May nobody light a lamp on your dead threshold or Bakhadya's whose house you entered as a son-in-law.'

Bakhadya's son-in-law hurried towards her, his lips pressed together, his hand raised. But one look at Kautik's face and state, and his hand came limply down. His lips relaxed as he said, 'Don't make a scene here. A cow doesn't die with the curses of a crow like you. Come on, get up and go off quietly.'

Nama then helped his mother up saying, 'Let's go, ma. He might beat us.'

'He will, will he? He'll need to have span-long teeth to beat me.' Kautik went on her way ranting and shouting out such details of Bakhadya's deeds as even his son-in-law hadn't ever heard.

Lost in her own world, Kautik went well past Ganpat Brewer's house when Nama reminded her and they returned to his shop. As she sat down, she pulled a cloth bag from her waist and gave it to Nama, and pushed her betel-leaf pouch before Ganpat. 'That's your loan. Take it,' she said. 'Now give me back my machine first.'

'We'll do that later. Have some betel leaf first.' So saying, he moved his betel-leaf pouch towards her. Then he began untying every pocket of her betel-leaf pouch. Examining every little bundle in it, he said, 'You come as my guest and treat me to your betel leaf. That's not right.' He returned her pouch to her.

'That contains your money,' she said.

'What? Where is it?' Believing he'd made a mistake, he began opening the pouch again.

'Where's your younger brother?' Kautik began to chat.

'Sadashiv? Must be loafing in the village, what else,' he said, 'There's no money in this.'

'Are you looking for the money, uncle?' Nama asked, holding out the cloth bag Kautik had given him. 'It's in this bag.'

'Dear mother. And I thought it was in the pouch,' Kautik said.

When Ganpat had finished counting the coins in the cloth bag, he said in surprise, 'But sister, there's only ten rupees here.'

'Then?' Kautik said, shocked. 'I took only ten from you, no?'

'You're right to say you took ten. But what about interest and all?'

'You said nothing about interest and all.'

'Take that now. Do these things need to be told, sister? And I might have too, but think of the time when you came for the money.'

'So how much more do I give you?'

'If it was someone else, I'd have taken twice the amount.'

'Tell me what you want from me.'

'You can give me another five rupees.'

'Fine. Now keep this money and let me take the machine. In another two weeks…'

Kautik stopped speaking mid-sentence. Ganpat had been swinging his head from side to side like a determined pair of scales. When she stopped speaking, he said, 'Can't do. Bad blood comes of money deals between brothers.' He paused, waiting for Kautik's response. But suddenly her attention wasn't on the outer world. She'd withdrawn into her own. Ignoring that, Ganpat began in a tone of compromise, 'One thing we can do sister…' Hopeful again, Nama tried to bring Kautik back to earth. 'Maay, listen to what uncle is saying.'

'Let Bakhadya's son-in-law's corpse rot…'

'Sister, I was saying…'

'What?'

'Since you've come all the way here, I'll let you take the base half of the machine. Take the top half when you pay the interest.'

'Let's do that at least.'

'You agree then?' Ganpat asked, contentedly.

Nama hustled Kautik. Ganpat showed them the machine, saying, 'See how I've kept it. Isn't it exactly how it was when you left it with me?'

'It is and all,' Kautik said.

'No,' Nama said. 'When we left it here, it was threaded with white cotton; it's black now.'

Ganpat gave him a sharp look, but Kautik wasn't paying attention. She was busy threading the jute rope she had brought through the machine base. 'Nama, pull this from the other end,' she said.

'Sister, how will you take the machine?' Ganpat asked. 'You could take my cart. The bullocks are at home. You can pay hiring charges—just two rupees—along with the interest.'

'My back's still strong,' Kautik said, forcing herself to smile.

'Suit yourself.'

Kautik finished binding the base. She lay a thick wad of folded sari on her head, pulling it down over her forehead.

She placed the knot of the jute rope on the wad, as do coolies carrying rice and wheat sacks. Then, she pressed her hands down on her knees to lever herself up. As she rose, she asked Nama to give her a hand.

Kautik set off directly for Tivase. They'd hardly crossed the village boundary when they saw Sadashiv, Ganpat's younger brother coming from the other side. He noticed Kautik carrying just the base of the machine and asked why.

Then he said, 'Sister, wait here for a while. I'll go home and come back in a tick.' He strode off at a rapid pace towards his house.

Kautik didn't heed what he'd said. She continued to walk on with Nama. They'd not gone more than half a field further when they heard Sadashiv call out. She stopped when she saw the machine head on his shoulder. Sadashiv came up to them and held out the head, saying, 'Take it. Your whole machine.'

Kautik took the head of the machine from him, talking non-stop about his goodness. She spoke of gods and devils, in which Sadashiv was a god and Bakhadya's son-in-law the devil himself. Then she said, 'I'll pay you the interest in a couple of weeks.'

'Don't bother, sister. We used your machine. To tell the truth, we should be paying you rent.' With that, he turned and walked off.

Kautik placed a tight coil of cloth on Nama's head. She placed the upper half of the machine on that, and, so loaded, they continued on the road to Tivase.

Kautik walked determinedly as far as the derelict temple that stands halfway between Talegaon and Tivase. By then she had begun to find it difficult to put even a single foot forward. So she said to Nama, 'Put down that machine top and give me a hand here.'

'Why?'

'Quick, you corpse. Something's cutting into my back.'

'But, maay, I can't lift this off by myself. It's way down in my neck.'

'Can't you try?'

Nama tried. Concentrating all his strength in his arms, he lifted the load. It barely rose an inch before his arms went limp and it came down on his neck again. Seeing this, Kautik exclaimed with the agony of her burden and the wound in her back, 'Now what can I do?'

'Can't see a single person around.'

'What's that coming this way?'

'That?'

'Yes.'

'That's a cow.'

'Thought it was a man.'

Kautik endured her load a while longer. She looked around to see if someone was coming. Then she made up her mind. Still standing, she began to bend forward little by little, her teeth biting on her tongue, till she could place her hands taut against her knees for support. As she bent, the rope knot on her forehead began sliding back till it reached the top of her head, and the machine base, which had hugged her back, crashed to the ground, breaking into two. Relieved of her burden, Kautik turned around. Seeing the two pieces of the machine base, she slapped her palm on her forehead, crying as usual, 'Dear mother, take that; now what's left to happen?'

Nama's dream lay broken in two, like the machine base. In pain and despair, Nama started saying, 'Didn't I tell you...' but he saw the look on his mother's face and changed his tone. 'Now help me put down the machine top.'

Kautik lifted his load and let it fall on the ground in such a careless manner, that Nama winced again. 'Take care or this too will...'

'So let it break,' Kautik said, as she slumped down. 'Whatever we do or don't, Lord Shadul's after us. Give. The tobacco pouch. It's with you.'

'Pouch? That was with you and who else?'

She groped at her waist and said, 'Left behind, I think. At Bakhadya's...dumped that too on his rotten corpse.'

'How could you leave it there? Did you even take it out there?'

'Then it's at Sita's.'

'No. You didn't take it out there either. You only took it out at Ganpat's.'

'That's it. I gave him the money didn't I?' she said. 'Must be there then. Will you go take a look?'

'Go all the way back?'

'Go, son. I don't have any tobacco.'

Nama grumbled as he walked away. But instantly Kautik called out, 'It's here, here. See it was in my pleats.'

'I was telling you…'

'You were and all. But I forgot.'

'You do that all the time these days.'

'Nama, good I remembered. Look, see what was cutting into my back.'

Nama looked at the place where Kautik lifted her sari and said, 'My God! Look how much blood's coming.'

Kautik waved at the blood on Nama's hand and said, 'Dear Mother. And is there so much blood?'

'There is. And didn't you feel it?'

'No, I didn't. Now…'

'Go on. Brood a little more.'

Kautik didn't say anything. She spat the plug of tobacco she was chewing on Nama's palm and said, 'Put that on the wound.'

'Tobacco? It'll sting.'

'Let it sting. When it stings is when the wound heals fast.'

Nama covered the wound with the tobacco while

Kautik put another plug in her mouth to satisfy her urge. Looking up into the dead tree above her head, she started muttering.

'Is your thirst quenched now?'

'Why? Who're you talking to?'

'My fate,' she said. 'Now when we get there, is that man going to have something more to say?'

'Who?'

'That man from Tivase.'

'I was thinking the same thing.'

'How far can a person look? Let it happen, whatever fate has decided.'

Kautik rose with renewed strength. She bound the two pieces of the machine base together one on top of the other, and carried them like a head-load of corn stalks. She helped Nama with the machine top and they set off again.

Sheshrao was happy to see the machine delivered at his doorstep. So overcome was he that he said to one of his apprentices, 'Go, Devrao. Order a cup of tea for sister.'

'Ugh dear mother. I don't drink tea-shop tea.'

'Then have a betel leaf at least.'

'That I will.'

Kautik opened Sheshrao's betel-leaf pouch and began making up a leaf. Sheshrao said in a frank voice, 'Should I tell you or not?'

'Now what do you want to tell me?'

'It's about Bhima.'

'Why? What happened?'

'Forget it. I won't tell.'

Kautik pressed him a little but Sheshrao wouldn't tell.

At last she said, 'Don't if you won't tell. Tell me what time in the morning to send Nama to you.'

*

Kautik and Nama were now on their way to Mozri, when Kautik asked, 'Tell me, how many miles is Umravati from here?'

'Maybe half-a-dozen. Why?'

'I'd like to walk there right now, and kick that corpse all the way home. That monster's ways have made us have no face to look our caste people in the eye. Nobody's for anybody here. There's no village for you and no neighbours for you. When they needed Kautik, they came to the house in the middle of the night with their "sister, sister".'

'Who are you talking about, ma?'

'I'm talking about that Sukhdev and his wife. I only asked them to say what they knew, and they brought up how I have moved home from village to village. That's fine. One day, I'll have you in my hands.'

'But you were talking about Bhima a while ago.'

'So? Am I afraid of his father? If he has a lakh, let him keep it in his house. What do I need him for that I should be scared of him? Lord, oh Lord.'

Back home, Kautik stopped as usual at Sakina's bellows. With hands on hips, she stood staring at the guest on the cot. He was wearing a fez cap and a waist-jacket. When she'd finished examining him, she walked to Sakina's door to ask her about him, Nama said, 'It's Bano's husband, isn't it? Don't you know even that?'

Kautik looked at him again and forced a smile. 'When did you come, son-in-law?'

'Just a while ago.'

A hand waved out at them from the gap in the curtain over Sakina's house. Nama noticed it and told his maay that Sakina was asking her to come in. Kautik went in. Looking at Yasodi lying on the floor asleep, thumb in mouth, she asked, 'When did she fall asleep?'

'Just now.'

'Did she eat?'

'Yes. Dal and roti.'

'That's good,' she said. 'I wasn't up to cooking anyhow.'

'And what will I eat, maay?'

'Eat me,' Kautik said. 'There's four armlengths of me! You can be well or ill but this monster doesn't care.'

'How you talk, poor soul,' Sakina said. 'Won't the boy get hungry in the whole day?'

'Let him eat then. There's leftover dal and half a bhakri.'

'And what will you eat?'

'I don't want to eat and all.'

'Why not?' Sakina asked. 'You didn't eat in the morning too.'

'I don't know what, but I'm feeling all strange.'

'Sit down then.'

'No sitting. I'll lie down home.'

Bano, sitting by the cooking fire, now said, 'Oh Kautik Aunty. Can't you hear, I've been calling you so long?' Kautik glanced that way. Bano was kneading flour. She said, 'You've forgotten me in such a short time?'

'No, dear Bano. How can I forget you? When did you come?'

'A while ago.'

'Husband and wife together, eh?'

Bano blushed. As Kautik walked towards her, she said, 'Aunty, don't come this way.'

'Why not?' she asked, reaching the fire. On Bano's right was an aluminium pan. The moment Kautik glanced at it, she screwed up her nose, looked out and made a spitting gesture, then hurried towards Sakina. 'Damn you both.'

Mother and daughter were smiling to themselves now.

Sakina stopped smiling and said, 'She was telling you not to go there.'

'It's a feast for the son-in-law, I suppose, eh?'

'What feast, dear sister?' Sakina said. 'I bought half a seer because you have to make something. And even that's only goat meat.' Sakina paused and said, 'Have a betel leaf.'

'Not now.'

'Why? Will you eat then?'

'No, poor soul. I'm getting the shivers.' She shuddered and said, 'See how fast the gooseflesh is coming up all over.'

'Go then and sleep.'

When Kautik entered her house, she asked Nama to have his dinner while she put two rugs together, pulled them over herself and lay down. A while later, she turned right around, her head where her feet were and feet where her head was. Then she turned again. She did this a few times more. Once she called Nama away from his dinner to inspect the wound on her back in the light of the oil lamp. She asked him to press it gently. The blood had dried now and a scab had formed; but below the scab was a swelling, which throbbed with pain. It couldn't take even a gentle touch. That's why Kautik kept turning over again and again, and yawning every few minutes, crying 'Ma, oh ma' or 'Oh God, no' before or after every yawn.

Nama would stop chewing then and ask her, 'What're you saying, ma?'

'Nothing, son.'

'Then why are you carrying on like this?'

'Have you eaten?'

'Yes.'

'But not enough to fill you,' she'd say. 'Never mind. It's night. Tomorrow I'll get up early and make bhakris.'

'All right.'

'Where's the girl?'

'At Sakina aunty's.'

'What's it doing there, that thumbsucker?'

'She's asleep, isn't she? You saw that.'

'Ma. Dear mother oh.'

'Ma, don't do that. Makes me feel bad.'

'When you've finished eating, put another rug on me will you?'

'Where's another rug here?'

'Then fold a sari in four and put it on me.'

'Yes.'

'Ma. Dear Mother oh!' she exclaimed. 'And press my arms and legs for me.'

'Yes.'

'Have Sakina's guests gone?'

'Now? How will they go at night? They'll go in the morning.'

'Call her over when they go. She'll have incense, no?'

'What for?'

'And camphor?'

'Yes, but for what?'

'Never mind if she doesn't.'

That's how she went on all night. Nama went to bed when it was time, but there was no sleep for Kautik. Nama got up earlier than usual next morning. He called out to his maay to get up and make him bhakris.

'Are you up, Nama?' she asked.

'Yes. Don't I have to go to Tivase from today?'

'What for?'

'Ma, to learn work.'

'Good I remembered.' She sat up. 'Wait, I'll make you some bhakris.'

'Never mind. You had fever all night,' he said, half heartedly.

'Dear Lord,' she said, getting up next moment. 'I'll give up work because I had fever at night, will I? And you'll earn our food for us.'

Nama said nothing. When she'd finished making his bhakris and was wrapping them up in cloth, he asked, 'Ma, you going to work today?'

'What's that? If I don't go, who's going to feed me?' she muttered to herself.

'I was only saying don't go a couple of days.'

'Of course. And this Tuesday, I'll knock out my teeth or yours for the market.'

Nama was silent. She continued talking to him, warning him. 'You're going to learn sewing. But if that Sheshrao starts yelling about anything at all, don't say I didn't warn you.'

'But I'm not...like that, am I?'

'You might be or you might not be. But when you want to learn any skill at all, you need to get into the teacher's gut and stay there. And you've got to tell me day to day what you did.'

'Every day?'

'Then? I won't feed you every day all twelve months for fun. I've worked hard all these days. I'll bear some more hardships another twelve months, why not!'

Sheshrao from Tivase let Nama off early on the first day. Joy gurgled and kicked in Nama's heart like a plump baby in a cot, more for the reason why Sheshrao had let him off early at the shop in the morning. Sheshrao had begun with the first lesson that tailors have given apprentices for centuries—buttons and buttonholes. He'd made four slits in a strip of cloth. He'd explained and shown where the needle had to go in and how the thread had to be looped over it. Nama had nodded to show he'd understood. The needle and cloth strip were handed over to him and he was shown to a dark corner of the shop where he had to sit and practise. He had practised diligently. The first three buttonholes had turned out uneven, but the fourth already showed skill. Sheshrao had been very happy to see this. Unable to stop himself, he had said to a customer, 'This is called learning. Someone who puts his heart into learning makes the teacher feel good. But his brother...now there was a needle.' Then he'd said to Nama, 'From tomorrow, you can put buttons and buttonholes on real garments.'

It was this that was making Nama's heart dance with joy.

He couldn't wait to get home and tell his maay about his great achievement. In case she didn't believe him, he'd brought along the cloth strip on which his first buttonholes and the last perfect one had been made to show her. As he hurried home, he kept checking his pocket for the strip, the way a man carrying his first salary in his pocket does.

As he walked, he was suddenly saddened at the thought that he'd have to wait a long time before Kautik got home from the fields. When he started learning English, he used to catch hold of the first person he saw, whether it was Yasodi or Bano, to practise his new words on. So now he stopped first at Qasam's bellows. But the house was in total silence. Only Qasam was there, sitting on his cot. Nama said to him, 'Uncle, uncle, where is Bano?'

Qasam said in a flat voice, 'She's gone back to Umravati, son.'

'Gone? When?'

'They left in the afternoon.'

'And Yasodi?'

'She'll be at your place.'

Nama turned into their side of the house. What he saw was the cot in the corner, Kautik on the cot and four or five rugs covering her. One of them came from Shevanti's house and one from Sakina's. The owners had come with their rugs and now stood around the cot. With all those rugs covering her, Kautik still thudded up and down like someone riding in a cart. The chatter of her lower teeth against the upper was clearly audible. The cot kept creaking with Kautik's quaking. Sakina held her down, saying, 'Didn't I say don't come to the field today? But has she heeded anyone in her life that she'll heed me!'

'Ma, oh ma,' Kautik kept saying.

Nama stood where he was, taking it all in. A while later, he spoke. 'Aunty, what's happened?'

'He's back. He's back. I think my Nama's back from Tivase.'

Hearing this, Shevanti winked at Sakina and said to Kautik, 'So? There's things you can hear quite well, eh?'

'Honestly. How she's been babbling, cursing that Bakhadya and abusing Ganpat over his mother and sister and God knows what else.'

Shevanti winked again at Sakina and said, 'That was all an act, sister.'

'No, my Shevanti. If I start acting, what will my little ones do? God's done much for them as it is. No one fore, no one aft, and the horse is a pauper's.'

'Keep quiet, sister. Don't blabber.'

'I'm not blabbering. I was telling you how it happened. That was the end of that corpse.'

'Which?'

'If the curse of this husbandless wretch doesn't work and someone is found to light a lamp at his threshold, Kautik's not my name.'

'Oh Brother Sadashiv. Why do you want to pick a quarrel with your brother for our sake?'

'Dear mother. You said nothing about interest when you gave the money!'

'Yes, I will. Don't you dare say things like that.'

'Go. Do what you like.'

Kautik went on rambling. Shevanti stood with her sari-end to her mouth, looking at Sakina to share her amusement. Sakina caught her eye and warned her with an out-turned palm to keep quiet. Then, with sad concern turning into a helpless threat, she said to Kautik, 'Now will you keep quiet or not?'

Her words made no breach in Kautik's meandering babble. 'It's no use now hoping to see my man again. You should have brought him back just once to meet me, shouldn't you, brother?'

'There's no vegetable in this, ma.'

'Let it be. Eat your bhakri with chillies for now.'

'Sakina, don't make the little girl eat chillies. She can have some jaggery from the pot if she likes. Or move. Move. Let me give it to her. It won't do for me to lie around like this. Come on, move.'

'Nobody's going to move. You lie down.'

'I will,' she said and threw off all her covers to sit up.

'Didn't I tell you to lie quiet?'

'I am. I am.'

'Then what're you doing trying to sit up?'

'Sitting up.'

'What did I say?'

'Did I say? Did I say?'

For a moment, everybody was silent. Kautik straightened her dishevelled hair and tried sitting up again. The other two found it impossible to restrain her. That scared Shevanti. She sprang away from the cot. Looking for male help, she began to call out to Qasam who was working at his bellows. The moment he appeared in the doorway, he glared at Kautik and said in an authoritative voice, 'Aren't you listening to me, Kautik?'

'Listening.'

'Then lie down.'

'Lie down.'

'Can't you hear what I'm saying?'

'What?'

'You have a fever. You must lie down.'

'You have a fever. You must lie down.'

'Don't you laugh, Shevanti,' he said solemnly.

'Don't you laugh, Shevanti.'

'Is that right?' he said angrily. 'If you won't listen to me like this, then I'm going to tie you down to the cot.'

'Let's see how. You need to have span-long teeth to tie me down.'

'Will I have to show you my span-long teeth then?'

Qasam shouted in real anger, never thinking Kautik would talk to him like that in front of others. 'No-good slut!'

'You're a slut maybe. Want to know what a slut looks like? I'll pull out your beard. Oh my God, dear God!'

Sakina saw trembling anger in Qasam's eyes. She hastened to protect Kautik. 'Best go away,' she said to him. 'She'll say anything that comes to her tongue.'

He went back. Sakina and Shevanti held Kautik close, tried hard to make her understand. But when they found nothing they did was of any use, they too went back to their homes.

Sakina had hoped that Kautik would mend in eight days or a fortnight. But soon she wrapped up her hope and put it away, and decided to speak out what was on her mind to Nama when he got back from Tivase. One day, she called him in when he returned, sat before him and began to speak.

'Nama, my son, you are an understanding child. But you won't feel badly about what I'm going to say, will you?'

''Course not. What about?'

'You can see how your mother is now.'

'Yes.'

'Nobody wants to give her work anymore nor can she work.'

'I know, aunty.'

'So how will you manage now?'

'Manage what?'

'Food and things.'

'I've written to my uncle.'

'No use waiting for him. Another man would have set off looking for you the minute he got the letter. But your uncle hasn't shown any sign of himself.'

'He hasn't too.'

'So how'll you manage your food?'

Nama didn't answer. When Sakina repeated the question, he simply looked up. So she continued, 'You'll take twelve or eighteen months to learn your trade.'

'No. I can start picking up small jobs in seven months or so.'

'Even so. Even seven or eight months.' She stopped, then said painfully, 'Who will feed you for that time?'

Nama's head suddenly went down. He was silent.

Sakina said, 'One could have managed one more stomach. But here it's three. Isn't that so?'

'Yes.'

'Now own blood won't show up. We at least did what we could all these days.'

'Then what do you say I should do? Unless I can do some small jobs, Sheshrao Uncle won't pay me.'

'We were thinking you'd be best off doing a job.'

Nama said nothing.

'What do you say?'

'But what job can I do? I hate working on the fields.'

'Forget farm work. Get a job in a tea shop for now.'

'Washing cups and saucers?'

'Why not? There's no shame in doing any kind of work for the belly.'

Nama was quiet again.

'You understand, don't you?'

Nama seemed resigned to the situation now. He said, 'But where will I find a job?'

'Don't worry about that. I'll tell uncle to ask around.'

'Ask who?'

'Our Nago at the bus stand. So you'll do it?'

'I'll have to.'

'You're an understanding child.'

'But I'll have to stop my learning, no, aunty?'

'That's not true,' she said, trying to put spirit into him. 'If it's written in your fate, you'll manage one way or another to study. You can never tell. You might get a letter from your uncle tomorrow, then?'

'But do you think it'll come?'

'You can't say. Maybe your uncle was busy with some work. As soon as he's out of it, he'll write...or he might come himself to take you people away.'

'Really?'

'Then?' she said. 'So shall I get uncle to ask Nago?'

'Yes.'

FOUR

These days, Nama wakes up while it's still dark. If Kautik's there, she's there. If not, she's not. Nama knows where to look for her. As soon as he gets up, he goes to the village boundary. Kautik resists coming back with him every step of the way home, but he holds her by the hand and brings her back. Then he brews some jaggery tea and divides it into three portions. If Yasodi's at home, she gets one portion. If she isn't, then Kautik gets two while he himself has one. After his tea, he gets into the grimy shorts that hang on a peg and, instead of the clean washed white cap that he used to wear, he runs a comb through his oily hair and leaves for work bare-headed. Kautik often asks him at such times, 'Where are you going, boy?'

He answers, 'To Tivase,' without looking at her.

'I thought so,' she says.

Nama goes back to Sakina's yard and calls out, 'Aunty, keep an eye out.'

Sakina doesn't remember. She asks, 'For what, son?'

'In case the postman comes.'

'Oh yes,' she says. 'I always do that.'

Sometimes Nama only half hears her, sometimes not at all. But he doesn't wait for her answer. He's already on his way.

After tea, Kautik makes a trip first to the village common. Generally, only a few people are there at this time. Some pass by on their way to or back from their ablutions. She addresses them in various ways as Uncle or Brother or Deewanji. She might suddenly accost a woman and appeal to her urgently, 'Is there work in your field today at least?'

Sometimes the person might say, 'No, Kautik, there's no work today.'

'Tomorrow then,' she asks. And the person answers, 'Let's see.'

Another might say, 'Work in my field got over a long time ago.'

And a third, 'I've sold off my field. There'll be no more work.'

Once in a while, someone might take her side and say, 'Please, Deewanji, give the poor soul some work. She has little ones to look after.'

Deewanji says nothing to this in front of Kautik, but once they've moved away, he might say, 'You want me to let her into my field and see it destroyed?'

Another man might point towards the bus stand, laugh and say, 'Go there. They're building Tukdoji's ashram. They need a lot of labourers.'

Kautik doesn't always believe such stories. She keeps on trying for work. When it's past midday, she even goes to the bus stand. She stops at the ashram site and her appeals for work begin. Much later, she walks to the stand. She stops in front of Nago's tea shop and snaps at Nama collecting cups and saucers inside, 'What are you doing here, you monster?'

At first, Nama hardly seems to notice her. Finally, he stops his work and goes out to her. He says in a confidential voice and a surprised expression on his face, 'Ma. You here?'

'Am I scared of you then?'

'I didn't mean that. It's because tatyaji just went home.'

'What? When?'

'A minute ago.'

'Really?'

'Ask Nagorao uncle.'

Nago instantly says, 'Of course, sister. Mahadev just got off a bus and walked into the village.'

Next moment, Kautik is walking rapidly towards the village. She glances at her house but doesn't see a soul there. So she moves on to the bellows. There, in place of Bano, sits Sakina. And where Sakina used to sit is Yasodi. Her thumb, which she once sucked only to fall asleep, is now permanently in her mouth. She pulls at the chain of the bellows with the other hand. In return for this, she gets to eat bhakri and other stuff regularly in Sakina's house. The sledgehammer that Bano used to wield is now in Sakina's hand. There's been no change in Qasam's place and work.

Kautik spends a lot of time there or none at all depending on how she feels. She might suddenly get up and begin to walk aimlessly, her mouth working as fast as her feet. 'I'll work another twelve months or so. Let Nama begin to earn, then I'm through.'

'I'll see how you tie me down. You need to have span-long teeth to beat me.'

'Nobody belongs to anybody, I tell you. There's no village folks and no neighbours. It was because I was there that I helped them. I brought that barber woman's baby into the world. I didn't say why should I help, she's only a barber woman.'

'I'm not mad. You may be. Let me tell you...God, oh God.

'What brother are you talking about? He's dead to me and I to him.'

When the last bus from Nagpur to Umravati has left, Nama trudges back home in the dark. He carries a cloth bag in his hand. He doesn't come straight home. He goes first to the Hanuman temple. If Kautik isn't there, he goes to the pilgrims' home. If she isn't there either, she has to be in Shevanti's or Sakina's yard. Wherever he finds her, he takes her by the hand and brings her home like a little child. In the early days, he would find it hard work. But now there's strength only in her mouth; there's none left in her body. Her struggle is futile. Nama can drag her after him with the greatest ease.

'So, did you go to Tivase?' she asks.

'Yes.'

'What did you learn today?'

'Jumper.'

'Really?'

'Yes.'

'Learn. Continue learning like this and start earning once and for all.' Kautik has much to say in the same vein.

Nama stays silent. He sits her down at home and puts a plate before her. Sometimes he puts stale bhakris and sometimes burnt rotis in the plate. There's leftover gravy from Nago's spice mix or broken fritter bits to go with them. If he's not carrying a bag, he brings these things home in the pockets of his grimy shorts. If the stuff's in the bag, it means it's been given to him by Nago. If it's in his pockets, it's stolen. Whichever way he's come by the food, he sets it down before his maay and says, 'Eat, maay. Eat. I've brought it for you.'

Kautik stuffs the food in her mouth and gulps it down greedily. He says to her, 'Eat slowly, ma. There's more of it.'

When Kautik has settled down to eat, he draws other things out of his bag or his pocket—flour, lentils, vegetables, cooking oil, tea and jaggery. While he's putting them away, his ears are pricked for sounds from outside. As soon as he's finished, he goes to Sakina's house. He stands in the yard and asks after Yasodi. Usually she's had her dinner and gone to sleep. Then he turns towards home, but his feet won't move.

He asks because he can't help it, 'Aunty, is there a letter or something?'

'No, Nama, my son.'

'Maybe he came when you weren't home and went away?'

'No. I was at home all day, dear.'

'Are you sure?'

His voice is resilient.